When Terran and Comyn meet. . . .

From the Darkovan underground classic "The Other Side of the Mirror," never before published in book form, to Marion Zimmer Bradley's own powerful tale of Tower and Domain, "Oathbreaker," here are memorable stories from that age when Terrans and Comyn sought to find their road to mutual survival on Darkover.

In this new volume from Marion Zimmer Bradley and the Friends of Darkover, you'll discover previously unrevealed moments in Darkover history and in the lives of key members of the Aillard and Ardais lines. So journey now to this excitement-filled era on Darkover, when technology and mind power, Terran spacer and Comyn lord seek to mold the course of Darkover's future.

AGAINST THE TERRANS
—THE FIRST AGE (Recontact):

After the Hastur Wars, the Hundred Kingdoms are consolidated into the Seven Domains, and ruled by a hereditary aristocracy of seven families, called the Comyn, allegedly descended from the legendary Hastur, Lord of Light. It is during this era that the Terran Empire, really a form of confederacy, rediscovers Darkover, which they know as the second planet of the Cottman IV star system. It is not apparent that Darkover is a lost colony of the Empire, until linguistic and sociological studies reveal that Darkovans are of Terran extraction—a concept not easily or readily acknowledged by Darkovans and their Comyn overlords.

THE SPELL SWORD
THE FORBIDDEN TOWER

AGAINST THE TERRANS
—THE SECOND AGE (After the Comyn):

With the initial shock of recontact beginning to wear off, and the Terran spaceport a permanent establishment on the outskirts of the city of Thendara, the younger and less traditional elements of Darkovan society begin the first real exchange of knowledge with the Terrans—learning Terran science and technology and teaching Darkovan matrix technology in turn. Eventually Regis Hastur, the young Comyn lord most active in these exchanges, becomes Regent in a provisional government allied to the Terrans. Darkover is once again reunited with its founding Empire.

THE HERITAGE OF HASTUR
SHARRA'S EXILE

THE DARKOVER ANTHOLOGIES:

These volumes of stories written by Marion Zimmer Bradley herself, and various members of the society called The Friends of Darkover, strive to "fill in the blanks" of Darkovan history, and elaborate on the eras, tales and characters which have captured their imaginations.

THE KEEPER'S PRICE
SWORD OF CHAOS
FREE AMAZONS OF DARKOVER
THE OTHER SIDE OF THE MIRROR

The
Other Side
of the Mirror

and other Darkover stories

by
Marion Zimmer Bradley
and
The Friends of Darkover

DAW BOOKS, INC.
DONALD A. WOLLHEIM, PUBLISHER

1633 Broadway, New York, NY 10019

DAW Book Collectors No. 698.

DEDICATION:
To Eileen and Linda
Muses of many talents

First Printing, February 1987

1   2   3   4   5   6   7   8   9

PRINTED IN THE U.S.A.

CONTENTS

Introduction

Almost since I published the second or third Darkover novel, other writers—usually young—have for some reason wanted to write about Darkover, too. I am and always have been a little baffled by this response; I am a great lover of J. R. R. Tolkien, but only once have I yielded to the desire to write a pastiche Middle Earth story; and although a Star Trek fan, I have in general refrained from adding to the voluminous apocryphal lore of the *Enterprise*.

On the other hand I would not go so far as one admirer of the Darkover stories proclaimed; that he would never be able to bring himself to read one word about Darkover except from my hand; he proclaimed them "tainted" and felt that they damaged the pure vision of Darkover.

Personally, I have always felt that it clarified my vision of Darkover to see it through someone else's eyes; and a special case in point is the story "The Other Side of the Mirror," by Patricia Floss. I remember seeing Patty as a dark-eyed wisp of a girl dressed in a Keeper's crimson robe and veil at an early Darkover convention; and when "Other Side" appeared in the mail, although it was too long for the Darkover anthology I was considering, and even too long for our fiction magazine *Starstone*, during the brief life of Thendara House Publications, we were able to sell a few hundred copies of a pamphlet edition of "Other Side" and distribute it to hard-core fans.

During this time I had begun writing *Sharra's Exile*, and had decided that the events described in Pat Floss's story made somewhat better sense than those I had envisioned as taking place "between the acts" as it were. I decided that Pat's version was henceforth to be considered the "official" version of events on Darkover between the end of *Heritage* and the beginning of *Exile*.

However, not having DAW's printing facilities nor distribution mechanism, there was no way to bring "Other Side" before the public which should have read it. The only possibility would have been to print it in one of the anthologies of short Darkover fiction—*The Keeper's Price, Sword of Chaos*—but Pat's story, though excellent, was nearly 30,000 words long; and one does not, whatever the story's quality, allot nearly a third of the available wordage to a single piece; so with considerable regret I was forced to refuse it for that anthology.

After the good sale of the first two anthologies made it possible to discuss a further volume with DAW Books; I envisioned a possible group of a few longer stories; by this time I had also received, without much hope of professional publication but because it was a good story which I had found pleasure in reading, "Blood Hunt," by Paula Crunk and Linda

Frankel. The idea was to form an anthology of three stories; that I would write a short novel, not long enough for a major Darkover book, but of sufficient length to round out a respectably-sized volume; such a volume might serve to please readers between major novels. The novelette—perhaps better classified as a novella (about 40,000 words)—is an episode referred to in *The Shattered Chain*, which various fans of the Free Amazon stories had urged me to write; I felt it was not important enough to merit a novel on its own but was possibly too hefty for a subplot in a work the size of, say, *Stormqueen*.

Having written the said novella, I felt it proper to enclose it in a bracket of somewhat tangential short stories. The first, "Bride Price," was a small "out-take" from some peripheral writings, which I felt cast some light on the characters of Rohana and Dom Gabriel Ardais and the curious nature of their marriage; very much according to the Tolstoy epigram which heads his famous novel *Anna Karenina*. ("Happy families are all alike; but every unhappy family is unhappy in its own way.")

The other story, "Oathbreaker," deals with the enigma that one of the few villains I ever created, Dyan Ardais, promptly became a favorite, and quite a number of fans and readers felt compelled to write stories about Dyan and his love life; especially they felt compelled to write about his love affairs with women . . . in the nature, I suppose, of the Star Trek fans who have felt compelled to entangle the chaste Spock in tormented love affairs with almost everyone except Darth Vader. While I prefer to leave Dyan's love life in decent obscurity (since I suspect that to investigate it too closely would be unedifying in the extreme), I had no particular objection to investigating the reason why a telepath of his proven abilities would have been banned from a Tower. This was the result; and it seemed a fitting cap to the brief portrait of Kyril Ardais in "Everything But Freedom."

I do not regard this handful of stories as a major addition to the literature of Darkover; but for the fans who want to know more about the private lives of their favorite characters, I hope it may prove of interest.

—Marion Zimmer Bradley

The Other Side of the Mirror

By Patricia Floss

Marius Lanart stood on the edge of the cliff, wondering if it would be best to jump off and save himself a good deal of misery. Certainly no one would regret his death. If he had been twelve, instead of nearly fifteen, he would have wept. He stared down at the blue stone towers of Comyn Castle, wishing they would fall and crumble into dust, and gradually the misery was replaced by a hot, furious anger that he had never felt before.

He clenched his fists, remembering the day's events. Andres, the Terran ex-spaceman whom his father had appointed Chief Steward of Armida more than fifteen years ago, had brought Marius to Comyn Castle late last night. This afternoon, Lerrys Ridenow had accompanied them to Lord Hastur's audience and championed Marius's right, as the son of a Comyn Lord, to join the elite Comyn Cadets.

Dyan Ardais, Commander of the Guards, had not even looked at him. He had said in a bored voice,

that Kennard Alton's "other bastard" had already
proven the fallibility of their mother's Terran blood.

Gabriel Lanart-Hastur, who was kinsman to Marius as well as Cadet-Master, had been patronizing:
"Marius looks even more Terran than Lew did, with
his dark hair and eyes. And some people still blame
Lew for the Sharra rebellion. It would be cruel to
expose Marius to the ridicule and the hatred his very
presence would incure among ignorant boys who share
the prejudices of their elders. I will personally instruct
him in swordsmanship and fighting techniques—but
not among the Cadets."

Then Lord Hastur had ended the discussion in his
usual fashion, raising a frail white hand and calling
for silence. The old man had calmly addressed Marius: "My boy, we have nothing against you personally, you must understand that. But the Comyn
Council ruled long ago that neither you nor your
brother had any claim to Comyn privileges. We gave
Lew those privileges because your father had no
other children, and his domain needed an heir. But
since your father took Lew and left our world, there
has been much resentment. . . . Believe me when I
say I wish it could be otherwise; but I cannot permit
you to enter the Cadets at this time."

More than anything in the world, Marius wished
that his father and brother had not gone away. *And
why haven't they come back?* he asked himself, for perhaps the hundredth time. *I know Lew was very sick,
and Father hoped the Terranan could help him, but it's
been years since they left. Is Father still so worried about
Lew that he's forgotten me? Even if Lew hasn't gotten
better, Father could come back to visit . . . he'd be Commander again, and send Dyan crawling back to Ardais,
and Hastur wouldn't dare deny me a place in the Cadets.*

And then I'd show them all! He let the fantasy sweep him up; but only for a moment. *No. Who am I trying to fool? It's been too long. Father and Lew will never come home. They don't want me any more than the Comyn does. How I hate them! Gabriel Lanart-Hastur, that filthy boy-chaser Dyan, and all the rest of the Comyn Lords! If I could pull that dungheap of a castle down about their ears—I would begin by pushing old High-and-Holy Hastur off the parapet—I swear by Aldones I'll make all of them pay for casting me out!*

The wind was colder now as the sky grew dark. He hugged his knees and stared his hatred at the castle. *Somehow, I will make them pay!*

From far off, a man's voice called, "Marius!" Probably Andres come looking for him. He didn't want to return to the castle, but he was not going to run and hide like a child afraid of a reprimand. Much as he hated the indifference and the cold stares of the Comyn Lords, he knew the only way to resolve the situation was to face it. *Father and Lew went away, but I will not. I am the last Alton, and I won't give up my heritage.*

He stood up and watched the faint glow of torch-light grow brighter, discerning the form of a man on horseback on the trail below him. The man dismounted, tethered the horse, and began to climb. It was Andres, scowling fiercely. Marius smiled; behind Andres Ramirez's habitual grimace was the man who had been his second father.

"Are you all right?" Andres growled, looking at Marius's torn sleeve and dirt-smudged face. "You lit out of the Castle like a rabbithorn in a brush-fire."

"How did you know where to look for me?"

"Lew used to come here often, his first summer in the Cadets, when the Comyn brats and Lord Dyan made his life miserable. He never wanted anyone to see him crying."

Three of Darkover's four moons had risen by the time they reached the castle. Marius suppressed a yawn as they approached the Alton quarters. A hot supper and a long sleep looked very attractive to him. If he *could* sleep, with Hastur's polite denial burning in his ears!

In the main hall of the suite, servants divested him of wet cloak and boots. A huge fire spread cheerful warmth through the hall, and Marius felt his taut muscles relax. During dinner, he noticed that everyone seemed solicitous toward him. Andres had not said one word of reproach for his flight that afternoon. Even Bruna, the gruff old woman who tyrannized the kitchen-maids and traded insults with Andres, asked if Marius wanted a third helping of stew. At that, he turned to Andres and said, "The condemned man eats well, eh?" Marius spoke half in jest, but Andres did not respond at all.

"Andres, what's the matter?" Then he clenched his fists. "Did the old man say anything after I left?"

Andres sighed heavily and looked at his callused hands. Marius had never seen him look so grim.

"Look at me, Andres. What happened? Have they excluded me from Council again?"

"Worse than that, I'm afraid. Lord Hastur has decided you're to go to the Terran Zone."

For a few seconds Marius thought he'd heard wrong. "And do what?" he spat out.

"There's a school that their government runs for the children of Terrans stationed here in Thendara. You'll be taking classes with them and with a private tutor in the HQ building. Hastur said you can live there, too, if you like."

Marius shook his head. He felt numb. How could this be happening to him? Not satisfied with rejecting him from the Comyn Cadets, Hastur and his puppets were now tossing him away like a dirty rag. He turned away, afraid that if he saw pity on Andres's face, he would start to cry.

"Are you sure that Hastur *ordered* it; that it wasn't just a suggestion? I know he's a politician, but Father was his strongest ally, and his friend. How can he do this to me? Am I held so worthless, to be thrown to the *Terranan?*" His voice shook, and he was unable to go on.

"Hastur ordered it, personally. I told him that your father gave you into my charge when he left, and I wouldn't permit this—this arrangement. But he reminded me that you and I are both subject to the will of the Council. Ha!" Andres snorted. "I don't think 'the will of the Council' had anything to do with it. You're an embarrassment to Hastur; he's unable to give you your rightful place in the Comyn, so he decides to introduce you to Terran culture, whether you're willing or not. That way you'll be out of sight, and. . . ." He stopped, seeing that Marius was barely hearing him. The boy sat quietly; one fist loosely clenched, his dark face as bleak and hopeless as an old man's.

Andres swore, then placed a hand on Marius's shoulder. "Look, son, this isn't as bad as it seems. Hastur didn't say you'd have to spend the rest of your life there, just one summer. The Terrans aren't monsters, you know. I'm Terran—spent half my life in Spaceforce, and I'm still trustworthy, aren't I? Marius, your own mother was born and raised on Terra, and a finer woman never breathed, God rest her soul. At least you'll get the chance to explore that side of your heritage ... you'll learn all about the stars, mathematics, science ... I know a few Comyn lordlings who'd break their arms for such an opportunity!"

Marius looked up at the Alton banners that hung from the ceiling. There was no hope there, nor anywhere else. "I can't fight Hastur. I'll go to the Terran Zone and learn whatever they want to teach me there. But I'll sleep here at night, even if Hastur sends you and the staff back to Armida."

Andres seemed cheered by this. "That's the spirit! I'll stay on, too. Armida can do without me for a few tendays." He rose from the table. "Hastur's already made the necessary arrangements; I'm to take you to the Zone tomorrow morning."

Marius fought a ripple of panic. "So soon?" He smiled bitterly. "The old man was pretty sure of me." To himself, he added, *He shouldn't have been. He may regret what I do with this Terranan education. And here is one more wrong to be avenged—the worst of them all.*

Later, after the rest of the household had retired, Marius sat alone by the empty hearth. He was very tired, but he could not sleep. Finally he lit a candle, placed it on the table, and knelt before its tiny flame.

Avarra, Dark Mother of Birth and Death, he prayed silently, *the peace of Your healing sleep eludes me. Grant that it may be thus with those who have cast me out, this night and all the nights to come, that they may never know peace again.*

The next day began badly. The pity in the servants's eyes continued to set Marius on edge, and he ignored his breakfast. Andres was not much better; he looked as if he were anticipating a funeral. When the time came to leave, Marius was almost glad. He put on his finest cloak and a new pair of suede boots and followed Andres through the castle. As they passed by the barracks, he heard the clanging noise of sword-play and harsh voices calling out orders. *The Cadets start training today,* he thought. *I should be there, too.* He gritted his teeth and composed his face into a blank slate. *No one must know what I am feeling, not even Andres. I will not be the object of anyone's pity or mockery.*

When they reached the square that marked the boundary of the Old City, he turned and said, "You can leave me now, Andres. I've been to the Zone before and I know the way to the HQ." He pointed to the enormous building that dwarfed both Comyn Castle and the gaunt structures of the spaceport. "They call it a skyscraper, right?" he added, pronouncing the Terran word with conscious ease.

"Don't get smart with me, Marius," Andres growled. "I'm taking you right up to the spaceport gates. The Terrans will have someone there to take charge of you."

"I'm not exactly a babe in arms," Marius said angrily, as they turned up a wide avenue of cafes, bars, and souvenir shops. "Just tell me who I report to in the HQ and I'll find him."

"Look," Andres answered, a little too loudly, "you may be nearly a man by Darkovan law, but to the Terrans you're still a minor, a child. And by the time you get to your first class, you'll be grateful to have someone showing you around. The HQ is like a gigantic anthill, and Terran bureaucracy is even worse."

The gates of the Spaceport Complex lay ahead. Andres stopped short and stared at the shining edifice that rose above them like a small mountain.

Marius looked, too; and, involuntarily, in a sudden wish to be close to Andres, he felt the familiar vibration of telepathic rapport ... *I never thought I'd be bringing Kennard's son here.* There was a bitterness there that nearly matched his own. Andres cleared his throat, and Marius felt the contact dissolve. "This is as far as I go, lad—" Andres pointed at the gate. "Good luck. I'll see you tonight." He turned around, but not before Marius had seen his eyes moisten.

Left alone, Marius walked forward, more than a little frightened. In conscious imitation of Kennard Alton, he squared his shoulders, lifted his head, and strode on proudly. The burly guards in black leather shifted their weight as he passed them, and he suppressed a grimace at the blasters they wore.

A slight man in a silvery, shining coverall stepped up to meet him. "You're Marius Alton?" he inquired in a nasal voice.

Stupid Terranan, Marius winced inwardly, and answered, "I am Marius Montray-Lanart." He hardly heard the Terran identify himself as Claude Sorrell, the "Public Relations" man assigned to take him through the HQ. It was like a cruel joke to be called 'Alton,' the name that Comyn Council had refused to give the sons of Elaine Montray. *One can't expect Terranan to be aware of such subtleties,* he told himself, and dismissed the incident from his mind.

The next few hours were the most confusing of Marius's life. Sorrell led him through what seemed an endless maze of glaring lights and windowless cubicles. Over and over again he answered impertinent questions on identical papers and signed his name to them, until he thought his hand would fall from his arm. He submitted to the indignity of having his body inspected by a pompous Terran healer and was rewarded with one more piece of paper to add to the pile that Sorrell carried for him. By the time they had finished testing him, he understood the remark Andres had made about "bureaucracy." The walls seemed to press in on him, and he wanted desperately to run back outside, away from all the people who infested the Terran base.

Sorrell took him to a vast room that reminded Marius of the Guard Hall at Comyn Castle, save that it was jammed with people eating at circular counters. They joined a long line before a machine that was twice the height of Marius. He was fascinated by the dials, buttons, and throbbing hum of the contraption—until Sorrell handed him a tray and utensils. "See the pictures next to the buttons?" Sorrell directed. "You pick whatever you want to eat and press the button beside it."

Marius felt sick to his stomach. *Eat food that comes from a machine? No wonder the Ridenow brothers say the Terranan are barbarians!*

"No, thank you," he said politely. "I'm not hungry."

After Sorrell had finished eating, they took the elevator to the Academic Placement Office on the thirty-first floor. "Well, Marius," Sorrell announced in the overly-cheerful tone that Marius was beginning to dislike, "you did very well on your tests. Your knowledge of Terran Standard is close to the norm, your grasp of basic mathematics is unusual for a Darkovan, and you show an affinity for historical analysis."

Marius wasn't surprised. He and his brother had learned to speak the Terran language early in life; their father had also insisted that Andres teach them the rudiments of mathematics. Sorrell continued to chatter. "You'll be studying Life Sciences, Basic Algebra, Empire Geography, Advanced Terran Standard, and, of course, Physical Fitness. You'll also see a tutor for an hour every other school day. Now we'll go pick up the textbooks that you'll need for those classes."

At last they let him go. Once outside, Marius nearly cried for joy. The air was sharp and keen, the first stars glimmered above him as the setting sun's red glare purpled the oncoming clouds. He had almost forgotten there were such things as wind and darkness. The day spent in the hot, constantly bright arc-lights of the HQ had seemed to last forever. He hurried through the Terran Zone, elated to be walking free again. The candle-lit windows of the Old City houses spurred him on his way.

In the days that followed, Marius found that life in the Terran stronghold was more difficult than he had anticipated. He was familiar with loneliness, having been shunned or scorned by most of the Comyn ever since he could remember; but the bulk of his life had been spent at Armida, the hereditary estate of the Alton lords. There, from the great house and stables to the villages and Ranger Stations in the hills, he was known and cherished as Kennard Alton's son.

Now he was thrust against his will into a world strange and frightening, and his was the loneliness of both exile and alien. Sorrell and Andres warned him of "culture shock," but that ancient cliche hardly described his own confusion. Inside the walls of the HQ, Marius felt like a child, learning the mechanics of existence for the first time.

In the first tenday alone, he mastered the use of elevators, slide-walks, push-button lights, video machines, microscopes, and Terran plumbing. He had thought himself fluent in Terran Standard; yet the effort of speaking and reading it each day tired him, and the concepts it carried were often completely foreign to his understanding. Also, the regulations that governed a Terran student's life were a constant irritant to him.

His claustrophobia increased with every day spent behind walls. He held himself aloof from his fellow students, and concentrated on learning what their teachers set before him. The only Terran with whom he felt at all comfortable was his tutor, a slender young woman who spoke perfect Cahuenga and insisted he call her by her first name, Elena. Marius was tempted more than once to unbend and confide some of his problems in her sympathetic ear; but he did not.

Hardest of all was changing worlds each day: leaving Comyn Castle when the sun had barely risen, sitting still throughout the day in the Terran base, and walking back to the castle under the sun's last rays became a torturous routine. If he had followed Hastur's suggestion, however, and lived in one of the windowless cubicles of the HQ dormitories, he would have gone mad. To climb the hill up to the castle was to return to Darkover from the horrors of exile. But whenever he passed the barracks, he heard the noise of the Cadets at swordplay, reminding him of all that he had lost.

Sometimes he encountered the Cadets when they were off-duty. Most of them ignored him, sneered, or made remarks that were not worthy of reply. Felix Aillard, an arrogant boy a head taller than Marius, stopped him one evening, to grab his books and rip out several pages. Infuriated, Marius had knocked him breathless to the ground with a quick jab to the solar plexus that he'd learned from his Physical Fitness teacher.

In the familiar comfort of the Alton rooms, he evaded Andres's questions and attempted counsels—but beneath his mask of equanimity, a terrible anger smoldered like the forge of Alar.

Marius had counted almost two tendays in the Terran Zone the day his luck changed for the better. His Terran Standard class seemed to stretch out in an unendurable catalog of grammatical minutiae. Marius did not need the sound of knuckles cracking from the rows behind him to perceive that the others shared his boredom. The only reason he could tolerate this class was the window near his seat, through which he could see the spaceport and the purple-tinged Venza Hills beyond the city. As Horton's heavy voice droned on, Marius sought distraction in the perfect view.

From the corner of his eye, a metallic blur arched upward, cleaving the sky like an arrow. *Probably one of their Mapping and Exploring expeditions, gone to spy on us from the air,* he thought. In a fit of resentment, he wished the craft would turn in mid-flight, fall from the sky, and crash into the spaceport. Though he knew his own matrix was not strong enough to accomplish this, he focused all his telepathic force into a mental image of the spaceport bursting into flame.

Without warning, he was interrupted. A wave of mental protest hit his unprepared mind, as strong and as loud as if the outsider had screamed that *NO!* in his ear. A garbled succession of images rippled across his mind, images that were not his own: a castle wall wreathed in golden flames, a woman-shaped form of fire towering above it; within the thing, a girl in a blue gown stood unafraid, and near her a man gripped a sword with a large blue stone in its hilt, and writhed, as fire lapped the hand that held the sword. There was agony on the scarred and haggard face—the face that Marius recognized as his brother Lew. Shocked, he slammed down his barriers to stop that barrage of horror, but not before he'd seen the girl crumple in the fire, and felt terror and grief like a raw wound in the mind that touched his.

Marius felt the back of his neck break into clammy sweat. The scene had been as real as if he'd stood on the burning parapet himself . . . whoever had broken into his thoughts had to be a gifted telepath. Was the intruder here, in the classroom?

He turned and scanned the bored, blank faces. He also scanned their thoughts, trying to locate the mind that had contacted his. *Where are you?* he beseeched the unknown. The only reply was the three chimes on the intercom, which signaled the end of the period. The Terrans rushed past him toward the door; and he wondered, *How could it have been one of them? All they're thinking about is getting to the cafeteria before it fills up. . . .* He waited until most of them had gone, then put his textbooks into his briefcase.

As he started toward the elevator, an unmistakable voice said, "Wait a moment." Turning, he saw a boy his own age, in the simple clothes and soft indoor boots fashionable among Terrans; otherwise he looked more Darkovan than Marius himself. Slender, with long, graceful hands, he had fair skin and reddish-brown hair. His eyes were of a color Marius had never seen before; amber, almost golden, like the eyes of a mountain cat.

"Marius Lanart," the stranger began, in the pure

Cahuenga of the far Hellers, "I must give account for my intrusion." He swallowed, looking uncomfortable. "You sent that—that daydream of yours all around the class. The other kids aren't telepaths—but I am, and I couldn't help seeing it, through your eyes. All that anger, and the fire you wanted to start—I guess it brought back too many bad memories to me. I couldn't stand it anymore—what you saw was a piece of those memories."

Marius had an odd sensation, a sort of empathy for the suffering that he felt in the other. Pity, and a sudden curiosity, moved him to ask, "Memories of what? I saw my brother in your mind."

"I was at Aldaran when Sharra broke loose." He frowned, then said abruptly, "We can't talk here. Do you have a lunch period now?"

Marius nodded and followed him. It was suddenly important that he know more of this strange *Terranan.* In an empty locker room they sat on the long benches, facing each other. Marius felt awkward, but his compulsion overcame his shyness. "How did you know my brother?" he asked.

"Lord Kermiac of Aldaran was my guardian; I grew up at the castle." He paused, then continued, "When Lew came to Aldaran, we made him part of our matrix circle. He saw that I had telepathy, like my sisters, and started to train me in its use. He was kind to me, like a brother . . . we were in rapport quite often, that's how I recognized you . . . he let me tag along after him and Marjorie. . . ."

Marius caught the mental image of Lew, walking through the streets of a shining city, smiling at the amber-eyed girl at his side.

"Marjorie was my sister," the other continued. "Our father was Terran, our mother the last of the

Darriels, an old mountain family. Maybe that's why Lew and Marjorie fell in love; they were both Terran-Darkovan hybrids and understood each other from the start—for all the good it did them." He shuddered, a feral grimace curling his lips. "When Lew finally shut down the Sharra matrix, he had to strike through Marjorie. And I couldn't help her, I was too frightened, and it all happened so fast. She died, and—and everything went up in flames. . . ."

Marius felt a thrust of pain as if it were his own anguish. Rather than dwell on it, he changed the subject. "You're as Darkovan as Lew and I. How did you come—here?" He swept the blank walls in a contemptuous gesture. "Did the *Terranan* take you by force?"

"No, I had nowhere else to go. My other sister, Thyra, fled with her lover, the gods alone know where; my foster father had died a few weeks before. I didn't know where Lew had gone—so I joined the Terran Empire, as my father's son." He brought the corners of his mouth up to form a faint smile. "I forgot to introduce myself. Rafe Scott, *z'par servu.*"

The fluid Darkovan phrase jarred with the Terran name—although "Rafe" was a Darkovan appellation, a diminutive for "Rafael" or "Rakhal." A fitting name for a son of Terra and Darkover. Here was one who might have been brother to Marius, so similar were their origins. *A son of Terra and of Darkover,* he repeated to himself. *Both have a claim on me, though I have tried to deny my mother's world.*

"I know," Rafe answered, with the astonishing awareness of a telepath. "At times I've felt that I'd sign away my soul to be truly a Terran, to belong only to the Empire—but I can't forget where I was born and those who raised me. Lawton, the Legate, says I'm lucky to have ties to both worlds. But I think it's more like a curse." He looked at Marius. "I could tell that you're very angry. It's something to do with Lord Hastur, Comyn Council, your father, and the Terrans. You didn't come to the HQ of your own free will, did you?"

Marius shook his head. Rafe's candor bewildered him, for he had always kept his emotions to himself; yet it was somehow very natural, as if he had known Rafe for a long time. So he told of the last few tendays, omitting only the extremes of his anger. To another telepath, such strong emotions were obvious, anyway.

When he finished, the other boy offered him a tentative smile and said, "It has not been easy. It never is, changing worlds. And you didn't want to in the first place." Marius sensed a surge of emotion behind that smile, an intense longing, echoed by Rafe's thoughts:

Like me, he is a hybrid, never truly a part of either world. We could be friends . . . Holy Bearer of Burdens, I have been alone too long!

On a warm afternoon several days later, Marius walked briskly through the Terran Zone, his brief-case swinging in his hand. It was not a school day, so he was going to meet Rafe in the library where they could work on their assignments together. Stopping at a street vendor's stall, he bought a meat-cake and continued on his way. As he nibbled at the hot, flaky crust, he felt a tingling anxiety on the edge of his consciousness. He stood still and concentrated; it was a scratching rudeness that made him feel like one of the caged rats in the school laboratory. He was being watched, by someone not very far from him. He was certain because the same thing had happened three times in the last six days—and he had had enough of it. He altered his route, changing direction from the HQ to the spaceport, hoping that the unseen watcher would be confused enough to reveal himself to Marius's outstretched senses. But when he reached the barricades surrounding the landing field, his pursuer was still on his track.

The crowd was growing larger, due to the influx of travelers from the just-landed *Southern Crown*. Marius had a momentary impulse to linger, as he had done once before on his way to the HQ. He enjoyed the sights and sounds of the massive complex: the roar of the huge starships as they rose into the air, the many varieties of people and other beings from hundreds of worlds . . . reluctantly, he turned and left the spaceport.

"You're late," Rafe commented when Marius met him by the fountain in the plaza in front of the HQ. "And angry. What happened?"

Marius was no longer surprised by the speed with which Rafe picked up his surface emotions. He was a strong telepath when he chose to use his power, and Marius had not barriered himself against him. It pleased him that Rafe cared enough about him to monitor his feelings. They had often entered the first stage of mental rapport without any deliberate effort; but when Marius had tried to probe deeper, for a closer bond, he had encountered such pain and fear that he had withdrawn, to Rafe's obvious relief.

"I was followed on my way here," Marius replied, "and it's not the first time. I don't know why the *Terranan* would want to spy on me, but—"

"Hold on," Rafe interrupted. "What makes you think the Terrans are responsible? I agree, most of the Spaceport officials are loud-mouthed fools, but the Intelligence people know what they're doing. Which wouldn't include chasing after a Comyn outcast who's got as good a claim to Empire citizenship as they have. It doesn't make sense."

"Maybe not," Marius said, and pushed the "up" button beside the elevator. "But who else could follow me all through the Trade City, and not be able to trail me to the Castle?"

"From what you've told me, your precious *Hali'imyn* are quite capable of it—either by using agents or their own matrixes. Perhaps they're worried that you'll spill some of their secrets to the Empire. . . ."

"That would serve them their due," Marius said sarcastically as the elevator doors opened at last. *Rafe's probably right,* he thought as they rode up. *If anyone has a reason to spy on me, it's the Comyn.* He was faintly surprised that he had not suspected them before; then realized he had not wanted to admit such a possibility to himself. A Lord of the Seven Domains, responsible for such a covert, petty, typically Terran activity as spying on him? *And yet. . . .*

The elevator jarred to a halt and opened its doors with mechanical precision. Halfway down the gleaming corridor, Marius stopped to quench his thirst at an auto-fountain. The cold water tasted of the shiny metal faucet and he spat it out. He shuddered suddenly, gripped by a total revulsion for every aspect of his comtemptible existence.

"Marius, take it easy!" Rafe said softly. "Things aren't that bad. I could be wrong about the Comyn having you followed—but even if I'm not, the honor of the Hasturs is a byword far beyond the Hellers. My foster father always spoke of Lord Danvan as a just and wise man, though their policies differed.

I'm sure he knows nothing of this nonsense and will put a stop to it the moment you appeal to him."

Marius thought, *The way I appealed to him to let me join the Cadets? Why haven't I done anything about that? I'll have to find the proper weapon and a way to use it.*

Before they entered the library, Rafe spoke again: "If we can finish by early afternoon, let's go down to the Spaceport. I know one of the mechanics, and he said he'll give us an inside tour of the whole Complex. It'll be a lot better than that phony *reish* the PR people give on their tours." He used the Cahuenga word for stable-sweepings, and in spite of his heavy mood, Marius smiled, thinking, *He saw that I was upset and tried to cheer me.*

The realization touched him, and he decided to show his appreciation. "I've got a better idea," Marius said aloud. "We'll leave here about an hour before dark and go to my rooms. We'll have dinner, and then I will personally guide you through every inch of Comyn Castle." A little surprised at his own daring, Marius paused. He could feel Rafe's pleasure like a tangible presence in the space between them. He tried to sound nonchalant. "Bring your books and an extra set of clothes, so you can stay the night if you like."

"I like," Rafe answered. "That is a princely offer, my lord Marius."

"*S'dia shaya, vai dom Rakhal,*" answered Marius, with the traditional Casta phrase. "Come on," he urged. "Maybe we'll be lucky and find a conference room that's empty."

They broke two or three pencils in their haste to finish the assigned problems, and left the HQ building as the evening clouds were rising above the hills. A cold rain froze the air, and Rafe shivered in his

light jacket. Nearing the castle, Marius slowed his
pace to a firm, deliberate tread. Under the massive
arch leading into the back courtyard stood three
young Cadets. The foremost was Felix Aillard, his
fair Comyn features twisted in a travesty of a smile.
He stepped up to intercept them, drawing his sword
as he moved."

"Let us pass," said Marius. It was not a request.
Felix simply stared, enjoying the situation. The wind
whipped his red-gold hair and flared his short black
cloak, making him look the epitome of a Comyn
soldier. "Why do you bar our way?" Marius asked,
and passed his briefcase to Rafe, so that he might
rest his hand on the sheathed dagger he always
carried.

"Oh, I don't bar *your* way, *com'ii*," said Felix, eyes
fastened on Rafe. "I see your new friends have provided you a servant. But no errand-boy of the
Terranan shall pass here!"

"Rafe Scott is not my servant. He is my friend.
You have no right to deny my guest and me entrance
to my home."

Felix laughed, an ugly, mirthless sound. Marius
was conscious of a wave of anger pouring like hot
pitch from the Cadet's mind toward Rafe. "You don't
think I have the right to forbid this Terran entrance?" Felix sneered. "Well, *chiyu*, you can stay
right here while I send for someone who does!" He
turned to the boy on his left. "Nicol, find the Commander, and tell him what Montray-Lanart is trying
to get away with."

Oh hell! Marius thought. *If he finds Dyan Ardais, that
damned ombredin will send Rafe back to the Zone just to
spite me!*

The Cadet ran off in the direction of the barracks.

Marius, seeing Felix's triumphant smile, longed to smash it through that handsome face. His indignation was not for himself alone, but for Rafe, and the embarrassment Felix was trying to cause him. Rafe wasn't even properly dressed for the weather, and this nasty little toy soldier was making him stand out in the rain like a beggar! It seemed natural that Marius should focus his indignation into his matrix; the power of his anger grew until it seemed to envelop him like a sheath of flame. Only a slight effort was required to strike Felix senseless, as he longed to do.

Felix faced him, suspicion and fear in his eyes as he gasped for breath, clutching vainly at his throat. Rafe turned also, with a horrified look. Marius heard him call, without words, *You don't know what you're doing! Stop it, before it's too late!*

Reluctantly, Marius slowed his onslaught. *It means that much to you?*

Yes!

Marius withdrew the destructive energy from his starstone. Revenge against Felix was not worthwhile if it caused Rafe such distress.

Now that he had back his voice, the Cadet was snarling like a catman. "I'll see you in Zandru's coldest hell—little *bre'suin!* Using a matrix to witch me! Why don't you fight me like a man, you damned Terran bastard!"

"Yes," Marius said quietly, "my mother was a Terran—but I was acknowledged by my father. You can't claim that distinction. Can you, Felix?" Bastardy was no disgrace in the Seven Domains, but the promiscuity of Felix's mother had earned him the epithet *six-fathered,* and Marius felt no compunction about turning it to his advantage. Felix, livid with rage, abruptly ran out of mocking words.

At that moment, Nicol returned; with him was a tall red-haired Guardsman whom Marius recognized as Lerrys Ridenow, his only supporter among the Comyn. *All thanks to the gods,* he thought. *Lerrys will put an end to this comedy.*

"I couldn't find the Commander," Nicol was saying, "but Captain Ridenow wanted—"

"To find out what exactly is going on here," Lerrys finished. "Cadet MacAran told me some tale of your apprehending a Terran spy being smuggled into the Castle by Marius Lanart."

"Captain, that is not true!" Rafe broke in. "I have been silent out of deference to your laws—but I will not have Marius abused further for my sake. He invited me here as his guest, and this talk of spying is ridiculous!" He coughed, then continued, "Sir, you are of the Comyn. Surely you have the means of knowing that I speak the truth."

Lerrys raised an eyebrow as he regarded Rafe. When he spoke, it was to the three Cadets, in the clipped tones of anger. "I find it hard to believe that a Cadet could be party to such foolishness. The Comyn is demeaned by such behavior. This lad is a stranger and the guest of Dom Marius; you have insulted him and broken the laws of hospitality. Return to your quarters; I'll deal with you later. Cadet Aillard—you will stay." He turned to Marius. "Will you wait for me in the Great Hall, cousin?"

"Gladly, kinsman." Marius led Rafe under the arch and across the small courtyard. A few minutes later they were inside the castle, at the foot of a marble staircase that curved its way up to the fourth floor.

"It's just like home," Rafe said. "Our Great Hall

had arc-light, but it was *just* as drafty—and we didn't have quite as many tapestries as there are here."

"Look over there, beneath the chandelier." Marius indicated a tapestry depicting a battle waged beneath the very towers of Comyn Castle, detailed enough for them to distinguish several Guardsmen and their leader, a dark-haired man engaged in single combat with a Drytown chieftain. The colors were so sharp one could make out the blood-spots on their boots. "Rafael Lanart was my ancestor," Marius explained proudly. "Three hundred years ago he led the Guards to victory against an invading Drytown army; after killing their war-chief! He won such great renown that many years later, when the King and his son were killed by treachery, it was Rafael who became Regent for the infant heir."

"Ah, Marius! There you are."

They turned, to see Lerrys Ridenow standing a few paces away, rainwater dripping from his cloak. "It's raining hard enough to wake the dead," Lerrys said irritably. "Sometimes I remember the old super-stition—such rain is a sign of the gods's anger at our arrogance." His voice softened. "You've certainly had your share of arrogance today, cousin. Please accept my apologies for the behavior of those Cadets—they will be strongly reprimanded, I assure you."

Surprised by the man's sudden solicitude, Marius shrugged and said, "It's all right, Dom Lerrys. They didn't hurt us. Besides, if you listen to dogs barking, you'll go deaf and won't learn much."

Lerrys smiled. "I fear we both have forgotten our manners. Introduce me to your friend, Marius."

"I am Rakhal Darriel-Scott—better known as Rafe Scott, *z'par servu*." Rafe was obviously tired of being dismissed as an ignorant Terran outsider.

"I bid you welcome to Comyn Castle, Rafe Scott. You look as if you're in need of a warm fire and a warmer drink—as I am myself. Won't you both join me in my quarters?"

"Thank you," Marius answered, "but we still have some schoolwork to do before dinner."

"At least let me see you to your door, since it's on the way to my own rooms."

As they climbed the stairway, Rafe asked, "Dom Lerrys, would you know why the Aillard boy hates me? Both Marius and I felt it, yet I've never seen him before."

Lerrys's fair face clouded. "It's a bad business. Felix had an elder brother, Geremy, who was a Captain in the Guards. He was on patrol on Midsummer Night last year . . . there was a brawl at a tavern, started by two Spaceforce men. Geremy intervened, and one of the Terrans shot him with a blaster. He died a few hours later, in Felix's arms. Felix has hated everyone and everything Terran ever since."

"I don't think I can blame him," Rafe said thoughtfully.

"I do," Marius snapped. "You had nothing to do with his brother's death, and he has no reason to hate you for it!"

Lerrys looked amused, but spoke gravely. "Your loyalty does you credit, Marius. And you're right. Unfortunately, men like Felix, who are poisoned by their hatred, don't think so clearly."

Marius caught an undercurrent of emotion: Lerrys was pleased by Marius's friendship with Rafe. It was not a vague feeling of kindness, but a strong, self-satisfied approval, as if Lerrys himself were somehow responsible for their relationship. Marius was glad he had refused the man's invitation, for his new interest was disturbing. *Perhaps he's an ombredin, and he wants both of us,* Marius thought; then stifled a laugh. It was impossible to imagine the casual, ever-elegant Lerrys prey to the excessive passions that had nearly disgraced Dyan Ardais three years ago.

Dinner was quiet, since Andres was not due back from Armida for two days. Afterward, true to his promise, Marius guided Rafe through as much of the castle as their feet could cover.

Later, Marius lay beneath the heavy coverlets of his bed; Rafe was already asleep across the room. Marius sighed, content for the first time since he had come to Thendara.

His euphoria continued for most of the next day. The clouds had parted, and the day was as warm as a Darkovan summer permitted. Rising early, they rode northward to see the *rhu fead,* the holy place of the Comyn. Although Rafe could not enter the ancient white sanctuary, he was enthralled by Hali, the lake beside whose misty shores it stood. They passed the rest of the morning riding northwest to the Plateau of Armida. After mid-day, they stopped and unpacked the food they had brought for the journey.

"I guess you haven't ridden in a long time," Marius said, observing Rafe's discomfort as he lowered himself to the ground. Rafe grimaced and reached for an apple. They ate quickly, scarcely speaking. Around them the trees rustled with the sounds of bird-cries and the fleet movements of the rock squirrels. Abruptly Rafe tensed, like a falcon poised for flight.

"What's the matter?" Marius asked.

Rafe stretched his arms above his head. "Marius, let's leave. . . ."

"Where to?"

"Anywhere—as long as it's light-years away from this planet! Terra and Darkover can do nothing but break their heads when they collide. I want to find a place where no one has any old feuds or grudges." He was smiling, but his eyes had a hungry, reckless look. "Let's just go—tomorrow, or next week. We're too young for Spaceforce, I know; but we could ship out as cargo boys. Maybe we'll become outlaws—living by our wits and our blasters, with prices on our heads. Or we could be Colonists. There are still plenty of new worlds to be explored and settled."

The colors of the forest wavered before Marius's eyes. The air seemed to ripple and he was gripped by the sudden shift in time that often possessed those of Alton blood. He saw Thendara Spaceport, and the open doors of a starship liner. Lew stood on the ramp, older, with gray streaks in his dark hair and resolution on his scarred face. He wore Terran-style clothing, as did the young blonde woman at his side; in his arms, Lew held a small girl-child. Her eyelids fluttered open, revealing eyes of liquid amber—eyes just like Rafe's. For a mere instant, Marius felt Rafe's presence in his mind, sharing the vision. Then he felt his friend's grief and heard him call, "Marjorie!" with a terrible yearning. The vision faded.

Rafe took a deep breath, waving away Marius's supporting hand. "I'm okay," he said quietly. "That kid you saw—looked just like my sister."

"Rafe, won't you tell me . . . more . . . about the night she died?" He hesitated, searching for words. "I can tell you've almost blocked off your *laran* because of the things that happened then. Maybe— maybe we should try for complete rapport . . . you

can't go on keeping it all locked up inside you."
Marius thought, *I have never given advice to anyone—
but I have known your pain, and I cannot remain indifferent to it.*

"Of course," Rafe replied, "you know all about hidden emotions! You keep your anger burning like a demon's cauldron. Isn't that a bit dangerous for an Alton, whose anger can kill?" Then he smiled, relaxing somewhat. "Oh, we're a fine pair! You with your rage, and me with my—my memories. Come on, let's put the rest of the afternoon to *good* use!"

A faint trepidation stiffened the hairs on the back of Marius's neck. *Something is going to happen*, he thought. *Very soon—perhaps this tenday. Something important. I know it.* He looked up at the cloudless sky, the tall evergreens swaying in the breeze; then at Rafe's expectant face.

"It is a warm day for Darkover." He rose. "If you're not too tired, I'll race you from here back to the Forbidden Road. My horse is spoiling for a good run."

Early the next morning Marius accompanied Rafe to the HQ, briefcase in hand. He felt like a mutineer awaiting punishment. It was hard to believe that just fourteen hours before they had raced their horses through the fragrant hills. *We're like fire-ants returning to the mound*, Marius thought angrily, *no spark of free will to distinguish us from a thousand others!*

Aloud, he asked, "What kind of life is this 'education' the Terrans are so proud of? Sitting on your backside all day, pressing buttons and scribbling notes like nearsighted clerks!"

"I wasn't forced to take the summer quarter, as you were," Rafe said. "I wanted to get some difficult subjects out of the way—the sooner I finish the school-ing required of all Terran kids, the sooner I'll be my own man, free to choose a direction. Besides, Mar-ius, if we're going to be space pirates, you'll have to know the Principles of Interstellar Navigation! So study that algebra!"

"I thought it didn't matter where we went," Mar-ius answered; but it was hard to joke in the swarming corridors and elevators of the HQ.

Once out of his Empire Geography class, Marius headed toward his locker room, but before he'd reached the elevator, a familiar voice that was not Rafe's called his name.

"What's your hurry?" the dark-skinned girl sa.d with a friendly smile. "I didn't think our automats excited you so much."

"Hello, Elena." He slowed his pace to match hers. He did not trust the tutor, and her pretty face unset-tled him; yet she was the only Terran he actually liked, except for Rafe. But then, Rafe was not really a Terran.

"You thought right," said Marius, "usually I bring my own lunch from home. Would you care to join me?"

"Thanks, but no. I've just clawed my way through the hungry horde, and I'm going back to my office for some peace and quiet." She glanced at him quiz-zically. "Your classroom is on my way—but that's not the only reason I came by it. I'm supposed to take you up to Administration."

Marius stopped short. "Why?" he asked warily.

"The Legate wants to talk to you." She lowered her voice respectfully, like a Darkovan mentioning Lord Hastur.

"And if I don't choose to accommodate him . . . ?"

"Marius, don't be childish. You don't have to lick the man's boots, but try to show him some respect in his own Headquarters."

Marius followed her without speaking. *Respect!* he thought. *What insolence! They send this slip of a girl to gull me with fair words, knowing I have no choice but to obey the summons. Sharra's chains! If my father were here, this Legate would beg for just one moment of my time!* His rage flamed up anew, and with it the pain and frustration that had begun the day his father had left him without even a farewell.

The Office of the Legate of Terran Affairs was a suite of five large rooms in the penthouse on the roof of the HQ building. Marius gave his name to the bored receptionist at the entrance.

"Marius," Elena said suddenly, "I may be just a cog in the machine, but I do care about you—please believe that I could never cause you harm." She squeezed his left hand quickly, then hurried away. Marius looked after her in some puzzlement.

"The Legate will see you now, sir," the receptionist said, not looking up from the piles of papers on her desk. "Please follow the servomech."

Marius trailed behind the slow, squat little robot to a closed door at the other end of the suite, where a brown-skinned giant in a Spaceforce uniform opened the door and ushered Marius inside. He was faintly surprised, having expected a Terran Legate's private office to be a garish blend of chromium and plastic, complete with an automatic bar and wall-to-wall video screen. This chamber had some Darkovan touches: wood paneling, a ceramic vase, a board used for the game of Castles, and a tapestry depicting a Midwinter Festival.

"Marius Montray-Lanart." The Legate rose from

his desk and executed a correct Darkovan bow. Again
Marius was surprised—he had thought that the high-
est Terran authority at Thendara Spaceport would
be as old and dignified as Hastur. The man facing
him with a disarming smile was younger than Lerrys
Ridenow; his bright red hair and fair skin could
have allowed him to pass as Comyn.

"Won't you sit down?" the strange figure urged.
As Marius complied, the man continued, in flawless
Cahuenga, "Dan Lawton, *z'par servu;* appointed Legate six months ago. One of the benefits of a very
taxing job is this private den, which has helped some
of my predecessors keep their sanity. I haven't had
lunch, and neither have you, I suspect, so I've taken
the liberty of having some sent up here. Can I provide you with a drink in the meantime?"

"No, thank you." Marius raised his eyes to meet
Lawton's blue ones; extending his senses slightly, he
perceived excitement beneath the Terran's casual
exterior. Curious in spite of himself, Marius relaxed
into an attitude of comfort.

"You must be wondering why I've asked you to
come here. Now, according to our files, you're a
telepath—so you'll know that I'm speaking as hon-
estly as I can." The Legate folded his hands in a
steeple. "I've watched you very carefully since you
first came to HQ. You haven't been too happy in this
environment, and I'm sorry for that. But you *have*
learned to function quite effectively in a world you'd
thought was beyond your understanding. Of course
I expected nothing less. . . .

"A Terran starship landed on Darkover," Lawton
went on smoothly, "something more than a hundred
of your years ago. The Comyn were horrified by the
intrusion of what they believed to be an alien race.

Scarcely twenty years after that first landing, one of those 'alien' invaders discovered he had *laran*—that telepathic ability so zealously guarded and prized by the Comyn. That spaceman was Andrew Carr, who married your own great-aunt and lived out his life as an Alton clansman, on Alton lands." The Legate smiled briefly. "I could list a hundred other Terrans who found happiness in Darkovan lifestyles: your uncle, Larry Montray; or Magda Lorne, the Intelligence agent who became a Free Amazon. Both are notable examples."

Marius shifted uneasily in his chair, wishing the Terran would get to the point of whatever he was trying to say. Just then, a large servomech glided into the room; Lawton pressed a button, and its upper portion opened, dispensing a tray laden with food. As the robot retreated, Lawton handed Marius a sandwich and poured him a cup of hot brown liquid. Marius lifted a hand in protest, thinking it to be coffee, the Terran beverage he had once sampled at Rafe's request.

"Don't worry," said Lawton, smiling. "It's fresh-brewed *jaco*. I have it brought in from a Darkovan food-stall every day—I don't like coffee either."

When Marius had finished a second sandwich, Lawton spoke again:

"What I've been leading up to is that the Comyn are the only Darkovans who are still blind to the advantages of mutual cooperation between our two cultures—with, perhaps, the exception of the Dry Towners or the bandits who infest the mountains. The Free Amazons have sent us their young women to train and employ for some three generations. In the past decade alone, we've established two medical colleges for Darkovans. We could do a lot more for this world—if the Council gave us the chance."

"A chance for Darkover to become another link in the chain of your Empire?" Marius interjected. "I do not think even the Free Amazons want that to happen, Mr. Lawton."

"Neither do I, actually." The Legate paused to see the reaction his remark had had, before continuing. "There are other alternatives, you know. Even a limited trade agreement would enrich Darkover with the best of Terra—medicine, science, an exchange of people and ideas—while protecting her from all the technocrats who'd like to remake another world in Terra's image. I am anxious to see Darkover reach a beneficial understanding with Terra. Because Darkover as you know it cannot last another twenty years."

"What do you mean?"

Lawton poured more *jaco* for himself. "There's only one force holding the Seven Domains back from the same kind of feudal anarchy that governed the Ages of Chaos; that's the Comyn. Unfortunately, they're disintegrating. Their birthrate has declined steadily for the last fifty years, and many of those who are left are succumbing to corruption and off-world decadence. Worse yet, the old telepathic gifts are being lost. Since your father went away, the Council's turned into a swarm of bickering malcontents. The next *real* crisis could finish them as a governing body. And then what will happen to Darkover?" Lawton swirled the liquid in his cup. "Would you like to see the Pan-Darkovan League take over?"

"Certainly not!" said Marius, his interest kindled, however reluctantly.

The Legate sipped *jaco*, and went on, "I can see a possible alternative to Darkover's exploitation by opportunistic businessmen from both worlds—and it involves people like you, Marius. For some time, I've been recruiting what could be called a future task force; young men and women who are the products of Terran and Darkovan environments. Terrans like your tutor, Elena, who have a little Darkovan blood and were raised on this world—and Darkovans with Terran ancestry. Even a few of your Comyn relatives, who can see beyond their own noses . . . some of them are off-world now, learning about the Empire and its government. I have others working here in Thendara; helping to rebuild Caer Donn; and some teaching our medical techniques in the Arilinn Guildhouse. When your over-bred Council chokes on its own bile and dissolves, my group will be there, to ease this world's transition from Terra's poor stepchild to her equal and ally. Eventually, Darkover will be ready to govern itself, either as a democracy or a constitutional monarchy." He looked directly at Marius. "You would be an ideal addition to this company. That's why I've had an eye kept on you. I made Elena violate her professional integrity to send me reports on your progress, both academic and emotional. I saw to it that you shared two classes with Rafe Scott." Lawton paused, then smiled. "Rafe is another of my future hopes. I wanted to see how you reacted to each other's rather unique backgrounds. . . ."

"Another controlled experiment?" There was ice in Marius's voice. "It *was* you who had me followed, then."

The Legate had the grace to look embarrassed. "Yes—and you may be right to despise me for such subterfuge. But there's an old Terran saying: *the end justifies the means.* I would happily give up my posi-

tion and everything I own to make Darkover an
active member of the interstellar community—and
that on its own terms, and not the Empire's."

Marius leaned back in his chair. If he were not a
telepath, he would have doubted the veracity of such
a statement; but he knew that Lawton was sincere
and could only wonder at the man's fervor.

"Right now," he said, "I have only one question.
Why do *you*, a Terran politician, care what could
happen to Darkover in twenty years?"

Again Lawton smiled. "Because, like you, I am a
son of both worlds. My mother is Darkovan—in fact,
she is half-sister to Lord Dyan, though he is not
quick to acknowledge the relationship. I gave my
allegiance to the Empire; but Darkover is my home."

The implications of the Legate's words dizzied Marius like strong wine. *What a vengeance this would be*, he
thought. *To aid a Terranan conspiracy, perhaps to hasten
the end of Comyn rule . . . but much as I may hate my
kinsmen, can I spy on them like a skulking bandit?*

Lawton stood up, in an attitude of dismissal. "I
can't promise that you wouldn't dirty your hands a
little as my agent—but no Darkovan could call you
traitor! You will not be paid. And I don't want an
answer from you yet. Think about what I've told
you; weigh the alternatives carefully. When you reach
a decision, you can tell the man waiting outside my
room; he's one of my key operatives, and you'll always be able to find him. Meanwhile, if you ever feel
that you're not getting a fair shake here at HQ, or if
you'd like to talk to someone older than Rafe, please
feel free to come see me."

Marius had become inured to surprising circumstances in the last half hour; otherwise he would
have been severely shocked when he left Lawton's

den. The man waiting at the door was Lerrys Ridenow.

"Hello, Marius," he said casually. "I gather that Dan's finally enlightened you as to our purposes."

"He called you one of his 'key operatives'," Marius countered. "I should have expected it, in view of your sudden interest in my welfare."

For an instant, Lerrys was somber. "You really don't trust anyone, do you? Believe it or not, my interest in you is genuine. Kennard Alton was the best of us, and I admired him. I disapprove of the way the Comyn have treated his only remaining son— it's another symptom of their degeneration. If you join Lawton's network, you can build yourself a future worth living."

Marius went reluctantly to his last two classes. The hour passed slowly, as if some malevolent godling had altered the track of time for the purpose of torturing him. He tried to listen to the instructor, but his mind remained on the interview with Lawton. Over and over again he seemed to hear the Terran's words: "The Comyn is disintegrating . . . the next real crisis could finish them." Somehow he knew the words were true. At this realization, time and space flickered and changed; he visualized a slender young man with strange white hair and familiar Comyn features blurred by tears, looking down at two babies pale and breathless in their tiny coffins.

Before he could identify the mourner, a terrible thought thrust itself ahead of all other considerations: Lawton had spoken of Rafe as one of his hopes for the future and had engineered his friendship with Marius—or claimed to have done so. Could it be that Rafe had knowingly participated in Lawton's scheme to recruit him? *Oh, gods, no!* Marius tried to negate the idea, but like the fast-falling night that gave this world its name, the thought was inescapable. All the pieces fit together neatly: Rafe's quick acceptance of him, the long hours spent together, even Rafe's fear of telepathic rapport. If Rafe had become Marius's friend on Lawton's orders, he would have concealed the fact far below the surface of his mind—he might even have been a skilled telepath and probed Marius's mind too deftly to be noticed. It was frighteningly plausible that the only one of his peers that Marius had ever called friend could have played him false from the moment they had met. He pulled himself together abruptly. *I'll see Rafe after school,* he reminded himself, *and try for a complete rapport . . . it would be impossible for him to conceal anything under the full impact of an Alton mind, impossible. And then we'll understand each other.*

At 1500 hours the last chime rang, and Marius fairly leapt from his seat. As usual, Rafe had preceded him to their meeting place and was busy throwing stones into the fountain. He smiled as Marius approached. Marius envied the other boy's ability to show emotion. He had never been able to laugh or cry with the many children living on Alton lands, or join in their horseplay when they grew older.

"How was your Life Sciences class?" asked Rafe—then his eyes widened in consternation. "Marius, what's the matter? You're upset about something."

Marius told of his meeting with Lawton and the subsequent encounter with Lerrys. Rafe gave a long whistle. "Well, that clears up the mystery of your unknown tracker."

He doesn't seem at all surprised, Marius thought dully. In a detached voice he asked, "Is that all you can say?"

"No, of course not—I'm not sorry it came as such a shock to you. Lawton's always had a bee in his helmet about a Terran-Darkovan Compact. It doesn't surprise me that he's trying to involve you in his crazy schemes. With your background you'd be a perfect agent."

"So would you," said Marius, looking directly into the other's eyes.

"What do you mean?"

He paused, hoping Rafe wouldn't notice how his hands were shaking. "Lawton spoke of you as if you were one of his group. He called you one of his future hopes." Suspicion flooded his thoughts. "And you seem familiar with his aims."

Rafe flinched and stepped back. Words froze in Marius's throat, but mentally he cried out in frustration, *I know not what to think—you have lived among these Terranan for three years, they could have changed you.*

Rafe's mind went suddenly dark, hidden behind a strong mental barrier, as if a window had been pulled shut, the shutters and storm-locks closed.

"Rafe, don't block me off!" said Marius, close to desperation. "If you could open your mind to me totally just once—we can straighten out this mess! I won't hurt you, and it might do you good." He stopped; Rafe was staring at him with a bewildered expression that quickly turned to one of furious outrage.

"How dare you!" he shouted. "You want to put me through a living hell so you can be rid of your filthy suspicions! And yet—" Rafe's voice cracked. "You've already convinced yourself I've spied on you for the Legate! No!" he shouted as Marius tried to interrupt, "Don't say any more. I think you should leave.

Maybe you'll be able to think clearly when you're back in your own environment." He turned away.

Marius grabbed his arm. "You didn't even try to deny it!"

"Take your hand off me." Rafe's chill voice was worse than anger. He turned on his heel and walked back into the HQ.

All right then! Marius snarled to himself. *So he crawls off and reports to Lawton. I should never have let myself put so much trust in him—and I never will again!*

Thunderstorms battered the city for the next four days. On the third night, Marius sat by the fireplace in the main hall of the Alton suite. He finished the last page of algebra problems and began to read his Empire Geography textbook.

A shadow darkened the page. He looked up to see Andres glowering at him. "It's getting late," the older man said. "You should go to sleep soon."

"I have fifteen more pages to read."

"Marius, there is such a thing as studying too hard. You'll ruin your eyes reading in this wretched light. Besides, you need a decent night's sleep. If you have trouble with your studies, get your Terran friend to help."

It took all of Marius's restraint to keep his face calm. The quarrel and Rafe's angry dismissal were things he had tried to keep from his thoughts—unsuccessfully, of course. Not even the anticipation of joining Lawton's network and ensuring the destruction of the Comyn could dispel the pain of losing what he had thought was a friend. *But in a few months I'll hardly remember him,* he assured himself. *I'll be living only for my chosen mission. It's better that way. People can betray you, but ideals are constant.* He stretched his legs and yawned. "Rafe has other things to do. What did the Hastur servant want?" he asked, to change the subject.

Andres kicked a burning log back into the centre of the fireplace from where it had fallen. "He brought a message that might interest you. Lord Hastur's compliments, and an invitation to the Ball on Festival Night."

"Well—that is kind of the Regent! I think I'll disappoint him and accept his invitation. The lords and ladies of the Comyn should know that I am still alive." It would also provide a perfect opportunity to inform Lerrys of his decision.

Suddenly, there was a heavy knock at the door. Andres opened it. A burly Guardsman said, "Sorry to trouble you at this hour, but there's a fellow here that wants to see Lord Marius." He indicated a slight figure in a gray cloak standing in the corridor.

"Let's see who it is, then," Andres growled. The cloaked figure entered the suite and drew back his hood.

"Rafe," said Marius coolly, inwardly cursing the whims of fate.

"I know it's late," Rafe said. "But I wanted to return this cloak you lent me—and I have to talk to you, alone." His constrained voice carried a message of urgency.

"Very well," Marius said, "I was tired of studying anyway." He dismissed the Guardsman and glanced pointedly at Andres. When the hall was empty, Rafe moved to the fireplace and warmed his drenched limbs.

"All right, so we're alone now. What can I do for you?" Marius spoke in Terran, without looking at Rafe.

"Just enough time for you to hear me out," Rafe answered in Cahuenga. "Then I'll go, if that's what you want."

"Talk, then."

Rafe took a deep breath. "It has never been easy for me to reverse a decision, once made—but that is what I've done. I don't know who has the right or wrong of this situation, but we were both too angry to think clearly . . . you've been too proud to even look at me in class, but I, too, was guilty of pride . . . when I drove you away. I realized tonight that it can't go on like this." He paused; Marius sensed the tension in him—and in himself. It broke as Rafe said, "You've been badly treated, so I guess it was easy to believe that I'd lied to you. Do whatever you have to in order to convince yourself that I truly am your friend. If a total rapport will make the difference—then—then—let's attempt it, and soon—so that neither of us will have any more doubts. You owe me that much." He stopped speaking. In the firelight Rafe looked very tired, almost at the end of his strength, and it hurt Marius to see him look that way.

Using his matrix, Marius approached the edge of Rafe's consciousness: fear and hope alternated at a high pace, and he caught the tail end of a thought: *He must believe me, he must! I can't lose him as I've lost everyone else. Oh, Bearer of Burdens, let me be strong for what we must do together!*

Marius was shaken: all his carefully constructed indifference toward Rafe melted like wax from a burning candle. He knew that Rafe was terrified of telepathic rapport—yet willing to endure it for his sake. What better proof of friendship could he ask for? He crossed the room and laid his hand on

Rafe's shoulder. "There is no need to subject you to such pain. I know your willingness. It is enough."

"No," Rafe replied, "it is *not* enough! Let's grind this stone now. This very night—if you wish it."

If it is that important to you, Marius thought. Aloud, he added, "But not now. We are both too tired. Stay here tonight, and we can try it tomorrow morning. To hell with school! Even grave-diggers are entitled to sick-leave. Besides, we might both be feeling sick after we finish."

After breakfast, Marius foraged through the supply room until he located a reserve of *kirian,* the drug used to lower resistance to telepathic contact. He measured out a safe dosage into a small vial.

Rafe awaited him, sitting cross-legged and tense on Marius's bed. He smiled faintly as he raised the vial in ironic salute and drank it all in one swallow. Moments later, his pupils dilated as the *kirian* took effect. It was time to begin.

Marius took his starstone out of its protective coverings and laid it on his open palm. His awareness sank into the stone, and he let its current carry him to Rafe. He sensed the other boy's even breathing, the steady hum of his heartbeat, the rush of blood through the arteries. They drew closer, in shared mental images: two boy-shadows embracing, lake-kestrels darting in and out of the fountain outside the HQ building. Thought-words sprouted like flowers from Rafe's awareness: *This is not so bad.*

Rafe drew in Marius's frustration, the old shame of undeserved bastardy, the peace he had left behind at Armida, his deep-rooted anger at the Comyn. *How can you live with such hatred and stay sane?* Rafe wondered.

Easily. It has become part of me.

Marius seized control again and probed deeper
into his friend's consciousness. A few glimpses of
Rafe's childhood warmed him: though both of his
parents were dead by his seventh year, Kermiac, the
old Lord of Aldaran, had been a kind foster father
to Rafe and his orphaned sisters. He had been a
happy child, known and liked by Terrans and
Darkovans alike.

Before Marius could see any more, Rafe's mind
jumped forward to his recent past, the three years in
the Terran Zone, where he'd tried to excise all traces
of his Darkovan background. Marius tried to find
the years between and encountered the familiar
resistance—a closed book, a high wall, the smell of
terror on the mind-winds. Rafe was incapable of
opening that portion of his memory.

"I do not know if I have the Alton Gift of forced
rapport, so you must help me break this deadlock.
At least, don't fight me."

Rafe relaxed in a moment of complete acquiescence. In that instant Marius focused all his telepathic power like a beam of light, piercing the barrier.
He thrust himself into that memory and felt Rafe
accept their new closeness. Then all barriers were
down. He was Rafe, living again the horror of the
dark time. . . .

They were a close-knit group at Castle Aldaran:
Rafe, Marjorie, Lew, Thyra, Bob and Beltran—united
in strong ties of kinship and love. Rafe had not even
been jealous of Lew's love for his adored sister Marjorie because Lew had treated him like a little brother.
Together, they had linked in a telepathic Circle, and
raised Sharra. *Sharra!* The ancient Forge-Goddess,

whose earthly focus was a gigantic matrix embedded in the hilt of a sword.

Soon after, Rafe collapsed in the first throes of Threshhold Sickness, and his foster father, Lord Kermiac, had died in his sleep. Rafe's wavering mind had sought his kindred, only to see the demonic force of Sharra twist them and turn them against one another—Marjorie screaming as Bob beat Lew's face with his long ringed hands. Rafe felt Lew's heart wrench and falter in hot agony as Bob pulled the matrix from about his neck.

Then two days (maybe two tendays to Rafe's sickness-blurred mind) of nightmares of Sharra's flames magnified as his burgeoning *laran* expanded his sense. Many strangers assembled at the castle, their minds in thrall to the Forge-Goddess. Waves of hatred, flowing from Sharra in a monstrous out-pouring of telepathic energy, encompassed all those gathered minds. That was when Beltran had come to Rafe, looking like a ghost, and warned him to stay in his room and feign the sickness that was already leaving him.

And then the nightmares had come true.

Hidden in his room, Rafe maintained a constant rapport with Sharra's Circle. The Goddess was at the back of every mind he touched, and he could not hide from Her. She drew him closer to Her fiery heart. While he shivered in his blanket, Sharra's flames blasted the city of Caer Donn—and the next night they loosed Her once more on the stricken city. As the terrible fire raged, Lew struck a fatal blow to Sharra, thrusting into the matrix itself. In so doing, he struck through Marjorie, who was Keeper of the Circle.

The Sharra-entity was gone, leaving only the fire,

a remnant of her fury. From a great distance, Rafe felt Marjorie's unbearable pain and merciful death. Something broke inside him, and he followed her into darkness.

Rafe awoke to a castle reeking with smoke, aswarm with Terran soldiers and Guardsmen from the Comyn lowlands. Bob and Thyra were gone, and Beltran wouldn't look him in the eye. Rafe begged the Terrans to take him away from Aldaran, and they had done so; halfway around the world to begin a new life as a child of the Terran Empire—though the demon shape of Sharra often shattered his peaceful dreams. Then he'd met a boy of his own age, whose very existence was a link to those half-buried memories: Lew's younger brother, who became his friend. . . .

"As I am still," Marius assured him, as he detached himself from the memory-experience. "Rafe—is your involvement with Sharra, and the destruction She caused, the reason why you've cut yourself off from Darkover?"

The very fiber of Rafe's being seemed to unravel. In a searing crescendo of emotion he cried out in the mental voice of a terrified child. *Darkover? I hate Darkover! Darkover perverted those I loved, Darkover destroyed my home, Darkover took Marjorie away from me! I want to get as far away from this forst d'Zandru world as I can and never come back!*

Marius felt himself drowning in Rafe's anguish, and desperately, he reached out again, opening his mind to the full impact of his friend's emotion.

We are as one—each to take a share of the pain, so to let it flow. I am the mountain, you are the stream. You will mold my surface, I will carry you. We will be as one for all eternity!

Countless years seemed to pass while their minds blended; they were transfigured in that special oneness. Briefly, an image passed between them of Marius standing in front of a full-length mirror, hands outstretched as Rafe, on the other side of the mirror, advanced until their palms touched through the cold glass. In a swift rush of clarity and self-knowledge they realized that for all their differences they had been hammered into similar molds.

I've been so afraid, these last three years, that if I came to know and love anyone, they'd be snatched away, like Marjorie—

And I, responded Marius, *never dared reach out. I've kept myself alone, thinking that if I ever let myself trust in anyone they would abandon me, like Lew and Father.*

The old loneliness, the bewilderment, surged between them.

It is all right, Marius. You can never be alone again. I am here.

Midsummer Day fell eleven days later. Rafe agreed to be Marius's guest at the Festival Ball—the annual gathering of the Comyn and the lesser nobility of the Seven Domains. In a spirit of holiday, they skipped their last class and bought pastries from a vendor in the Old City.

"It's going to be a warm night," Marius said between mouthfuls. "Are you ready to dance until dawn?"

"I left my dancing shoes at Aldaran," Rafe answered, "but I'll try to remember the steps, at least . . . don't tell me you asked me to this ball to take your place on the dance floor?" He paused, then projected his question into Marius's mind: *Just why did you invite me? I am a stranger to your lowland ways and kindred.*

The bond between them was so strong that Marius was unsure whether he answered in words or thoughts. "I've always tried to stand—or dance—on my own feet. But I know I'll need your support tonight when I face the usual Comyn derision."

That evening, in the Alton suite, Rafe watched a tailor make the final adjustments on Marius's costume. Most of the younger members of the nobility wore unusual garb on Midsummer Night. For himself, Marius had ordered the flamboyant dress uniform worn by a Commander of the Guard during the Ages of Chaos.

"Aren't you a fine figure!" Rafe exclaimed. Marius's outfit consisted of a green velvet tunic with flared sleeves and silver trim, with fur-lined boots and a full-length black cloak.

"I found it in an old book about Varzil the Good," explained Marius, once the tailor had gone. "My ancestors wore this uniform. Tonight it should serve to remind the Comyn of how much they owe the Altons."

Rafe frowned, and Marius caught his unspoken question: *Where do you think all this anger will take you to?*

Marius tensed—then relaxed. Rafe, at least, had a right to question him. "Lord Hastur, in his infinite wisdom, sent me off to the Terran Zone. No doubt he was hoping that I'd stay there, instead of lingering at Armida under Gabriel's Regency ... Hastur, Gabriel, and the other Comyn tyrants would prefer to see Kennard Alton's Terran bastard vanish into obscurity. So I'll join Lawton's operation and help prepare this world for a change in government. I'll have ample opportunity to make sure the Comyn destroys itself! When they do, I'll take what's mine— the Alton Domain. And to Zandru's coldest hell with anyone who tries to stop me!" Marius felt truly strong, filled with the purpose and the fire of his righteous anger.

Rafe dropped their contact as if it were a red-hot iron, turning his attention to the lacings on his costume. He had chosen to dress as a mountain hunter, complete with wolfskin cap.

Just then Andres appeared. "Aren't you ready yet?" he asked, with obvious impatience. "Marius, anyone would think you a nervous maiden getting dressed for her handfasting! As long as you've accepted Hastur's invitation, you'd better honor it by arriving on time!" His tone softened. "Enjoy yourselves, both of you. And Marius—be careful not to drink too much before you eat."

Marius's cheeks turned red. *Damn it if Andres isn't the only man in the world who can make me feel like a little boy again.*

"I've never seen you blush!" Rafe laughed. "I didn't think you could. You're always so well controlled." Rafe's good humor was infectious, and Marius had to laugh, too.

The professional dance troupes had begun their exhibitions when Rafe and Marius entered the huge ballroom. The first dance, an intricate carole, was succeeded by the rousing eight-man ring dance of the Kilghard Hills.

"Gods, it's been long since I saw people dance!" Rafe exclaimed as he watched the whirling forms.

"After we pay our respects to old Hastur, I'll find you someone to dance with," Marius promised as he led Rafe through the crowd.

Danvan Hastur of Hastur was an impressive figure, with snow-white hair and piercing eyes. At least, Rafe was impressed. Marius was unmoved by the old

Lord's facade of dignity and kindliness. He introduced Rafe in turn to Gabriel Lanart-Hastur, a well-
built redhead of soldierly bearing. Gabriel was quite
courteous, but his wife Javanne did not trouble to
hide her antipathy.

"Gabriel is a distant cousin of mine," Marius explained to Rafe as they headed for the buffet table.
"A telepath, and the husband of Hastur's granddaughter. When my father went away with Lew, the
Council made Gabriel Regent of the Alton Domain.
That sets up Gabriel's oldest son in an excellent
position to inherit Alton if Father dies off-world—"
He stopped, aware that his unspoken anger troubled
Rafe. "It looks like every Comyn and minor noble in
the Domains managed to get here tonight," Marius
remarked more calmly. "I'll point out a few. Those
two officers by the window, fending off all those
matrons and dowagers, see them? The handsome
redhead is Regis Hastur, the old man's grandson
and heir. The darker one's Danilo Syrtis, who was
made Regent of Ardais a couple of years ago. There's
Lerrys Ridenow talking to that little blonde girl—
Guardsmen usually wear their uniforms to this Ball,
even if they're off-duty. Look—Dyan Ardais, in full
regalia as Commander!"

Marius had no sooner mentioned Dyan's name
when the Ardais Lord made his way to the corner
where he and Rafe were standing. At his elbow, like
a house cat, stalked Felix Aillard.

"A joyous Festival to you, young Lanart," said Dyan,
raking Marius from head to toe with his oddly colorless eyes. "Or should I say, 'young Commander'?
This gathering of bluebloods is well protected indeed, with not one, but two Commanders of the
Guard!"

Marius relaxed, somehow enjoying Dyan's verbal fencing, although the mountain lord was known for making people uncomfortable. Rafe's thought echoed in his own mind: *He's sizing us up as if trying to decide which is the prize stallion!*

Marius said politely, "Lord Ardais, may I present my friend Rakhal? He is a far kinsman of mine, from Aldaran."

Dyan bowed gracefully, but Felix chose that moment to speak. "Sir, he is lying! This fellow is a Terran from the Trade City."

"Consider your words carefully when you accuse an Alton of lying," said Marius. "I have spoken the truth and will happily repeat it before any Tower-trained telepath."

"You can hardly call yourself an Alton," Felix began, his face bright with anger and wine.

Dyan cut him off with an abrupt gesture. "Felix, you need a bridle on your mouth." Before Felix could say another word, Dyan cuffed him on the cheek, very gently. "My throat is quite parched. Fetch me a glass of white wine." After Felix skulked away, Dyan turned to Marius. "It's been a long time since I've seen you, kinsman. You've grown well. Have you had news of your father . . . ?"

Sadistic bastard, Marius heard Rafe think, and answered, "No, I have not."

For an instant, there was honest regret behind Dyan's falcon gaze. "A pity. The depths of space are deep, the gulfs between the worlds immeasurable." This last was a recent addition to Darkovan folk sayings. "Enjoy yourselves, lads," he added, dismissing them.

The first dance was a sedate pavane. Lord Hastur opened the measure, choosing as his partner a fragile, dark-haired woman in the crimson draperies of a Keeper.

"That's my cousin, Callina," Marius informed Rafe. "She's Keeper at Arilinn Tower and Lady of the Aillard Domain." A welcome thought struck him. "Callina's younger sister Linnell was fostered at Armida. She grew up with me. When my father left, the Council gave her into Callina's charge. Maybe she's here tonight."

Marius helped himself to sarm-nuts and melon balls from the buffet. After seeing that Rafe's plate was filled, he continued to identify those of the dancers whom he recognized. Unfortunately, none of the young girls were familiar to him—and no maiden of the Domains would dance with a total stranger, even on Festival Night. Even if he identified himself, they would presume that a young man of his caste who was not in the Guards must have some grave defect. *Damn the Comyn's collective eyes!* Marius swore for the hundredth time at least.

All around them, he saw Guardsmen and Cadets bowing to young women and leading them onto the dance floor. For himself, he did not care; he was used to being outcast among the Comyn. But he wanted Rafe to have a good time, to drink and dance as a Darkovan. Although their mental barriers were raised in the telepath's reflex against large crowds, Marius felt Rafe's sympathetic reaction. He abhorred pity, but his friend's emotion warmed him like an added cloak.

"Don't worry about being a proper host," Rafe assured him, "I could hardly enjoy myself more." He laughed. "Between the food, the music, and the dancing, I'm like a child at Carnival! There's so much to do I don't know where to go next." Suddenly he froze. "Marius, look over there, in the corner by the curtains. No, not right now, do it casually! That woman in the white dress has her eye on us."

With due caution, Marius looked across the long table. A tall, auburn-haired woman was indeed watching him and Rafe with more than idle curiosity. "I told you that you look like a different man in that get-up," Rafe joked. "These lowland women seem to like men in uniform. Let's go over and talk to her."

"Rafe, she's at least ten years older than us! She probably has a jealous husband who'd call us out just for looking at her—or even thinking about her!"

"Still, we could greet her and wish her a joyous Festival. There's no harm in that. Besides, I can claim immunity, being *chaireth* and ignorant of valley customs. And no one can call *you* out, you don't come of age for another three tendays."

Just then a feminine voice called, "Marius!" and a slender girl in the traditional green gown of Midsummer approached them from the other side of the ballroom.

"Our luck is changing," said Rafe appreciatively. "I'll go bring us some wine."

The girl's skipping tread was familiar, but Marius did not recognize her until she had reached his side and taken off her mask. Then his heart leaped. Reddish brown hair, large blue eyes, hesitant smile on a heart-shaped face—*Linnell!* He took her by the shoulders and kissed her on both cheeks.

"Lord Hastur told Callina you were here," she said breathlessly, "so I couldn't sit still until I'd found you." She ruffled his hair and smiled. "You're a head taller! I can't believe it, you're nearly a man now." In a lowered voice, she murmured, "I heard about the Council's refusing you admission into the

Cadets. That was shameful! But tell me, what have you heard from Father and Lew?"

"Nothing," he answerd; then forced some cheer into his voice. "Andres says it's very difficult to send messages through space."

Linnell's face was wistful, the way it had been the day Lew had left Armida to join the Tower Circle at Arilinn nearly seven years ago. Memories of carefree days spent romping through Armida's pastures with Lew and Linnell made him seek her hand and hold it.

"I wish those days were back again," she echoed his thoughts in a small, little-girl voice. "I wish Lew and Father would come back, so we could all go home together. . . ."

"*Chiya,* so do I—I cannot say how much. But the world will go as it will, not as you or I would have it," he said, firmly closing the door on those sunlit hours of childhood. "I did not know you have *laran,*" he went on, releasing her hand.

"It was a long time in coming. I had Threshhold Sickness after Mid-winter, so I was packed off to Arilinn. I've been there ever since. I don't have anything near Callina's power, though. Just enough empathy to make a good psi monitor."

Marius grinned. "In one respect you haven't changed at all, Linna. You're still overly modest."

Rafe returned, with two glasses of white wine and a broad smile when he saw Linnell. "Sister," said Marius, his fingertips poised on the girl's shoulder, "this is my friend Rakhal. Rafe, may I present my foster sister, Linell Lindir-Aillard?"

"*S' dia shaya, Damisela,*" Rafe replied, bowing low. The unseen orchestra chose that moment to begin a new dance. Rafe looked quickly at Marius, took a noticeable breath, and asked, "*Damisela*—will you further honor me with this dance?" Linnell assented with a gracious smile.

Rafe was a good dancer, despite his lack of practice; more than one envious head turned to watch as he led Linnell through the intricate steps. Marius was the only one to know how nervous his friend felt each time he encountered Linnell's deep blue eyes. *Too bad Linnell's already betrothed*, Marius thought. *Rafe couldn't find a sweeter girl in all the Seven Domains!*

"Excuse me, young sir." A female voice cut into his reverie. "Have you seen Lady Aillard?" Marius raised an eyebrow in polite surprise. His questioner was the woman in white, whose attention Rafe had remarked earlier. Although obviously twice his age, she was easily the most beautiful woman he had ever seen.

"Lady Callina was dancing with Lord Hastur," he answered, "but I don't see her on the floor now. May I offer my services in her stead?"

The woman's smile was mechanical. "Thank you. I wanted to wish her a joyous Festival before I left."

Marius felt pain, like a throbbing wound, in the woman's mind; in a curious telepathic overlay, he heard a fragment of her thought: *A year ago this very night ... it happened while I was here, dancing. . . .* Then her mind closed in one incisive stroke.

"Forgive me," she said softly, her face suddenly pale. "I had no right to expose you to my private grief. I am a disgrace to my Tower, to let my barriers slip like that." She turned, as if to leave.

"Lady, you need not go," said Marius. "I am a telepath, though not Tower-trained. I can't help picking up random thoughts sometimes. And in a crowd this size, it's not easy to keep myself completely barricaded. It was more likely my fault than yours."

After a moment, she smiled again. "You are kind
... were you not here on Festival Night last year?"

"No, this is my first—" Marius cursed himself.
Now she would know how young he was!

"I'd have thought you were older," she said, esti-
mating his appearance in one sweep of her long
eyelashes. To cover his sudden discomfort, Marius
bowed and introduced himself. He was relieved when
she evinced neither shock nor disdain. "I knew your
brother," she said, "when he was at Arilinn. Our
minds touched often in the relays. I am Coryssa
Aillard, psi monitor at Dalereuth Tower."

Marius summoned all this courage and asked, "Now
that we know each other, do you think we might
dance?" He was aware of the surprised glances of
nearby Guardsmen as Coryssa took his proffered
arm, and rejoiced inwardly. *Let those toy soldiers gape!
The best-looking woman at this Ball is dancing with ME!*

The music started. Marius and Coryssa took their
place on the floor. All around them were similar
couples—flushed faces, sparkling eyes, flaring cloaks,
the women's gowns rustling as they brushed the
floor. Marius was acutely conscious of Coryssa's body,
of his own, and the joyous rhythm that swept them
onward. In an easy mental motion, he reached for
Rafe, and found his own excitement reflected in his
friend's mind.

The pipes sounded a last flourish. Reluctantly,
Marius took his hands from his partner's waist.
Coryssa's hand tightened in a fist on Marius's shoulder, and he caught the direction of her troubled
gaze: Felix Aillard was watching them from a corner—
but not merely watching, staring. There was something very ugly in the set of his mouth.

"It's too warm here," Coryssa said. "I'm going to

sit down by that open window near the archway. Could you bring me a glass of *shallan*?" Before Marius could say a word, she had gone. It was clear that Felix's insolent stare had upset her. He looked around the room for Rafe and was relieved to see him chatting with Linnell and two other young girls.

Coryssa sat on the window bench, waving a fan across her face. She smiled brightly when Marius presented her the glass. "Please sit down," she said. "It's been years since I've spent more than a few days in Thendara. Dalereuth is so far south that we wait for months to hear the news that doesn't come through the relays. Tell me, is it true that the Council has managed to keep peace with the Terrans for a whole year, with no incidents?"

Marius launched into an explanation of the present boundaries between Old Thendara and the Terran Trade City. Coryssa's green eyes seemed to glow as he talked, which made it difficult to speak clearly. Rafe's sudden appearance was a welcome relief. After introducing himself, Rafe extended a plate of sweets to Coryssa.

"Do you want to make me fat?" she asked mockingly.

"*Vai Domna*, there is small chance of that!" Rafe reassured her. She laughed and reached for the plate.

"Well, isn't this a pretty picture!" a harsh voice interrupted. Felix Aillard was standing somewhat unsteadily above them.

Marius rose, but Coryssa spoke first. "It is, and you can be a part of it, Felix," she said gently, offering him the plate. Felix struck it from her hand and it crashed on the floor. Marius put one hand on his dagger, but Coryssa motioned him to restraint.

Let her try to deal with him, came Rafe's thought. *Evidently she knows the boor. And there is something here that we do not know.*

"That was bravely done, Felix," Coryssa said coolly. "I suggest you take a walk outside, until you're sober enough to stand up straight. Unless you'd rather disgrace your uniform by passing out in full view of the Hasturs!"

"So you think I'm a disgrace to my uniform?" Unlike most drunks, Felix did not slur his words in the slightest. "Fine words, Lady. You don't wear a uniform, so no one can call you out, or give you demerits. But *your* conduct is a disgrace to your womanhood!"

"You have not the right to talk to me that way." Coryssa's voice was calm, but Marius saw her hands tremble, even as she clenched them in her lap. "I am a grown woman, with no husband, responsible only to my Tower and to myself."

"Tell me who has a better right than I! Do you realize the spectacle you're providing for the Comyn tonight? Talking, laughing, *dancing* with these—" He pointed at Rafe and Marius. "These *Terranan!* Members of the same race that killed your son! By Zandru, have you no shame?"

Marius remembered what Lerrys had told him about Felix's older brother; killed by a Terran on Midsummer Night. Then Coryssa must be Felix's mother! That would explain her distress at the memory of Festival Night a year ago.

"Felix, speak your grievance to me alone," Coryssa was saying, "not in public, and without involving Dom Marius, whose only crime was to befriend me."

Felix turned to face Marius. If looks could inflict harm, then Marius would have been a dead man twice over. "You," Felix grated. "You filthy Terran interloper! How dare you even speak to my mother!"

"Control yourself!" Coryssa interjected. "You're the

one making the spectacle now." But she might have been a statue for all the notice Felix took of her; the focus of his wine-muddled grief and anger had shifted from his mother to Marius.

"Everyone tells me to be quiet—to leave well enough alone!" Felix went on, "Well, I'm tired of it. I am fifteen and a man, by the laws of the Domains. And by that law I call challenge upon you, Marius Montray-Lanart!"

"And I refuse," answered Marius. "You are too drunk to think clearly. Your allegations are ridiculous—as usual. Such wild talk only embarrasses you and your mother. And she does not deserve such treatment. If you still wish to fight me when you are sober . . . then you're a bigger fool than I thought, and I will be happy to teach you a lesson."

Felix tensed like an *oudrakhi* about to charge. "Trying to get out of it, aren't you! Trust a *Terranan* to evade responsibility!" Marius could hear him thinking, as loudly as if he'd screamed it. *Like those animals who shot Geremy!*

Aloud, Felix shrilled, "You'll face me now whether you wish to or not!" He launched himself at Marius, a long dagger shining in his hand.

Marius began to reach for his own weapon, then stopped, as a wall of sudden darkness crashed down upon him. Time itself seemed to stop. Marius saw himself in a thick forest, surrounded by moving forms. Pain in his leg, he dropped to his knee. A furred non-human towered above him, a long knife in its upraised hands. There was death on that blade. His death? He tried to dodge, but the terror of death paralyzed him and he could not move. Then a body thrust in front of him, shielding him from that inevitable stroke. He was safe . . . someone screamed, and he could see again.

Felix was standing quite still, and the dagger was not in his hand. Rafe, standing directly in front of Marius, with his back to him, turned suddenly, and Marius saw where the dagger had gone. He caught Rafe as he staggered and eased him to the ground. *When that premonition, or whatever it was, gripped me and I couldn't move, Rafe must have pushed himself in front of me.* But had it been a premonition? No. *He would not die by a knife.* He *knew* that and shuddered, blaming himself for that crucial moment of inaction.

Looking up, he saw Rafe's assailant still standing. He felt the salt of tears burning to be shed, but another emotion consumed him entirely, and he heard glasses crack and break all over the ballroom. Felix fell without a sound.

Then a mental call that was more like a sob reached him: *Marius, stop it. Please, stop it!* There was no mistaking that voice. Rafe was alive!

Marius squeezed his friend's hand gently, then turned his attention to the crowd of people surging toward them. He held up his other hand and they stopped. His demonstration of the telekinetic Alton anger had served to enforce obedience. Fighting to keep his voice level, Marius said, "No one comes any closer. No one."

Regis Hastur stepped to the front. "This should not have happened." His barriers were down, revealing sincere regret. "But please, let us help him."

"You Comyn have helped him enough already!" Marius retorted. At this point, he did not want any fair-faced Hastur within arm's length of him. *Wasn't it enough for you Comyn to cast me out? Now you've struck down the only friend I ever had!*

At Regis's side, Danilo Syrtis winced as if he'd been hit; Lerrys's face went bone-white. Oblivious to their empathy, Marius spoke again. "What I need now is a horse and a litter made ready, and a message sent ahead to Terran Medical."

Dyan Ardais knelt by Felix's prone body. "The fool's all right," he said a moment later. "Just a sore head—luckily. I'll take him back to barracks." He lifted Felix in his arms and strode from the ballroom.

"Let me through, *Com'ii*." The crowd parted as Callina Aillard passed through their midst. "Marius," she said quietly, "your friend is bleeding. If you move him, he could die. I am a Keeper. Let me see what can be done for him here."

Marius looked at Rafe. His face was gray, twisted in pain; the red stain below the heart was spreading. Unable to speak, Marius nodded.

Callina and Coryssa pulled off Rafe's heavy shirt and monitored the wound intently, while Danilo Syrtis dispersed the onlookers.

"It's not good," Coryssa said at last. "The blade struck between the ribs, into the lungs . . . there's some internal bleeding."

"Can it be stopped?" asked Marius, feeling helpless. Rafe's hand stirred in his as he regained consciousness.

"I think so," Callina answered. "That is, if we can get through to the damaged lung. Lord Regis—see that we are not disturbed!"

Rafe jerked his head up suddenly, and saw the blue matrix stones bare in the women's palms. "No!" he gasped. "Keep those demon's tools away from me!" He struggled, until Marius touched his forehead.

"Lie still!" he commanded. "I know you're afraid of starstone craft, but you were able to sustain rapport with me. If I link my mind to theirs, will you let the Keeper and Coryssa stop the bleeding? You know I won't let anyone harm you, *Brédu*."

Rafe sighed, like a tired child, and gave his mental consent.

Have you the strength for this undertaking? Callina's thoughts dropped into Marius's mind like stones falling into a pond. *The Circle at Neskaya said your laran was minimal.*

Neskaya was wrong! Marius retorted. *They didn't look for anything more in a "Terranan half-caste"—they didn't even have a Keeper. But you are one. Probe my mind if that will convince you, but hurry! My friend could be dying. . . ."*

Callina withdrew, and concentrated on her matrix. "Coryssa, you will monitor me; and Marius, you will follow us in."

Marius sensed the women's downward mental motion: Callina in a straight dive, Coryssa cometlike with a fiery trail. Then Callina extended her reach to include Coryssa and Marius. It was as if they formed an edifice—roof, pillars, floor—Callina pulled them into Rafe's consciousness. The boy's entire being seemed to erupt in fear of the alien minds, a fear that threatened to shake Callina's precarious hold.

Easy, Rafe, Marius soothed. *Be calm, there will be no pain.* He slid into an intermediary position between Rafe's awareness and that of the women.

The Keeper's touch was skillful as she fastened on the ruined tissues. The crucial cells, the very walls of the lung, were torn and bleeding. Marius controlled his initial panic; felt Coryssa steady him.

Callina began the difficult task of closing the severed vessels. Rafe's heart did not falter, so delicate was the force she exerted. Then Rafe lapsed into unconscious peace. Marius focused all his psychic power through Coryssa into Callina's mind. A mental image flashed: three hands linked around a broken string. Blue matrix-light flared on those torn fibers, and Marius became a weightless shell, raw power flowing through him . . . all at once, the rush of blood was stemmed, the vessels whole, as if they'd never been cut, and Callina was bringing them up, out of the tangled cellular jungle.

Marius paused, to verify Rafe's easy breathing—but his own equilibrium was shaky at best. He felt Coryssa's presence beside him. "Come on," she encouraged. "I've steadied your heartbeat, lean on me the rest of the way. Don't be silly—you haven't failed. You're only a novice at matrix work, and this operation is strenuous enough to tire a Keeper like Callina."

There was a swift sensation—almost of flying—and Marius was flung back to the physical reality of his own body. But something was wrong because the walls of the room were blurred. He tried to see where Rafe was, but he could not raise his head. Unrecognizable voices boomed in his ears: "He's exhausted himself. . . . We'd never have managed it without him, the Terran lad had such strong barriers. . . ."

Someone slipped an arm under Marius's shoulders and helped him to walk. "Where's Rafe?" he asked, hardly hearing his own voice. Then his grip on reality was lost in an oncoming tide of darkness.

A foul-tasting liquid burned his throat, and he awoke. He was lying on his bed in the Alton rooms. Andres was looking down at him concernedly. "Captain Ridenow brought you here," he said. "White as a lost soul, you were. But a snack and a good night's sleep should put you to rights."

Marius put his hand to his head, remembering.

He jumped up in bed. "Where is Rafe? I must go to him!"

Andres's iron hand pushed him back. "Your friend's sleeping soundly in the Aillard rooms. Lady Coryssa's watching over him. Tomorrow he should be strong enough to be removed to Terran Medical."

Marius lay back docilely, letting Andres feed him honeyed fruits from a tray. The sweet juice was cool and it cleansed his mouth of the heavy aftertaste of sickness. He felt his strength returning. The memory of Felix's hate-crazed face would not leave him; and he thanked all the gods he knew that Rafe was alive and out of danger.

"I've got to get some air," he said, sitting up.

Andres frowned, and Marius saw, as if for the first time, the older man's great strength. Andres extended his hand as if to push him back again; instead, he rested it on Marius's shoulder. "All right, Mario, if it's what you need. But don't go too far. You've had enough excitement for one night."

It had been years since anyone had called Marius by that nickname. He clasped Andres's hand briefly and left the room.

A soft breeze stirred the banners that emblazoned the parapets of the castle. Far below, the entire city was bathed in the light of the four moons; but Marius took no solace from the beauty of the scene. He felt empty, drained. Ever since he had left Armida on that far-gone day in late spring, his emotions had been centered on one goal. First there had been the hope of becoming a Cadet; then the raging desire for retribution against the Comyn for their many rejections of him. Now, that fierce hatred that he had fed like a sacred fire was gone from him.

I cannot have forgotten, he mused in bewilderment.

*For so many sleepless nights I have thought of nothing but
my rightful vengeance against those who cast me out. The
shock of Rafe's near-death must have unsettled me.*

Yet he knew that was not the answer. Try as he
would to rekindle the fires of rage, it seemed that a
gulf of many years stretched between this moment
and the time when he had longed to kill every Comyn
who came in sight. Was it only minutes that had
passed since he had struck down Felix?

*Why is it that I don't even hate him any more—that
arrogant bastard who nearly killed Rafe? Can emotion be
like a coin; and when I vented my anger on Felix, I spent
all that I had? Aldones, Lord of Light, God of my fathers,
what have I lost? I do not know what to do now, or what I
shall become. . . .*

An hour went by as Marius paced back and forth.
There was no answer to his dilemma, no matter how
many times he reviewed the events of the summer.
He felt as lonely as he had during those first days in
the Terran Zone. No, that was not completely true.
He had Rafe as his friend. The East Tower bell
tolled midnight. Marius yawned and realized how
tired he was.

At that moment a cloaked figure stepped out of
the shadows. A patch of moonlight illuminated the
blond head of Felix Aillard. Marius felt like laughing, as if he were watching a comic performance.

"Well, Felix," he said mildly. "You pop up again,
blocking my way as usual. What are you here for this
time?"

Abruptly Felix dropped to his knees and extended
a dagger, hilt forward. Absent-mindedly Marius took
it—then nearly dropped it when he discerned the
dark stains on the blade.

"Yes," Felix said. "It is marked with the life-blood

of your friend. I give it to you and beg your pardon
for a blow wrongfully struck. And if you will, take
his blood back with my own. It is your just right—
and my just doom." So saying, Felix loosened his
cloak and bowed his head.

This can't be happening! thought Marius, stunned.
*After weeks of baiting me and stabbing Rafe in a fit of
drunken rage, Felix kneels here calmly asking me to kill
him! In another minute Danvan Hastur will appear and
make me Commander of the Guards, and I'll know this is a
dream. . . .*

Then he remembered having heard his father tell
of an ancient Comyn ritual: if a man killed another
man by treachery, or a woman or child, and his
victim had no adult male relative to avenge him,
then the murderer could be obligated to offer the
dead one's kindred or friends a chance to kill him
with the very weapon he had used unjustly. The rite
was no longer in use, except in some parts of the
Kilghard Hills—and Valeron. Exasperated, Marius
thought, *Doesn't the fool know that Rafe is alive?*

Felix must have had *laran*; he raised his head and
answered, "I know that he lives. But if my mother
and Lady Callina had not been there, he would likely
have died. And my challenge on you was not valid.
You are still a minor by Comyn law. And your
friend—"

"Did your mother put you up to this?" Marius cut
in.

"No!" The old arrogance surged in Felix's voice.
"You're a telepath, damn it! Listen to my words and
judge the truth behind them." He drew a breath that
was more like a sob. "Your friend was unarmed, had
no weapon at all. When he fell, and you rushed to
his side, I wanted to run. But I couldn't. I watched

the two of you, and it was like reliving Midsummer Night last year. . . ." The sudden pain in Felix's mind made Marius want to cry out, it was so intense. Felix struggled to keep his voice from breaking. "When I knelt by my brother, and he dying from a coward's weapon—in the barracks, I saw what I had done. I am lower than the cursed *Terranan* who shot Geremy. At least he did not shoot out of mindless anger but from fear alone!" Felix's eyes brimmed with tears.

He said no more—but Marius heard his thoughts only too clearly: *For years I thought myself virtuous and damned my mother for the shame her wildness brought upon me and our house . . . what I did tonight was far worse a crime; nearly killing an innocent stranger. I was like a madman, striking at shadows. . . .*

At last Felix spoke again. "If you take my life now, I can redeem some shred of honor."

Marius closed his eyes, putting the other boy's torment out of his mind. He placed his hands on Felix's shoulders in the traditional stance of lord to paxman. "I will not take your life, Felix. I give it back to you, as a penance." Felix raised his head, obviously surprised. Marius continued, "Nor will I call challenge upon you. Now get up. Here is your dagger."

"But—you were furious," Felix said. "The way you attacked me—"

"I *was* furious, yes. But there are more important things to think about. For one thing, my friend is alive." He smiled grimly. "Besides, I think you'll punish yourself much more than I could."

Watching Felix depart, Marius pondered the sudden change that Festival Night had wrought in their lives. *Felix spent all his anger tonight, as I did. Though I can't say that he was as justified in his hatred as I was in mine, perhaps there was some kinship. . . .*

The steps he had taken merged in a clear pattern. He remembered the strange comfort he had derived from his vows of vengeance; how noble they had made him feel. *It was easy to be angry,* he mused. *Much easier than confronting the circumstances that motivated that anger. But my hatred didn't improve my position.*

He shivered as he thought of what he had shared with Rafe—the frightening visions of Sharra's fire. *In my self-satisfaction I was as blind as Felix. Rafe tried o show me, through our rapport, just how dangerous the power of hatred can be—and he nearly died before I was rid of the delusion that I was an avenging god. Even then, if he had not stopped me, I might have killed Felix.* Marius understood, then, why his father had always warned him about unleashing his Alton anger. If Rafe had died, he would have lashed out at the assembled Comyn like a mad dog, blaming them for Felix's misdeed.

Anger had ceased to consume his soul; but he felt too much bitterness to spend another year moping at Armida. Oddly enough, he felt some pity for the Comyn. Their ranks were already diminishing, and they were losing their hold on the world they had ruled for centuries. *No wonder they despise me. My Terran blood, even my brown Terran eyes, are constant reminders that they will be supplanted by men from other worlds. Still, they need not be supplanted, if they could learn to cooperate a little. There are many Comyn traditions worth preserving.* . . . He thought of the matrix operation that had probably saved Rafe's life. For all the Terrans's vaunted science, there was nothing on all their worlds that could match the potential of Darkover's matrix technology.

Thankfully, Marius realized that he had found the direction he had sought. He would continue to press his claim on Armida, to hold the Alton Domain for Lew. He knew, with the certainty of his *laran*, that Lew would return one day.

And when he came of age next month, Marius would tell Lerrys that he had chosen to join Dan Lawton's network. *But not out of anger*, he assured himself. *Or at least, not because of any hunger for vengeance. Lawton was right—Darkover and Terra have a lot to give each other. And this way I can be a part of that sharing.*

He laughed aloud, feeling that an unbearable weight had fallen from his shoulders. Then he reached with his mind into the night-covered castle, until he had located Rafe's peaceful, unconscious rhythm. *Sleep well, my brother*, Marius called. *When you are strong again, I will open my mind and show you what I have learned.*

Bride Price

by Marion Zimmer Bradley

Around her the chapel of Comyn Castle was silent; empty save for herself and the painted figures of Camilla, Hastur, and Cassilda on the walls, painted in the old style; Camilla with her arms filled with fruits of summer, Cassilda with starflowers in her hands, Hastur silent and motionless before the women; as unresponsive as Gabriel before her on his bier. The body was covered with heavy velvet draperies in the Aillard colors, gray and crimson, and Rohana, dry-eyed, could only remember the filmy draperies in the same colors, laid out on her narrow bed on the morning of their wedding.

"It looks like a Keeper's funeral," she quipped. "All that for a wedding? And for me?"

"Rohana," her mother said solemnly, "It is a good marriage. I cannot understand you; your sisters, if they had been given to the Head of a Domain, would have been beside themselves with delight. Yet you act as if all this had nothing to do with you. One would think—" Lady Liane stopped, and Rohana knew that her mother had been on the point of asking a question to which she really did not want to know the answer. *One would think you had really wanted to stay in the Dalereuth Tower for the rest of your life.* But that could have been arranged, after all. Instead Lady Liane asked, "Is Gabriel Ardais not to your liking, you ungrateful girl?"

"How could he possibly not be to her liking?" asked Dame Sarita, who had nursed all three of the Aillard daughters and had been present at both previous marriages. "He is so tall and handsome, strong, well-spoken—"

"What a pity that you cannot marry him, Nurse, if he is so much to your liking," Rohana said, but her heart was not really in the teasing.

"No, but really," said her mother, frowning a little, "I swore no daughter of mine would ever be forced unwilling to her bride-bed, and if you dislike Gabriel, you had only to say so before things had gone this far."

Rohana sighed, taking pity on the dismay in her mother's face. "No, no, it is not that I dislike Gabriel; he is certainly no worse than any other who has been offered to me. But you can hardly blame me for thinking that this day is for the pleasure of my kin, and not for mine, or even for Gabriel's. Every day since the handfasting it has been drummed into me early and late—how rare it is to unite two of the greatest Houses in the Domains, to join hands, Ardais Heir to Aillard daughter, till the wedding sounds more like a stock-breeding fair than a bridal." She looked down into the courtyard where smoke was rising from the pit where two great beasts were being roasted in the coals; the smell was savory and good but somehow it sickened her. "I am only surprised

you do not have rope-dancers and jugglers and the
three-legged man from Candermay to divert the
crowds while they await the main event; or are you
planning to return to the customs of the Ages of
Chaos, when the bride and groom gave the star
performance and the crowds stood around to cheer
them on?"

"Rodi, for shame!" Dame Sarita reproved, blushing.

"Well, it is not my pleasure being done, nor Gabriel's," Rohana said. "Somebody should get some amusement out of it, after all. It is Aillard being married to
Ardais, not Rohana to Gabriel. I have learned my
part as well as any lyric performer on any stage in
Thendara, and I dare say I will do it as well but
without the applause."

"Silly girl," reproved the nurse, "every woman on
her bridal day is a queen."

"Oh, yes, said Rohana, "a bride is allowed to queen
it for a day." She stood in her light shift, her coppery
hair falling loose and straight to her waist, looking
with level brows raised, at the finery spread on her
bed. "In the hope that a day's queenship will help
her forget that from that day she is forever subject
to some man and has given up even her own name."

"But Rohana, that is not so," said Lady Liane. "Do
you truly believe I am only subject to your father?"

"No, mother, but you are Aillard, and you married a man you knew your inferior; and my father
knew from his wedding day that his bride was also
his Lady to be served and obeyed. I wed with a
Comyn Lord from Ardais, where they reckon even
inheritance in the man's line; his wife will not be his
superior or even his equal. I have no heart to enforce my will by strife, Mother, and so—" she

shrugged, "I doubt I will enforce it at all." She let herself drop into a chair.

"Come, my babe, don't be dismal," said Dame Sarita, chucking her under the chin. "A day will come when you will remember this as the happiest day of your life."

"Does that mean that all days after this will be less happy?" asked Rohana with a sigh.

"By no means, child; I know days like this are a strain, but this will soon be over, and then you will know all the delights that are in store for a bride. I remember my own dear good man—" she began reminiscently, but Lady Liane interrupted her.

'Sarita, the child's hardly breakfasted. Go down to the pantry and find something tasty, a mug of soup, you know what she will like best," she said, and when the nurse went away, Lady Liane drew Rohana against her stroking her hair.

"Child, I can't bear to see you so wretched," she said. "I truly thought that you liked Gabriel."

"And so I do, Mother; I like him as well as I could like any man I have seen only once for an hour or so."

Oddly, the Lady blushed. She said in a stifled voice, "Daughter, do you know how much custom was violated for that much; I had to explain to Lord Ardais that you were a *leronis* and accustomed to much freedom; I dare say he thought you immodest for asking actually to meet your promised husband."

"Or is it only that you are shy of being the center of attention? It is true that in the Tower you did not learn to live with all eyes on you as a Comynara must. Or perhaps— Rodi, is it your woman's time? If so, I shall ask your father to have a word in private with Gabriel, and make him understand that he should let you alone for a day or so—"

Rohana grimaced. "Nurse is already ahead of you, Mother; for half the last cycle she has been dosing me with her midwife's messes to prevent that very thing."

Lady Liane smiled and for the first time in her entire life Rohana felt that her mother spoke to her as an equal.

"I could wish my mother or nurse had shown that much foresight; but in those days no one would have spoken to a young maiden of such things. Though I must say that when I had courage to speak, your father was most kind and understanding."

It was hard to think of her stately mother and father as an embarrassed young bride and a considerate young bridegroom. "How old were you then, Mother?"

"Fifteen," said Lady Liane, "Sabrina was born before I completed my sixteenth year; I was so pleased that my first child was a daughter for Aillard; your father was sorely disappointed, but he was kind and brought me flowers. And Sabrina had two children before she was your age. And your sister Marelie also wished to marry young; too young, I thought, which was why I asked that she should spend a year first in Dalereuth Tower before you. But she had no talent for *laran*. This was why I was proud when you displayed that talent; and Lord Ardais, too, is pleased, since it seems Gabriel has but little of it. If you wished to spend your life in a Tower, Rohana, you had only to say so."

Rohana had had a private wager with herself that her mother would say exactly this, and in these words;

but the heart had gone out of the game. She sighed and shook her head.

"No, " she said, "I have not the gift. Of our group it was Leonie who had it; and Melora." She swallowed and covered her face with her hands. Her eyes filled with tears.

"Melora," she said, weeping. "From the time we were little girls, we promised one another that whichever of us married first, the other would be her bride-woman. Why will no one tell me what has happened to Melora, Mother? Is she dead? Did she elope with a groom, or a stable-sweeper, or a charcoal-burner?"

Lady Liane sighed and shook her head. "No, my love; we would have told you that, that you might avoid such a catastrophic choice. You are now old enough to know; she was taken by Dry Town bandits, and those who went to seek her vanished and were never heard from again. We hope she is dead."

Rohana flinched with dread, and her mother embraced her and stroked her hair. At that moment it almost seemed possible to pour out all her fears and questions; but Sarita came back into the room with a tray of food and the opportunity was gone, perhaps forever.

"You must eat well," she urged, "for you'll get but little in your bridal dress. I brought you a mug of soup with noodles, and a slice of roast rainbird, and blackfruit cakes; look, love, have you seen the *catenas*?" She held up the beautifully filigreed copper marriage bracelets.

Lady Liane rose, kissed Rohana carefully on the brow, and the moment's intimacy was gone. She said, "I will see you when you are dressed, my dear," and withdrew.

Dressed like an exquisite doll in the Ardais colors, Rohana moved through the lengthy ceremonies; the bracelets were locked on her wrists, she exchanged a ritual kiss with Gabriel; his lips, too, seemed cold as ice. He made over to her the keys of his Great House, and introduced her to his paxmen; she accepted the ritual kiss on her hand from each of them. Through all this he was as remote and withdrawn as she was herself; had they forced this marriage on him? And yet he was not indifferent to her; now and again she would notice his eyes fixed on her.

Rohana knew that she was beautiful; young as she was, men had desired her. She had learned to seem indifferent to it; in the Tower, where she could not possibly be unaware of it, she had learned to shut it out; now there would be no way to remove herself from it. She knew that was what marriage was all about, and felt a certain fastidious distaste for the whole thing. Well, she would do what was expected of her, no one could ask for more. But the intensity in Gabriel's eyes frightened her.

By the time they were led to the bedding, she was really afraid. She knew that the country jokes, the roughhousing, were only traditional; the girls expected her to giggle and struggle, perhaps to cry and be ashamed. Well, they should not have any fun from her; she remained perfectly composed, smiling faintly at the worst of the jokes, lifting her brows a little when they were too vulgar. The witnesses had been prepared to keep it up for hours, but Rohana's cool withdrawn face made it seem pointless; one by one the songs and laughter died away and they were left alone.

Gabriel turned to her and said, "I have never seen

so young a bride so composed; where did you learn that, my Lady?"

"You know I was a *leronis* in Dalereuth; the first thing we are taught is self-command, under circumstances far more trying than this. I did not want them to treat me like a freak at Festival Fair."

He said, "By your leave, my Lady?" got out of bed and threw the bolt of the door. Returning, he came and sat on the edge of her bed. He was not quite so tall as she thought, but stockier and more broadshouldered; his face was pale and through her own nervousness she thought, seeing beads of sweat falling and rolling from the crisp red curls at his hairline, *why, he is nervous, too,* and for the first time she thought of this unknown young man, not as an unknown conspirator in this unwanted bridal, but a victim like herself. She held out her hands to him.

"Talk to me a little, Gabriel. I know so little about you . . . it seems strange that by custom a husband and wife should meet as strangers. I do not even know how old you are."

"I shall be twenty-six at spring sowing," he said. "I know my father told yours that I was twenty-three because he was afraid they would think me too old for you; but I want to be honest with you, Rohana." It was the first time he had used her name. "I do not think they told you, either, that I had been married before. She died in childbirth when we had not been married a full year."

Rohana thought, *that could happen to me.* But the thought was distant and dreamlike and she *knew*—with the *laran* which was still mysterious to her sometimes—that this was not the death allotted for her. She wondered if he had loved the dead woman and if this marriage was an unwelcome to him as it had been to her.

He said, touching her hand lightly through the folds of lace at her wrist, "I wish to ask you—I know this is a strange request for a marriage-night—" and stopped.

Rohana bracing herself against some unspeakable request—if it embarrassed *him*, what could it be? —said gently "You can always ask. Speak, my husband." She was still too shy to say his name.

"I would ask you—to be kind to my daughter. She is only two years old, and I fear she has known but little kindness in her life. I have seen her but a few times. I brought her a doll but perhaps she was too small to pay much heed to it."

Rohana said, "I certainly would never be unkind to a little child who has done me no harm. I know little of children—I had no chance to see much of them in the Tower—and I have seen little of my sister's children. But I promise I will never be cruel to her—I will not beat her or be rough with her even in words, I promise you that. What is her name?"

"Cassilda," he said, and she was startled; on the plains of Valeron where she had been brought up, the name Cassilda was regarded too reverently to give to a human child.

"You are schooled in a Tower, Rohana? Were you to be a *leronis*?"

"So I thought for a time; but when the time came for me to leave to marry, no one protested. My gift is not so great."

He said, not looking at her, "Rohana, I know that within the Tower—some women are free to take lovers. If you have loved before, I swear I will never reproach you. Is there another who owns your heart?"

"No," she said, startled; she had never believed that a man, and a mountain man at that, could understand this. Yet she was troubled by the memory.

Melora's cousin, Rafael. He had wanted her and they had come so close to being lovers. Not because she desired him—she had hardly even understood what desire meant, till she felt it burning in him; he had wanted her so much that she had herself been tormented, sharing his hunger and his need; she had wished to give him this, to comfort him; she had been distressed by his suffering but at the same time helplessly reluctant; and he had sensed her reluctance and would not take her against her innermost will; nor accept her only as a gift of kindness.

She reached now for Gabriel's hand and said gently, "No, my husband; I am grateful to you for your understanding, but I have never felt more for any man than friendship, and no man can say of me that he has had more of me than a dance by moonlight and the tips of my fingers to kiss."

Gabriel squeezed her hand. He said "I am almost sorry for that," he said. "Since you must be married to a stranger, I think it would have been a good thing to know what it is to—to love someone you had chosen, before you were married off to—to someone you could not be expected to love that much." He said it without sadness.

Curiously Rohana was dismayed. She thought, *I do not want him to love me. It is enough that I must leave my home and live among strangers, hard enough to be a wife in a strange land without that burden, too. I wish we might do our duty to one another and ask of each other no more than that. It would be easier if I could be always indifferent to him, with no bond further than the children we have; if I could be as indifferent to him, as cold and unmoved as I was to those girls teasing me when we were bedded. And at* the same time some perverse instinct of contrariness demanded, *Why is he so sure I will never love him?*

He said after a moment, so that she wondered if he had some *laran* after all and read her mind, "Rohana, this was not altogether an arranged marriage; I asked my father to seek your hand, though I knew you were too young for me."

She stared in surprise; why should he have done such a thing? She did not remember ever laying eyes on him, though she supposed they must have seen one another now and then in Council season, perhaps when she was a little girl and he already a young man.

Ah, Blessed Cassilda, I could endure this if only I could be altogether indifferent to him. She heard the hostility in her own voice as she asked "Why, Gabriel?"

He said, his words stumbling, "Not only because you are beautiful, do not think that."

So he knows that would offend me, she thought. At least he did not think she was one of those women offended unless they are flattered and complimented for their looks. She had known so many of them.

"Because," he explained, stammering a little, "Once when I came to visit your brother, I saw you singing and playing a *rryl.* I love music more than anything else—except perhaps my horses—and the thought that we could have that in common—"

"Are you fond of music?"

"I have little skill to play any instrument," he said. "I was born with clumsy hands that will not do my will; but until my voice broke I was first treble in the choir in Nevarsin. I am said to have a pleasant voice still, and I love singing. It would please me above all things if one of our children might be musical. I hold that a gift higher than any *laran.*"

"I heard you singing tonight," she confessed—*one of those dreadful rowdy drinking songs*— "And it is true you have a pleasing voice."

"I am glad that something about me pleased you," he said, and looked at her with a faint hopeful smile, "I never saw a bride look so wretched and I could not bear to think you already hated me."

She said quickly, impulsively "I find nothing in you that I could hate." And he smiled—she was reminded of a puppy trying to be friendly.

"Do you think less of me because I cannot carry my drink like a man? My brothers are always making fun of me that I cannot carry my wine and that often it makes me ill—they said a bridegroom insults his bride if he will not drink to her and I should get properly drunk at least once in my life."

"You need never drink on my account; I despise drunkenness," she said, and found herself wishing he would stay like this.

He smiled faintly. "I was afraid if I had too much to drink, I should lose myself and—handle you roughly," he said. "When I was married to Catalina—" he looked away from her, "they persuaded me to go to her drunk—I was afraid, too—and it was a long time after that before she could overcome her—her fear of me; I do not think she was entirely free of it when she died."

"How dreadful for you!" Rohana said without stopping to think.

"And for her, poor girl; I wished to run no risk of frightening you."

She said, warmed by an impulse, "I do not think I could ever be afraid of you, Gabriel."

"God forbid you should ever have cause." He said after a moment "If a man can court a—a mistress,

or a courtesan, and bring her to care for him, I see
no reason why a husband should not woo his wife
for a lover. You might come to care as much for me
as for a man you had chosen yourself." His eyes
were filled with what she recognized incredulously to
be tears. "I have been married to the most beautiful
and noble lady in the Domains, after all—the one I
would have chosen anywhere."

And as had happened in the Tower, she could feel
the swelling surge of his desire, and as it had done
then it half-frightened her, half-excited, sweeping
her away into intense awareness of him.

*This is what it is then, to touch the mind without fear or
hesitation, I need not hold myself back from him, it is right
to want him, to share his passion; it is even my duty.*

Still she felt a touch of sadness. *How can I ever know
whether this is what I want or whether I am simply caught
up in sharing his passion, his wishes, his desire? Is there
nothing left of my own?* As she laid her hand in his and
then raised her arms to embrace him, she wondered
if it mattered.

The important thing was that they were joined as
one; did it matter which first desired? *Yes,* she thought
sadly, *it matters, but not enough for me to resist this
sharing, since whether I will or not, I have been given to
him. And since we are given to one another, it is better we
should have one another willing than unwilling.*

*I could remain myself, and resist this—I did it in the
Tower; why give Gabriel what I denied Rafael then, just
because our families have joined us without our own wishes?
Or rather without my wish—for Gabriel wishes to love me. I
could remain aloof from him—but there would be none of
the happiness I feel we might have together. I could remain
myself, and have an unhappy marriage. Is that too great a
price to pay for my own integrity? Or I can let myself be*

*caught up into this overpowering emotion and perhaps be
very happy—at least for a time—and never more know
what it is to be myself.*

*But how can I be other than myself? Is this not myself,
too?* she wondered, and then Gabriel was kissing her,
and she had forgotten what it was to wonder.

And now he lay dead before her, and she could
only ask herself if she had ever known what it was to
love, or if there was such a thing. This man she had
sheltered, tended, to whom she had borne children,
with whom she had lived for more than half a lifetime. *Now*, she thought, *I am alone, and forever.*

*But I am myself again—if I can remember who I am. Or
why.*

Everything But Freedom

By Marion Zimmer Bradley

"I did not say that I had no regrets, Jaelle," Rohana
said, very low, "only that everything in this world has its
price. . . ."

"So you truly believe that you have paid a price? I
thought you told me but now that you had had everything a
woman could desire."

Rohana did not face Jaelle; she did not want to cry.

"Everything but freedom, Jaelle."

—The Shattered Chain, *1976.*

I

"Look," Jaelle cried, leaning over the balcony, "I
think they are coming."

Lady Rohana Ardais followed her from inside the
room, her steps slowed somewhat by pregnancy. She
moved slowly to the edge of the balcony to join her
foster-daughter Jaelle and leaned to peer down from

the balcony, trying to see past the bend in the tree-lined mountain road that led upward to Castle Ardais.

"I cannot see so far," she confessed, and Jaelle, troubled by the angle of the older woman's leaning forward, seized her round the waist and pulled her back from the edge.

Rohana moved restlessly to free herself, and Jaelle confessed, "I am still afraid of these heights. It makes my blood curdle, to see you standing so close to the edge like that. If you should fall—" She broke off and shuddered.

"But the railing is so high," said the third woman who had followed them from the inner room, "she could not possibly fall, not even if she wished! Look, even if I climbed up here—" Lady Alida made a move as if to climb up on the railing, but Jaelle's face was whiter than her shift, and Rohana shook her head. "Don't tease her, Alida. She's really afraid."

"I'm sorry—did that really bother you, *chiya?*"

"It does. Not as badly as when I first came here, but— Perhaps it is foolish—"

"No," Rohana said, "not really; you were desert-bred and never accustomed to the mountain heights." Jaelle had been born and reared in the Dry Towns; her mother a kidnapped woman of the Comyn, her father a desert chieftain who was, by Comyn standards, little better than a bandit. Four years before, a daring raid by Free Amazon mercenaries had freed Melora and the twelve-year-old Jaelle; but Melora had died in the desert, bearing the Dry Town chief's child. Rohana had wished to foster Melora's children; but Jaelle had chosen to go to the Amazon Guild House as fosterling to the Free Amazon Kindra n'ha Mhari.

Jaelle peered cautiously over the railing again. "Now

they are past the bend in the road," she said. "You can see—yes, that is Kindra; no other woman rides like that."

"Alida," Rohana said, "Will you go down and make certain that guest-chambers are made ready?"

"Certainly, sister." Alida, many years younger than Lady Rohana, was the younger sister of Rohana's husband, *Dom* Gabriel Ardais. She was a *leronis*, Tower trained, and skilled in all the psychic arts of the Comyn, called *laran*.

"You will be glad to see your foster-mother again, Jaelle?" Alida asked.

"Of course, and glad to be going home," proclaimed Jaelle, heedless of the pain which flashed across Rohana's face.

Rohana said gently "I had hoped that in this year, Jaelle, this might have become your home, too."

"Never!" Jaelle said emphatically. Then she softened, coming to hug Rohana impulsively. "Oh, please, kinswoman, don't look like that! You know I love you. Only, after being free, living here has been like being chained again, like living in the Dry Towns!"

"Is it really as bad as all that?" Rohana asked. "I do not feel I have lost my freedom."

"Perhaps you do not really mind being imprisoned; but I do." Jaelle said. "You will not even ride astride, but when you ride you burden the horse with a lady's saddle—an insult to a good horse. And—" she hesitated, "Look at you! I know, even though you do not say it, that you did not really want another child, with Elorie already twelve years old and almost a woman, and Kyril and Rian all but grown men. Kyril is seventeen now, and Rian as old as I am!"

Rohana winced, for she had not realized that her

fosterling understood this. But she replied quietly "Marriage is not a matter for one person to decide everything. It is a matter for mutual decision. I have had many choices of my own; Gabriel wished for another child, and I did not feel that I could deny it to him."

"I know better than that," Jaelle replied curtly; she did not like her kinsman Gabriel, Lord Ardais, and did not care who knew it. "My uncle was angry with you because you had brought my brother Valentine here to foster, and I know that he said that if you could bring up one baby who was not even of your own blood, there was no reason you should not give him another."

"Jaelle, you do not understand these things." Rohana protested.

"No, and I hope I never do."

"What you do not understand is that Gabriel's happiness is very important to me," Rohana said, "and it is worth bearing another child to make him happy." But secretly Rohana felt rebellious: Jaelle was right; she had not wanted another child now that she was also burdened with Melora's son. Little Valentine was now nearly four years old. Her own sons had not been happy about having an infant foster-brother, even though her daughter treated the baby—now a hearty toddler—like a special pet, a kind of living doll to play with. Rohana was grateful that Elorie loved her fosterling; she herself found it a heavy burden, having a little child around again when she had already reared all of her own children past adolescence. And now, at an age where she had hoped childbirth and suckling all behind her, she must undergo all that again; and she was no longer strong and tireless as she had been when she was younger.

She sought to change the subject, although for one equally filled with tension.

"Are you still determined to take the Renunciate Oath as soon as possible?"

"Yes; you know I should have taken it a year ago," Jaelle said sullenly. "You stopped me then, but now I am fully of age and I cannot be prevented in law."

Jaelle knew it had not been only Rohana's disagreement that had prevented her from taking the Oath which would make her a Free Amazon—a member of the Sisterhood of Renunciates. It had been Kindra herself. She remembered, as she watched Kindra riding toward Castle Ardais, how they had ridden up this road together a year ago, Jaelle sullen and furious.

"I am of age, Kindra," she protested. "I am fifteen; I have a legal right to take the Oath; and I have been two years within the Guild House, I know what I want. The law allows it. Why should you stop me?"

"It is not a matter of law," Kindra protested. "It is a matter of honor. I gave the Lady Rohana my word; is my word nothing, is my honor nothing to you, foster-daughter?"

"You had no right to give such a word when it involved my freedom," Jaelle protested angrily.

"Jaelle, you were born daughter to the Comyn, Melora Aillard's daughter; nearest heir to the Domain of Aillard," Kindra reminded her, "Even so, the Council has not forbidden you to become a Renunciate. But they have insisted that you must live for one year the life of a daughter of the Comyn, if only to be certain we have not kidnapped you nor unlawfully denied you your heritage."

"Who could believe that?" Jaelle demanded.

"Many who know nothing of the Renunciate way, who do not trust in our honor," Kindra said. "It was a pledge I was forced to make as the price of having you for a fosterling in the Guild House; that when you were of age to be married, you should be sent to Ardais, there to live at least a year—they tried to argue for three—as a daughter of the Comyn, to know—not as a child, but as an adult—just what heritage and inheritance it was that you were renouncing. You should not, they felt, cast it away sight unseen and unexperienced."

"What I know of the heritage of Comyn, I do not want, nor respect, nor accept," Jaelle said stormily. "My life is here among the Guild-sisters, and I swear I shall never know any other."

"Oh, hush," Kindra implored. "How can you say so when you know nothing of what it is that you have renounced?"

"What good was it to my mother that she was Comyn?" Jaelle demanded. "They let her fall into my father's hands and dwell there as no better than concubine or slave—"

"What else could they do? Would you have had them plunge all the Domains into a war with the Dry Towns? Over a single woman—"

"Had Jalak of the Dry Towns kidnapped the heir to Hastur, they would not have hesitated a moment to make war on his account; I know that much," Jaelle argued, and Kindra sighed, knowing that what Jaelle said was true. Kindra herself had no great love for the Comyn, although she genuinely admired and respected Lady Rohana. It had taken much persuasion for Jaelle to agree to spend a year at Ardais as Rohana's foster-daughter, to learn what it was to be born daughter to the Comyn.

Now the year was ended; and Kindra was coming, as she had promised, to take her back to the Guild House, to take the Oath and live forever as a free woman of the Guild, independent of clan or heritage.

She brushed hastily past Rohana and ran down the stairs; as she reached the great front door, Kindra was just riding up the long path. Jaelle, cursing the hated skirts which she had to wear at Ardais, bundled them up in her hands and sped down the front pathway, to fling herself at Kindra, even before the woman dismounted, almost jerking her from her saddle.

"Gently! Gently, my child," Kindra admonished, dismounting and taking Jaelle into her arms. Then, seeing that Jaelle was weeping, she held her off at arm's length and surveyed her seriously.

"What is the matter?"

"Oh. I'm just so—so glad to see you!" Jaelle sobbed, hastily drying her eyes.

"Come, come, child! I cannot believe that Rohana has been unkind to you, or that you could have been so miserable as all this!"

"No, it's not Rohana—no one could possibly have been kinder—but I've been counting the days! I can't wait to be home again!"

Kindra hugged her tight. "I have missed you, too, foster-daughter," she said, "and we shall all be glad to have you home to us again. So you have not chosen to remain with the Domains and marry to suit your clan?"

"Never!" Jaelle exclaimed. "Oh, Kindra, you don't know what it's been like here! Rohana's women are so stupid; they think of nothing but pretty clothes and how to arrange their hair, or which of the guardsmen smiled or winked at them in the evenings when we dance in the hall—they are so stupid! Even my cousin, Rohana's daughter—she is just as bad as any of them!"

Kindra said gently, "I find it hard to believe that Rohana could have a daughter who was a fool—"

"Well, perhaps Elorie is not a fool," Jaelle admitted grudgingly. "She is clever enough—but already she has learned not to be caught thinking when her father or her brothers are in the room. She pretends she is as foolish as the rest of them!"

Kindra concealed a smile. "Then perhaps she is cleverer than you realize—for she can think her own thoughts without being reproved for it—something that you have not yet learned, my dearest. Come, let us go up, let me pay my respects to Lady Rohana; I am eager to see her again."

"When can we go home, Kindra? Tomorrow?" Jaelle asked eagerly.

"By no means," Kindra said, scandalized. "I have been invited to make a visit here for a tenday or more; too much haste would be disrespectful to your kinfolk, as if you could not wait to be gone."

"Well, I can't," muttered Jaelle; but before Kindra's stern glance she could not say it aloud. She called a groom to have Kindra's horse taken and stabled, then led Kindra toward the front steps where Rohana awaited them.

As the women greeted one another with an embrace, Jaelle stood at a little distance, looking at them side by side and studying the contrasts.

Rohana, Lady of Ardais, was a woman in her middle thirties; her hair was the true Comyn red of the
hereditary Comyn caste, and was ornately arranged
at the back of her neck, clasped with a copper
butterfly-clasp ornamented with pearls. She was richly
dressed in a long elegant over-gown of blue velvet
almost the color of her eyes; her thin light-colored
undergown was heavily embroidered and the over-
gown trimmed at the neck and sleeves with thick
dark fur. Now the rich garments looked clumsy, her
body swollen with her pregnancy. By contrast to
Rohana, Kindra appeared frankly middle-aged; a
tall lanky woman in the boots and breeches of an
Amazon, which made her long legs look even longer
than they were; her face was thin, almost gaunt, and
her face, as well as her close-cropped gray hair, looked
weathered and was beginning to be wrinkled with
small lines round the eyes and mouth. Almost for
the first time, Jaelle wondered how old Kindra was.
She had always seemed ageless. She was older than
Rohana—or was it only that Rohana's relatively sheltered and pampered life had preserved the appearance of youth?

"Well, come in, my dears," Rohana said, slipping
one arm through Kindra's and the other through
Jaelle's, "I hope you can pay us a good long visit.
Surely you did not ride alone all the way from
Thendara?"

Jaelle wondered scornfully if Rohana thought
Kindra would be afraid to make such a journey
alone—as she, Rohana, might have been afraid. To
her the question would have been insulting; but
Kindra answered uncritically that she had had company past the path for Scaravel; a group of moun-

tain explorers going into the far Hellers, and three Guild-sisters hired to guide them.

"Rafaella was with them, and she sent you her love and greetings, Jaelle. She has missed you, and so has her little girl Doria. They both hoped you would be with them another time."

"Oh, I wish Rafi had come here with you," Jaelle cried. "She is almost my closest friend!"

"Well, perhaps she will be back in Thendara by the time we are able to return there," Kindra said, smiling. She added to Rohana, "Mostly it was a group of Terrans from the new spaceport; they are trying to map the Hellers—the roads, the mountain peaks and so forth."

"Not for military purposes, I hope," Rohana said.

"I believe not; simply for information," Kindra replied. "The Terrans all appear to have a passion, from what I know of them, for all kinds of useless knowledge; the height of mountains, the sources of rivers and so forth—I cannot imagine why, but such things might be useful even to our people who must travel in the mountains."

They were now well inside the great hallway, and Jaelle noted, standing in the corner where a heap of hunting equipment was piled, Lord Gabriel Ardais, Rohana's husband and the Warden and head of the Domain of Ardais. He was a tall man with a smart military bearing that somehow gave his old hunting clothes the look of a uniform.

"You have guests, Rohana? You did not warn me to expect company," he said gruffly.

"Strictly speaking, the lady is Jaelle's guest; Kindra n'ha Mhari, from the Thendara Guild House," Rohana said calmly, "but though she journeyed here to bring Jaelle home, she is my friend and I have invited her to stay and keep me company now I must be confined so close to house and garden."

Dom Gabriel's mobile face darkened with disapproval as his gaze fell on Kindra's trousered and booted legs; but as Rohana spoke on his face softened, and he spoke with perfect courtesty. "Whatever you wish, my love. *Mestra*," he used the term of courtesy from a nobleman to a female of a lower class, "I bid you welcome; any guest of my lady's is a welcome and a cherished guest in my home. May your stay here be joyful."

He went on, leading the way into the upper hall, "Did I hear you speaking of *Terranan* in the Hellers? Those strange creatures who claim to be from other worlds, come here in closed litters of metal across the gulf of the stars? I thought that was a children's tale."

"Whatever they may be, *vai dom*, theirs is no children's tale," Kindra replied. "I have seen the great ships in which they come and go, and one of the professors in the City was allowed to journey with them to the moon Liriel, where they have set up what they call an observatory, to study the stars."

"And the Hastur-lords permitted it?"

"I think perhaps sir, if we are only one of many great worlds among the stars, it may not be of much moment whether the Hastur-lords permit or no," Kindra returned deferentially. "One thing is certain, such a truth will change our world and things can never be as they have been before this time."

"I don't see why that need be," *Dom* Gabriel said in his usual gruff tone. "What have they to do with me or with the Domain? I say let 'em let us alone and we'll let them alone—hey?"

"You may be right, sir; but I would say if these folk have the wisdom to travel from world to world, they may have much to teach us," Kindra said.

"Well, they'd better not come here to Ardais trying to teach it. I'll be the judge of what my folk should learn or not," said *Dom* Gabriel, "and that's that." He marched to a high wooden sideboard where bottles and glasses were set out and began to pour. He said deferentially to Rohana, "I'm sure it would do you good, but I suppose you are still too queasy to drink this early, my love? And you, *Mestra?*"

"Thank you, sir, it is still a bit early for me," Kindra said, shaking her head.

"Jaelle?"

"No, thank you, Uncle." Jaelle said, trying to conceal a grimace of disgust. *Dom* Gabriel poured himself a liberal drink and drank it off quickly, then, pouring another, took a relaxed sip. Rohana sighed and went to him, saying in a low tone, "Please, Gabriel, the steward will be here with the stud-books this morning, to plan the seasons of the mares."

Dom Gabriel scowled and his face set in a stubborn line. He said, "For shame, Rodi, to speak of such things before a young maiden."

Rohana sighed and said "Jaelle, too, is country-bred and as well acquainted with such things as our own children, Gabriel. Please try to be sober for him, will you?"

"I shall not neglect my duty, my dear," *Dom* Gabriel said. "You attend to your business, Lady, and I shall not neglect mine." He poured himself another drink. "I am sure a little of this would do your sickness good, my love; won't you have some?"

"No, thank you, Gabriel; I have many things to see

to this morning," she said, sighing, and gestured to her guests to follow her up the stairs. Jaelle said vehemently as soon as they were out of earshot, "Disgraceful! Already he is half drunk! And no doubt before the steward gets here, he will be dead drunk somewhere on the floor—unless his man remembers to come and get him into a chair—and no more fit to deal with the stud-books than I am to pilot one of the Terran starships!"

Rohana's face was pale, but she spoke steadily.

"It is not for you to criticize your uncle, Jaelle. I am content if he drinks alone and does not get one of the boys to drinking with him; Rian already finds it impossible to carry his drink like a gentleman, and Kyril is worse. I do not mind attending to the stud-books."

"But why do you let him make such a beast of himself, especially now?" Jaelle asked, casting a critical look at Rohana's perceptibly thickened waistline.

"He drinks because he is in pain; it is not my place to tell him what he must do," Rohana said. "Come, Jaelle, let us find a guest chamber near yours for Kindra. Then I must see if Valentine has been properly washed and fed, and if his nurse has taken him outdoors to play in the fresh air this morning."

"I should think," Kindra said, "that Jaelle would have quite taken over the care of her brother; you are a big girl now, Jaelle, almost a woman, and should know something of the care of children."

Jaelle's face drew up in distaste.

"I've no liking for having little bawling brats about me! What are the nurses good for?"

"Nevertheless, you are Valentine's closest living kin; he has a right to your care and companionship," Kindra urged quietly, "and you might take some of that burden from Lady Rohana who is burdened enough."

Rohana laughed. She said "Let her alone, Kindra; I've no wish that she be burdened too young with children if she has no love for it. After all, he's not neglected; Elorie cares for Valentine as if he were her own little brother—"

"The more fool she," Jaelle interrupted, laughing.

"He must be quite a big boy now; four, is he not?" Kindra asked.

Rohana replied eagerly, "Yes, and he is such a sweet quiet little boy, very good, biddable, and gentle. One would never think—"

She broke off, but Jaelle took it up.

"Never think he was my brother? For I know very well, Aunt, that I am none of those things, and in fact I do not wish to be any of those things."

"What I was about to say, Jaelle, is that one would hardly think him kin to my sons, boisterous as they are; or that one would hardly think him of Dry Town clan or kin."

Kindra could almost hear what Rohana had started to say; *one would hardly think his father a Dry Town bandit.* She was astonished that Jaelle, who was, after all of the telepathic blood of Comyn, could not understand what Rohana meant; but she held her peace. She liked Rohana very much and wished that the lady and her foster daughter were on better terms, yet it could not be amended by wishing. Rohana conducted her to a guest chamber and left her to unpack; Jaelle stayed, and dropped down on a saddlebag, her lanky knees drawn up, her gray eyes full of angry rebellion.

"You are still trying to turn me into a Comyn lady like Rohana! I should do this or that, I should look

after my little brother, and I don't know what all!
Why do we have to stay here? Why can't we start
back to Thendara tomorrow? I want to go home! I
thought that was why you were coming—to take me
home! You promised, if I endured for a year, I
would be allowed to take the Oath! Now how long
will I have to wait?"

Kindra decided it was time to hit this spoiled girl
with the truth of the situation. She drew the girl
down, still protesting beside her.

"Jaelle, it is not certain that Comyn Council will
give permission for you to take the Oath at all; the
law still regards the Comyn Council as your legal
guardians. Rohana was given your custody as a minor; a woman of the Domains is not like a com-
moner," Kindra began. "I dare not risk angering
your guardians. You know that the Guild House
Charter exists by favor of Council; if we let you take
the Oath without permission, our House could lose
its Charter—"

"That is outrageous! They cannot do that to free
citizens! Can they?"

"They can, Jaelle, but in general they would have
no reason for doing so; for many years we have been
careful not to infringe on their privileges. I am afraid
it is just as simple as that."

"Are you trying to say that for all the talk in the
Oath of freedom—*renounce forever any allegiance to
family, clan, household, warden or liege lord, and owe
allegiance only to the laws as a free citizen must* . . . it is
nothing but a sham? You taught me to believe in it . . ."
the girl raged.

Kindra said steadily, "It is very far from a sham, Jaelle;
it is an *ideal,* and it cannot be fully implemented in all
times and conditions; our rulers are not yet suffi-

ciently enlightened to allow its full perfection. One day perhaps it may be so: but now the world will go as it will and not as you or I would have it."

"So I have to sit here in Ardais and obey that drunken old sot and that spineless nobody who sits by and smiles and says he must do what he will because she will not stop him—this is nobility indeed!"

"I can only beg of you to be patient, Jaelle. Lady Rohana is well disposed toward us, and her friendship may do much with the Council. But it would not be wise to alienate *Dom* Gabriel, either."

"I would feel like such a hypocrite, to swarm about and curry favor with nobles—"

"They are your kin, Jaelle; it is no crime to seek their good will," Kindra said wearily, unequal to the task of explaining diplomacy and compromise to the unbending young girl. "Will you help me unpack my garments, now? We will talk more of this later. And I would like to see your brother; my hands helped bring him into the world, and I promised your mother that I would try always to see to his well-being; and I try always to keep my word."

"You have not kept your promise to me, that I should take Oath in a year," Jaelle argued, but at Kindra's angry look she knew she had exhausted even her foster-mother's patience, so she began helping Kindra take out her meager stock of clothing from the saddlebags and lay it neatly away in chests.

II

One of the few tasks confronting Jaelle at Ardais which she felt fully compatible with her life as a

Renunciate was the care of her own horse; *Dom*
Gabriel and even Rohana would have felt it more
suitable if she had left the beast's welfare to the
grooms, but they did not absolutely forbid her the
stables; and almost every morning before sunrise she
went out to the main stables to look after the fine
plains-bred horse Rohana had presented her as a
birthday gift; where she gave the beast its fodder
and brushed it down. She also exercised her own
horse and rode almost every day. Although she still
resented not being allowed to ride astride, she was
obedient to Rohana's will, suspecting that yielding on
this matter might be the price of being allowed to
ride at all. No one could have said or suggested that
Lady Rohana was not a good rider, although she was
to all outward appearances the most conventional of
women.

Jaelle suspected that Rohana was hoping to force
her to admit that she could find as much pleasure in
riding sidesaddle as in riding Amazon style in boots
and breeches; but this, she was resolved, she would
never do.

Perhaps, she thought, while Kindra was here—and
Rohana could not constrain a guest to follow her
customs—Rohana could be persuaded to allow her,
Jaelle, to ride as Kindra did. She was intending to
try, anyhow. Her own Renunciate clothing, which
she had worn when she came here, was too small for
her now. She had grown almost three inches, though
she would never be really tall. Perhaps one of her
cousins could be persuaded to lend her some breeches
until she would have proper clothing made on returning to the Guild House; she certainly did not
intend to ride back to Thendara in the ridiculous

outfit which Rohana thought suitable for a young lady's riding; the sort of riding-habit her cousin Elorie wore, a dark full-cut skirt and elegantly fitted jacket with velvet lapels, would be the mock of every Renunciate in the Guild House!

She took her horse out of the stall and began brushing down the glossy coat. She had heard Rohana and Kindra speak of hawking this day perhaps and meant to ask if she would be allowed to ride out with them. Before long, the horse's coat gleamed like burnished copper, and she herself was warm and sweating profusely, despite the chill of the stable—it was so cold that her breath still came in a white cloud. She began to lead the horse back into its stall when a hand touched her and she frowned, knowing the touch. Her first impulse was to pick the hand off her like a crawling bug, perhaps with a fist-sized blow behind it; but if she was to persuade her cousin Kyril to lend her his riding-clothes, she did not want to alienate him too thoroughly.

Rohana's elder son was seventeen years old, a year older than Jaelle herself; like his father, he had dark crisply-curled hair; many of the Ardais men were dark rather than having the true-red hair of the Comyn. She had heard that this had come from alliances with the swarthy little men who lived in caves in the Hellers and worked the mines for metals, worshipping the fire-Goddess; a few of the Ardais kin, it was said, even had dark eyes like animals, but Jaelle had not seen that; certainly Kyril's eyes were not dark, but blue as Rohana's own. He was tall and broad-shouldered, but otherwise lean and narrowly built; his features were heavy, and at least to Jaelle's eyes he had the same sullen mouth and weak chin as his father. Kyril would look better, she thought, when he was old enough to grow a beard and conceal it.

She shifted her weight a little so that Kyril's hand fell away from her, and said, "What are you doing out so early, cousin?"

"I could ask the same of you," Kyril said, grinning. "Have you stolen out this early to keep an assignation with one of the grooms? Which one has stolen your heart? Rannart? He is all a girl could desire; if he were a maiden I should swoon over those eyes of his, and I know Elorie seeks to touch his hand whenever he helps her into her saddle."

Jaelle grimaced with revulsion. "Your mind is filthy, Kyril. And already you have been drinking, early as it is!"

"You sound like my mother, Jaelle; a little drink makes the bread go down easily at this hour and warms the body. Yours would be the better for a little warming."

He winked at her suggestively, trying to slide an arm around her waist, and she said, concealing her annoyance and moving as far from him as the confines of the stall allowed, "I am as warm as I wish; I have been currying my horse, and I prefer exercise to drinking. I think you would be the better for a good run, and it would warm you better than whisky, believe me. I don't like the smell or taste of the stuff, and certainly not for breakfast."

"Well, if you don't want whisky, I can think of a better way to warm you in this cold place," Kyril said, and she realized that he had moved to block her exit from the stall. "Come, Jaelle, you need not pretend with me; you have lived with those Renunciates, and all the world knows how they behave about men; would any woman ride astride with her legs showing, unless she wished to invite any man who sees it to spread them?"

Jaelle tried to push past him. She had been a fool; she should have managed to keep the horse between them. "You are disgusting, Kyril. If I desired any man, it would not be you."

"Ah. I knew it; those lovers of women and haters of men have corrupted you! But try it with a real man, and I swear you will like it better." He caught her around the waist and tried hard to push her against the edge of the stall.

"Oh, what a fool you are, Cousin! Just now you said Renunciates were all mad for men, and now you will have it that we are all lovers of women. You cannot have it both ways."

"Oh, Jaelle, don't haggle with me; you know I've been hungering for you since you were only a skinny little thing, and now you'd drive any man mad," he said, pushing closer and trying to kiss the back of her neck. She forgot about not wanting to alienate him and pushed him away, hard.

"Let me go, and I won't tell your mother how offensive—"

"Offensive? A woman like you is offensive to all men," Kyril said, and she pushed hard again, driving two stiffened fingers into his solar plexus. He staggered back with a grunt of pain.

"You cannot blame a man for asking," he said, almost smugly. "Most women consider it a compliment if a man desires them."

"Oh, Kyril, surely you are not short of women to warm your bed!" she said crossly. "You are only trying to annoy me! I don't want to trouble Rohana; you know she is tired and ill these days! Just leave me alone!"

"It would serve you right if no man ever desired you, and you had to marry a cross-eyed farmer with nine stepchildren," Kyril snarled.

"What does it matter to you, even if I marry a cralmac?"

"You are my cousin; it is a matter of the honor of my family," he said, "that you should become a real woman—"

"Oh, go away! It is time for breakfast," Jaelle said furiously. "If you make me late, I swear I will tell Rohana why and risk making her as sick as I am when I look at you and smell your filthy breath!" She pushed to the door of the stable while Kyril rubbed his bruised rib.

As the two young people headed for the great hall, she saw *Dom* Gabriel riding up to the great gateway. He was not alone, but she was only vaguely surprised to see the Lord of Ardais out so early; she could not credit that he might have been only in search of fresh air and exercise on a morning ride.

I should not wonder that Kyril is already corrupt; with such a father, it would be a miracle if he were anything else. I only hope he did not awaken Rohana going out so early, she thought, and went up into the Great Hall for breakfast.

Rohana, in a long loose gown covered with a white apron not unlike the housekeeper's, greeted her with a smile.

"You are awake early, Jaelle; riding?"

"No, aunt, only grooming my horse," Jaelle said. Kyril slunk into his place at the table and Jaelle with a fragment of her consciousness heard him order one of the serving-women to bring him wine.

Ugh, he will be a drunken sot like his father within a year! Jaelle thought, and turned her attention to greeting her younger cousins. Elorie and Rian, with their governess, took their seats and attacked their porridge and honey with childish greed. Rohana had a little stewed fruit on her plate, but Jaelle noticed her kinswoman looked pale and was only pretending to eat.

Dom Gabriel made an entrance—any other way of describing it, Jaelle thought, would be an under- statement—followed by a slightly built, pretty girl of seventeen or so. She cast a look at Gabriel that was almost pleading, but he ignored her and she as- sumed a look of hard defiance.

Jaelle understood at once; this was not the first young woman that Lord Ardais had brought to the house under these circumstances; *at least,* she thought, *this one is not younger than his own sons.*

"Gabriel, will you name our guest?" Rohana asked with perfect courtesy.

He stepped to the girl's side and said "This is Tessa Haldar." The double name proclaimed her at least minor nobility.

Rohana said gently, "She will be staying?"

"Certainly," Gabriel said, not looking at the girl, and Rohana immediately comprehended. Jaelle was not much of a telepath, but she caught the edge of Rohana's emotion.

I suppose he thinks I care who he sleeps with?

Gabriel glared at her, and Jaelle also heard what he would not say aloud before the entire household; *well, you are no good to me now, are you?*

Rohana's face paled with anger.

Whose fault is that? It was you who wanted another child!

Jaelle fought to close her perceptions, flooded with a sick embarrassment; by the time she looked up, Rohana was helping the girl off with her cloak. *Poor child, none of this is her fault.* Rohana said aloud, "Here, my dear, you must be chilled by your long ride. Sit here beside *Dom* Gabriel." She beckoned to the hall-steward. "Hallard, set another place here, and take her cloak. Bring some hot tea; the kettle is cold."

"Forget that swill," *Dom* Gabriel said contemptuously; "After a ride like that, a man wants something warming." Rohana did not alter her cool gracious manner for a moment.

"Hot spiced cider for *Dom* Gabriel and his guest."

"Hot spiced wine, you imbecile," *Dom* Gabriel corrected her rudely. Rohana's carefully held smile flickered, but she gave the order. Her lips were pressed tightly together and there were two spots of color on her cheeks.

Kindra came into the hall and Rohana said good morning. She came to greet Jaelle and took a place among the children.

Dom Gabriel scowled and said quietly to Rohana, over the bent head of the girl Tessa between them, "What's this, Lady? Am I to have a woman in breeches at my own table?"

Rohana said between her teeth, "Gabriel, I have been gracious to *your* guest." He scowled fiercely, but he lowered his gaze and said nothing further. Jaelle gazed into her plate, feeling she would choke on her bread and butter. How could Rohana sit there calmly and allow *Dom* Gabriel to make her confront his new *barragana* at her own breakfast table. And when she was pregnant, too! Yet she sat there politely watching *Dom* Gabriel feed the girl sops of bread soaked in the spiced wine from his own goblet.

Rian asked, "Mother, may I have wine instead of more tea?"

"No, Rian, you cannot deal with lessons if you

have been drinking; I will send for spiced cider for
you; it will warm you better than wine."

"Rohana, don't make a mollycoddle of the boy! If
he wants to drink, let him," Gabriel grumbled, but
Rohana shook her head at the hall-steward.

"Gabriel, you gave your word that the children
should be wholly in my hands till they are grown."

"Oh, very well, do as you please. Listen to your
mother, Rian; I always do," *Dom* Gabriel said with a
sickly smile.

"If I were Rohana, I would . . . I would kick that
girl, I would scratch that smug smile off her face,"
Jaelle said to Kindra as they were leaving the Hall.
Kyril heard and said jeeringly "What do you know of
a man's privileges?"

"Enough to know I want no part of them," Jaelle
said. "I thought I had proved that to your satisfaction earlier this morning, cousin."

Rian, Rohana's younger son, a slenderly built boy
of sixteen with a perpetually worried look on his face
and red hair like Rohana's, said, "Mother is not
pleased, I can see that. But it is not the first time. My
father will do what he will, and whatever he does,
my mother will say before the household that whatever he chooses to do is well done—whatever she
may think in private. I agree with you, Jaelle, it is a
disgrace; but if she will not protest, there is nothing
you or I or anyone else can do."

Jaelle had seen Rian finish the goblet of his father's
spiced wine after *Dom* Gabriel left the table, when
Rohana was not looking; she looked contemptuously
at the boy and said nothing.

Kindra said quietly, "Come to my room, Jaelle; I
think we must talk about this."

And when they were alone in Kindra's room, she

said "By what right do you criticize your kinswoman Lady Rohana? Is that what I taught you, who want freedom for yourself, to refuse Lady Rohana her choices?"

"You cannot convince me it is by her own choice that she allows him to bring his mistress right under her roof and to her own table!"

Kindra said "Perhaps she would rather know where he does his wenching instead of wondering where he is when he is abroad? I know she is troubled about his health and fears something might happen to him if he goes forth from home. At least here she knows definitely what he is doing—and with whom."

"I think that's disgusting," said Jaelle.

"It is no matter what you think; you were not consulted," Kindra said sharply, "and it is not for you to complain if she does not. When she complains to me or consults me about his behavior, I shall not lie about how I feel; nor need you. But until she makes you the keeper of her conscience, Jaelle, do not presume to be so."

"Oh, you are as bad as Rian!" Jaelle said in frustration. "Rohana can do no wrong."

"Oh, I would hardly say that," said Rohana gaily, coming into the room in time to hear Jaelle's last words, "But I am glad to hear you think so, Jaelle."

"But I *don't* think so," said Jaelle crossly, turning her eyes away from Rohana, and slammed out of the room.

Rohana raised her eyes. "Well, what was that all about, Kindra?"

"Only a bad case of being sixteen years old, and knowing how to settle all the problems of the world, except her own," Kindra said wryly. "She loves you,

Rohana; she cannot be expected to be happy at seeing you humiliated at your own table."

"No, I suppose not," Rohana said, "but does she expect me to take it out on an innocent young girl who thinks she is loved by a nobleman? She will learn otherwise, soon enough, and my sympathy is all for her. Why, she cannot be much older than Jaelle."

"I think that may be what is troubling Jaelle, though she may not entirely realize it," Kindra said.

"Well, there is time enough for her to choose among men," said Rohana. "But it would trouble me greatly if she were to decide that all men are like her Dry Town father—or like Gabriel—and turn away from them forever."

"Do you really think she will learn otherwise here?" asked Kindra. Rohana sighed.

"No, I suppose not. Kyril is not much better than his father; I have tried to do my best by example, but it is only natural for a boy to pattern himself after his father. Perhaps I should send Jaelle to my Kinswoman, who is happy with her husband. But she has so many little children—there are six not yet eight years old—and they really have not room for another grown girl under her roof. But one way or another, I should make sure she knows that men can be good and decent. Perhaps she should go for a time to Melora's cousins in the lowlands."

"I had trouble enough getting her to come here," Kindra reminded her. "And that was because she loved and respected you. I doubt she wants to learn more about men."

Rohana sighed again. "It is trouble enough having trouble with my own daughter," she said, "but I wanted Jaelle here because she is all I have left of poor Melora. Perhaps I should have let her go to Jerana who was willing to make sure she would have the proper training of a Comyn daughter. Nevertheless, I do not want to think of her as turning entirely against men as they say Amazons do."

Kindra frowned and said seriously, "Rohana, would it really matter to you so much if she should become a lover of women? Are you so prejudiced on that subject?"

"Prejudiced? Oh, I see," Rohana said. "No, it would not trouble me so much; but I want her to be happy, and I am not yet convinced that there is any happiness for women outside marriage."

"I would find it hard to believe that there is happiness for women *in* marriage," Kindra said. "Certainly I found none; I told you the story outside Jalak's house in the Dry Towns.

Years slid away as Rohana remembered Kindra's words. Kindra's husband had felt her inadequate because she had borne him only two daughters; she had risked her life to have a third child and had borne the desired boy, after which he had showered her with jewels. "*I was of no value,* Kindra had said; *the daughters I had borne at risk of my life were no value; I was only an instrument to give him sons. And so, when I could walk again, I cut my hair, and kissed my children sleeping, and made my way to the Guild House where my life began.*" Yet Rohana knew this decision had not been made lightly, but with great anguish.

Now she was strengthened to ask what she had never dared before despite their closeness.

"But what of your children, Kindra? How could you leave them in his hands, then, if you thought him so evil?"

Kindra's face was colorless, even her tight lips white.

"You may well ask; before I came to that decision, I had wept through many nights. I thought even of carrying them thither with me or stealing them back when they were big enough. Avarra pity me, one night I even stood over them with a dagger in my hand, ready to save them from the life I could not bear; but I knew I would turn it first on myself." Her voice was flat, but her words came in a resistless rush which compelled Rohana's silent attention. "But he—my husband—was not an evil man; it was only that he could not even *see* me; for him I did not exist, a wife was but an instrument to do his will. And I spoke to many wives, and not one could understand why I was angry or dismayed; they all seemed well-contented with their lot. So what could I do but believe that other women *were* so content— Many of them could not see what I had to complain of. They asked, "He does not beat you, does he?" as if I should be happy just because he did not. So it seemed to me that the fault lay with me, that I could never be content under those terms, that I should die if I was no more than a mother of his children; but even that it was to his advantage to be rid of me and have a truly contented wife happy with her designated place in life, who could bring up my daughters to be happy as those other women seemed to be . . . in finding a husband and being his brood stock. And so I left him as much for his own good and theirs, as my own. And I have heard in the city that he married again and that my daughters married well, and they, too, seem happy. I have three grandsons I have never held in my arms; I am sure my daughters would draw away their skirts as if I

bore plague, should I make myself known to them."
She swallowed, Rohana could see tears in her eyes.
"But I have never looked back. And if I were there
again, I would do the same."

Rohana embraced her silently, and did not speak
for a long time. She felt touched by the other woman's confidence, knowing it was not lightly given,
even to her sisters of the Guild House; she had
enough *laran* to know Kindra had never told her tale
at this length to even the Guild-mothers.

"I would not swear that I would not have done so
in your place," Rohana said, "but the choice never
came to me; I bore my two sons *before* my daughter
was born, and by the time she was born Gabriel was
glad to have her. Gabriel already had a daughter by
his first marriage and loved her well. She is in
Dalereuth Tower; they say she has the Ardais Gift.
She dwelt under our roof till she was fifteen; she
had but lately left us when I learned of Melora's
plight."

*And you were rich enough and had enough servants and
ladies at your command that you could leave your own
children in the hands of others and go on such a quest,*
Kindra thought, but Rohana picked up the thought.

"It was not as easy as that, Kindra. Gabriel has not
yet forgiven me."

"And this child you did not want is the price of his
forgiveness? You pay highly for your husband's good
will, my Lady," Kindra said, and Rohana spontane-
ously embraced her.

"Oh, my friend, do not say, *my Lady* to me. Call me
by my name! I may call *you* my friend, may I not?
My house is full of women, but I have no real friend
anywhere among them! Not even Jaelle—she disap-
proves of me so much!"

"Not even *Domna* Alida? Not even *Dom* Gabriel's sister?"

"She least of all," Rohana said, still clinging to Kindra and looking up at her. "It troubles her that all things in the Domain have been given into my hands; she knows well that Gabriel is not competent to rule his own affairs, but she feels that since she is an Ardais and a *leronis*, if affairs must be in any hands but Gabriel's own, they should be in hers. I think she would kill me if she could think of a way to escape punishment for my murder. She watches me forever—" Rohana deliberately stopped herself, aware that she sounded as if she were on the edge of hysteria.

"So you can see I am in need of a friend. Stay with me, Kindra—stay at least until the baby is born!"

Impulsively, Kindra embraced her.

"I will stay as long as you want me, Rohana, I promise. Even if I must send Jaelle southward with a caravan before winter."

"She will not like that," said Rohana, smiling wanly. "And to say that is like prophesying snow in the pass of Scaravel at Midwinter—it takes not much *laran*." And having said this, she found herself wondering; did Kindra have *laran* after all? It was unheard of for her to be so much at ease with anyone outside her own caste.

Kindra grinned at her. She said "I told you once in the desert, I think you would make a notable Amazon, Rohana. You have the true spirit. When I go southward with Jaelle, why not come with us? Or if it troubles you to travel when you are pregnant, bide here beneath his roof until your child is born. If it is a daughter, we will take her south with us and foster her in Thendara Guild House; if it is a son, leave it with *Dom* Gabriel since he has other women and all he now desires of you is another son. I think you would be happy as one of the Oath-bound of the *Com'hi Letzii*."

She smiled, and Rohana knew that the offer had been made at least partly in jest; but suddenly Rohana was seized by a great wild desire to ride south with Kindra as once she had done, on their quest to the Dry Towns; to leave all this behind her, and follow Kindra anywhere, even to the end of the world.

"What a mad thought!" she said breathlessly, "but you make it sound very tempting, Kindra. I—" to her own shock and surprise her voice wavered, "I almost wish I could. Almost."

III

A little after Kindra had left her, after she had seen to the welfare of the younger children, and sought out Valentine in his nursery to make certain all was well with her fosterling, Gabriel came to her in the conservatory. He looked ill and tired, and Rohana's heart when out to him as always.

"Are you well, Rohana? You have been more sick with this pregnancy than any of the others. I did not know that, or I would have let you be."

She said irritably, "It is something late to think of that now." At his crestfallen look she repented her cross tone and said, "All the same, I thank you for saying it now."

He said shyly, "I thank you for your graciousness to poor little Tessa this morning. Believe me, I would not have affronted you; I did not mean you to take it like that. But she is in trouble at home and I did not think it right to leave her there to suffer when her trouble was all of my making."

Rohana shrugged. "You know perfectly well it matters nothing to me with whom—or what—you share your bed. As you made clear to me this morning, I am no good to you at present." She did not hear the bitterness in her own voice until she had finished; and then it was too late.

He reached impulsively for her hands and kissed them. "Rohana," he said breathlessly, "you know very well you are the only woman I have ever loved!"

She smiled a little and closed her hands over his. "Yes, my dear, I suppose so."

"Rohana," he demanded impulsively, still breathless, "What has happened to us? We used to love one another so much!"

She held his hands in hers.

"I don't know, Gabriel, she said, "perhaps it is only that we are both growing old." She touched his cheek in a rare caress. "You don't look well, my dear. Perhaps riding so early is not good for you. Are you still taking the medicine sent you from Nevarsin?"

He shook his head, frowning. "It does me no good," he protested, "and then when I drink wine, it makes me sick."

She shrugged. "You must do what you think best," she said. "If you choose to have falling seizures rather than giving up drink, I cannot choose for you."

The impatient look she dreaded came over his face again; as always, if she spoke about his drinking he was angry. He said stiffly "I came only to thank you for your kindness to Tessa," and stormed away again. Rohana sighed and went to the little room where she went over the business of the farm each day with the steward. She let the nurse bring Valentine to play on the floor with his blocks; her own unborn child had recently begun to move in her body, and she thought about what it would be like to bring up another child. Perhaps this son she could shield a little from Gabriel's influence, so that some day he could be some use to her on the estate; she did not feel she could trust either of the boys now. And Elorie was not old enough to know or care much about such things.

She spent the morning discussing with the steward the wisdom of replanting resin-trees at this season against the added dangers of forest-fire if there were too many resin-trees; and the necessity of dealing with the forge-folk for metal to shoe the best of the riding-horses. Of necessity she had learned a good deal about the business of processing resins for paints and wood-sealers to keep wooden fences and buildings from rotting away; the high quality resins could only be processed from the trees whose presence brought the greatest dangers of forest fire.

Not till late afternoon, when Valentine had been sent to the nursery for a nap and his supper of boiled eggs and rusks, was Rohana free to ride; she sent a message inviting Kindra to join her if she wished. She went quickly to her room and changed into a shabby old riding-skirt; when Kindra joined her, she found that she envied the other woman's freedom of breeches and boots, remembering how she herself had worn them on her adventure with Kindra's band.

They were preparing to ride through the gates when Jaelle came into the stable in riding things.

"Oh, please—may I ride with you?"

The question had been addressed to Kindra; she turned to Rohana. "It is for your guardian to say."

Jaelle said sullenly, "You are my guardian," but she turned politely to Rohana.

"Please, kinswoman?"

"Well, since you already have your riding things on—but we shall have no time for hawking; we will only be riding to the ridge to inspect the resin-plantings," Rohana told her. "Come, if you can keep up."

Jaelle ran to lead out her horse.

"Keep up with you? I will guarantee I can ride harder, faster, further than either of you—or both!" she exclaimed, jumping up swiftly into the saddle.

"Oh, certainly you can ride harder and further than I can now, Jaelle—or any pregnant woman," Rohana said, and pretended she did not see her ward's grimace of distaste.

"Doesn't it make you angry to be tied down that way?"

"Not a bit of it," Rohana returned equably. "Remember this is my fourth child and I know what to expect. Come, let's ride up toward the ridge; I need to see for myself what the winter has done to the resin-trees."

"Why doesn't *Dom* Gabriel see to that?" Jaelle asked.

"Because he has never had any kind of sense for business matters, Jaelle; do you think there is something wrong with the notion that a woman should administer the affairs of the Domain?"

"No, certainly not; but he leaves it all to you, along with all the other things that everyone else agrees are your affair—caring for the house, the meals, the children—so that you do a woman's work and a man's, too—"

"Because I have always been stronger than Gabriel; if I left it to him, all these things would be in a muddle and the estate in great financial difficulties. Or is it that you think I should make Gabriel diaper the babies and count linens, and perhaps bake bread and cake?"

The picture that created in Rohana's mind was so ludicrous that even Jaelle laughed.

"I feel he should do his share," Jaelle said. "If he does not, what good is a man, anyway?"

Rohana smiled and said, "Well, my dear, it's just the way the world is arranged."

"Not for me," Jaelle said.

"Would it surprise you, Jaelle, to know that when Gabriel was younger, before his health was so broken, he did indeed rock the children, sing to them, and get up with them at night so I could sleep? When we were first wed he was the kindest and tenderest of fathers. He did not drink much then. . . ."

Jaelle found that so disturbing that she changed the subject. "When do we go southward, Kindra, so I can take the Oath?"

Kindra opened her mouth to speak, but Rohana said first, "Surely there's not hurry. I had hoped you would give me as much time as you gave the Guild House; three years, to know what you want from life."

Jaelle's eyes flamed.

"No! You promised me, Kindra, that if I spent a year with my Comyn kinfolk, there would be no further delay. And I have given you a year, as you asked." She added scowling, "You spoke to me, at that time, some fine words about honor and the value of your word."

Kindra sighed. "I am not trying to delay you, Jaelle.

But I have pledged your kinswoman—who is my friend—that I will remain here until her child is born. You cannot take the Oath here."

Jaelle looked like a stormcloud. She said "Kindra—"

"I know, I had perhaps no right to make such a pledge in view of my word to you," Kindra said, and Rohana interrupted.

"It is my fault, Jaelle; I begged her. Will you deprive me of her company while I am so far from my usual health?"

Jaelle stared at the ground moving past under the horse's feet. At last she said sullenly "If it is your will, Rohana, then your claim on Kindra is the best." She did not believe this; she frowned even more darkly, thinking; grown-ups always made their own decisions, without the slightest concern for what younger people wanted.

Rohana understood all this as well as if Jaelle had said it all aloud, but she could not say so. As they rode up the ridge, she drew her horse neck and neck with Jaelle's and said, "I promise to you I will make no further obstacle to your taking the Oath if it is still your desire."

"Can you possibly have any reason to doubt it?" Jaelle asked, "Do you think your life is so fair I would wish to lead it?"

"Still, I would not have you take oath too young," Kindra said. "It would not hurt to delay a little; you might later wish to marry."

Jaelle looked her full in the eyes. "Why? So that I might have children first—and then abandon them, as you did?"

"Jaelle!" cried out Rohana, feeling Kindra's recoil of pain before the words were entirely spoken. "How can you—"

Kindra slapped Jaelle, hard, across her cheek. She said calmly, "You are insolent. Certainly it is better to prevent such a necessity; but I did not do it willingly, and it is better to take thought first. Would it be better to abandon the Oath should you later wish to change your mind and marry?"

"That will take place, kinswomen, when the Pass of Scaravel runs with fire instead of ice," Jaelle said angrily, and stared at the resin-tree stubs broken by the winds of the past winter.

"Well, are they salvageable, or must they be re-planted?" Kindra asked. "I do not know of such things."

"Now that I have seen, I can decide at leisure at home," said Rohana, turning her horse about on the trail. "No decision should ever be taken in haste, certainly not one like this."

They rode back silently toward the castle below.

IV

A few days later, Kindra woke early and wondered what had awakened her. Jaelle, in the next room, was sleeping; Kindra could hear her quiet breathing through the opened door. Outside in the corridors was a bellowing, a pounding, an unholy clamor; was it a fire, an attack by bandits? Outside the shutters she could see the dim grayish-pink light of the coming dawn.

Kindra slid her feet into fuzzy indoor boots and pulling a robe round her shoulders, went out into the corridor. Now she could recognize the bellowing voice as *Dom* Gabriel's; hoarse, almost frenzied, shouting, and quite incoherent. Kindra could not help wondering if he was already drunk at this unseemly hour and wondered for a moment if she should tactfully disappear so as not to embarrass Rohana, or whether the presence of a stranger might restrain some dangerous act.

Dom Gabriel came into view at the end of the corridor. Young Kyril, seemed to be trying to restrain his father, who was brandishing something and yelling at the top of his lungs about a horse-whipping.

Kyril said clearly, "I shouldn't advise you to try it, Father; you might find out it is not I who gets whipped. It is not my fault if your women find me more of a man than you."

Now Kindra could see the girl Tessa, scantily clad in a garment revealing even for a bedgown, clinging to Kyril's shoulders and trying to pull the two men apart. Rian came and skillfully in mid-yell wrenched his father off Kyril—evidently he knew some sleight or special skill at wrestling—and pushed his father, abruptly quiet as if he had been stricken dumb, down into one of the chairs placed at intervals along the hall. Lady Rohana, half-dressed, came along the corridor and her face turned sick at the number of people witnessing the scene. She said softly "Thank you, Rian. Please go and call his body-servant at once, or he may be ill. Gabriel, will you come back to bed now?" she asked, bending over the trembling man. "No, of course not; Tessa will go with you—won't you, my dear."

"Damned little slut," Gabriel mumbled. "Din' you hear? Should be horsewhipped an' I'm the one to do—" He made a half-hearted attempt to rise, but his legs would not carry him and he sank back.

Kyril stepped forward and put his arm round Tessa. "Lay a hand on her, father, and I swear you'll be the one to suffer!"

Gabriel struggled upward.

"Bastard! Le'me at him! Want to fight? Put yer fists up like a man, I say!" He lurched at Kyril, who launched a blow at him; but Rohana, flinging herself between them, received the heavy blow on the side of the head.

Kyril cried out in shock, "Mother!" and reached out to keep her from falling. Gabriel's reaction was almost the same, but on seeing Rohana dizzy and half-conscious in her elder son's arms, he staggered back and let himself fall into the chair, mumbling "Rohana? Rohana, you all right?"

"Small thanks to you if she is," Kyril said angrily and lowered his mother gently to the arm of an old settee. Rian had returned with *Dom* Gabriel's body-servant, who was fussing around Lady Rohana with restoratives. She raised her head and said "Kyril—"

"Oh, yes, blame everything on me, as usual!" the young man said, his arm round Tessa. "If I had had somewhere to take her, this would never have happened."

Dom Gabriel muttered "Should throw—little slut—right out o' here—"

Kyril looked almost heroic with his arm round the shrinking girl.

"If she goes, Father, I go with her; mark my words! And after this, keep your hands off *my* women—understand?"

Dom Gabriel raised his swollen blustering face, scowled and shook his fist, struggling to speak; then his body twisted into a frightful spasm and he fell, striking his head, twisted and lay with his body twitching, unconscious. Rohana sprang toward him, appalled, but his body-servant knew what to do; the man forced a twisted kerchief into *Dom* Gabriel's mouth so he would not bite his tongue, straightened his limbs a little as the convulsion died down, and knelt beside him, muttering words of reassurance as his eyes opened. Kyril flinched as his father stared sightlessly at him.

"It's all right, Kyril," said Lady Rohana wearily. "When he comes round, he won't remember anything about it."

"Look here, Mother, you can't blame me for this—"

"Not entirely; but you should know that when he has been drinking for days, this would be likely to happen and anything might set him off." She added to the body-servant, "Call one or two of the stewards and get him to his room and his bed; he will not leave it today nor probably tomorrow. And make sure that when he comes round there is soup or broth for him, but not a drop of wine, no matter how abusive he is nor how he raves. If you cannot refuse him, tell me and I will come and talk to him.'"

When *Dom* Gabriel had been carried to his room, she looked at the assembled family in the hallway.

"I suppose there is no use in telling people to go back to bed and sleep after all this," she said, and went to her daughter. "Don't cry, Elorie, Father has been ill like this before; he won't die of it, no matter how bad it looks. We must simply try harder to keep him from so much drinking or too much excitement." She turned to Kyril, who still stood with his arms round Tessa. She said to the girl in a clear icy voice, "You are not very loyal to your lord, my child."

"No, Mother," protested Kyril. "It's the other way

round. Father knew perfectly well Tessa was my girl. He brought her here to make trouble, that's all, maybe because he was hoping people would think it was *his* child! But how could anyone think an old goat like him—" he broke off abruptly, his voice strangling back in his throat as he looked at his mother. In her light gown, it was perfectly clear that Rohana's pregnancy was well advanced. He stared at the floor and mumbled. Jaelle snickered, her hand held tight over her mouth so only a suffocated sound like a fart escaped. Kindra scowled angrily at her, and Jaelle stared at the floor.

Rohana said wearily "Well, the girl should be monitored; if the child is an Ardais, no matter which of you fathered the poor thing, Tessa is certainly entitled to shelter here, and protection, and it is my business to see to it. Alida, will you have her monitored today?"

She beckoned to the *leronis*, who said, "Certainly; Gabriel had spoken to me about her child already—"

"Then he did not know—then he thought—" Rohana said half under her breath. She swayed on her feet suddenly, and Kindra supported her with a strong arm.

"Lady, this is too much for you," she said urgently.

"If everyone will—go and dress—I will see to breakfast in the hall—" Rohana said shakily.

Jaelle said in a firm voice, "No, Aunt, you are ill; *Dom* Gabriel is being looked after by his servants; you go back to bed, and Elorie and I will see to breakfast. Kindra, get her back to her room—call one of the women and carry her, don't let her walk! Aunt, for the baby's sake—"

"Why, thank you, Jaelle," said Rohana in surprise, letting herself fall back into Kindra's arms as the

wave of sickness threatened to overcome her. She
never knew who carried her to her room or her bed.

The light had strengthened considerably when she
woke again, and Kindra was sitting by her bed.

Jaelle was just opening the door. She asked in a
whisper "How is she, Kindra?"

"You needn't whisper, Jaelle, I'm awake," Rohana
said and was surprised at how shaky her own voice
sounded. "Is everything all right downstairs?"

"Oh, yes; everyone had breakfast; Elorie told the
cooks to make spicebread, and she had hot cider
served to the workmen. Rian told everyone the Master was ill, and the replanting of resin-trees would
begin at noon—he would come himself to oversee—"

"Rian is a good boy," said Rohana softly.

"Yes; he knows the estate well, and if Kyril would
let him, he could save his father much trouble,"
Jaelle said, "but Kyril is so jealous that Rian might
have some influence with his father—" she shrugged.
It was Kyril who took up some broth and was feeding *Dom* Gabriel; it was, I am sure, a touching sight,
but I heard *Dom* Gabriel shouting, as loud as he can
shout which is not very loud now, to take away that
swill and bring him some wine."

"Oh, dear," Rohana struggled to sit upright, "I
must go to him and explain—"

"No indeed," Kindra said urgently, "You must keep
your bed, my Lady—Rohana," she corrected herself,
"or you are likely to miscarry. And *Dom* Gabriel, at
least if he were in his right mind, would like that
even less than having the stewards refuse his orders."

Rohana sighed and lay flat again, knowing that
what Kindra said was perfectly true. Gabriel would
simply have to resign himself; though always irritable for days after one of these seizures, he dreaded

them enough that he might indeed heed a warning. "But tell him why I do not come to keep him company and sit by his bed," she said.

Jaelle said "I sent the healer-woman with a message already, Aunt. And I have sent for the midwife; she will know if there is danger."

Thus reassured, Rohana settled herself beneath the covers and lay somnolent, neither waking or sleeping all the morning. She hardly noticed the visit of the estate midwife, who examined her briefly and said she was in no immediate danger of miscarrying but a day or two of rest could do her nothing but good; that the lady was inclined to work too hard for her own good. When she woke in the late afternoon she found Kindra seated by her bed, her needle flashing in and out of a piece of fabric.

"What are you making? Jaelle does so little of this kind of work, I never connect it with a Free Amazon— a Renunciate."

"I find it restful; it is a collar," Kindra said. "I seldom have leisure to sit and do fancywork of this sort. If you like, I will make a piece of embroidery for a baby dress; then if your child is a girl—"

"Oh, no," Rohana said, "I would like a girl well; but it is a son, and Gabriel at least will be pleased."

"I suppose it is your *laran* that tells you that," Kindra said, and Rohana looked startled.

"Why, I suppose so; I never thought of it—I cannot imagine what it would be like to be pregnant and not know whether I bore a son or daughter. Are there women who truly do not know?"

"Oh, yes," Kindra said, "though I always was sure— but I thought perhaps it was my own fancy—at least I always had an even chance of being right."

There was a muffled knock on the door, and Lady Alida came in.

"Are you feeling better, Rohana? My dear, you must not trouble yourself about anything, anything at all; I can see to everything, absolutely everything," she said, smiling, and Kindra thought that the smile was not unlike a plump kitten who had fallen into the cream jar.

"I am sure of it," Rohana murmured.

"But there are a few things which must be settled at once," Alida said, "Kyril must be sent away immediately; this hostility against his father is very bad for both of them. He should go to Nevarsin; he needs discipline and some learning. It is not good for him to be here when you and Gabriel are at odds; he is almost a grown man."

"I suggested this a year ago, but Gabriel would not agree," Rohana said, and Alida smiled her cat-smile.

"Then perhaps there was some good in this morning's altercation; Gabriel will be glad to have him out of the house, I think. And there is something else; I monitored the girl Tessa; and it is indeed Kyril's child she is carrying." Her face took on an edge of fastidious distaste. "Will you really keep her under this roof?"

"What choice have I? If the child is an Ardais—even a *nedestro* has the right to shelter beneath his father's roof," Rohana said.

Alida grimaced. "I have seldom so resented the monitor's Oath," she said. "I was tempted to tell the girl she was lying—she wasn't, of course—and throw her out. I admit I don't have your charity, Rohana."

"I am not displeased at the thought of even a *nedestro* grandson," Rohana said, but Alida shook her head.

"Only a girl. I am sorry if that is not what you wanted."

"A granddaughter I will welcome, if she is healthy and strong," Rohana said. "At home she might be ill-treated, starved, or abused. Make arrangements, Alida: find her a room of her own and someone to look after her, and mind you, don't stint her of anything because Kyril will not be here to see. Anything else?"

"Yes." Alida had been moving about the room, now she came and sat down in a small upright chair. "Rohana, did you know that Rian is a full wide-open telepath, two-way, and probably a full empath as well? Gods alone know where he got it—it's not an Ardais trait."

"Oh, I am not sure of that," Rohana said. "Before he became so ill, Gabriel had a good touch of empathy; it was what I loved best in him." She paused to consider. "So Rian has it? No wonder he is torn so—"

"Between sympathy for you and for his father," Alida said bluntly, "the strife is tearing him to pieces. He should be in a Tower."

"I had hoped for a year or two of education for him in Nevarsin first—" Rohana protested.

"By no means," said Alida firmly. "He is too sensitive and scrupulous; he would heed every word they tell him. Surely you know that most boys hear only a little of what their elders say—Kyril has never heeded anything he is told—but Rian would take every word to his heart and dwell all his life a prisoner of *cristoforo* scruples. No, Rohana; the only safe place for him is a Tower, and I have already been in the relays; Arilinn will take him. Don't worry; they will educate him as well there as at Nevarsin, be sure of that."

I suppose I should be grateful, Rohana thought, *for Alida has spared no trouble for my sons, but her officiousness infuriates me; she really wants all things in her own hands. She is positively gloating that while I lie here ill, she has arranged everything as well or better than I could have done.*

But she attempted to barricade her thoughts from Alida and to thank her graciously.

"You have arranged everything so well, Sister-in-law, that now I will have all my children gone from me—except for Elorie, and she is betrothed—I shall be an idle old woman."

"Idle? You?" Kindra protested. "And you have still Valentine and Jaelle."

"Jaelle makes no secret of it that she is eager to be gone," Rohana said.

Alida said, "That cannot be allowed, Kindra. She must take her mother's place in a Tower; I am sure we could find one that would be glad to have her."

Rohana said "Have you ever seen any sign that she has enough *laran* for that? I think she would be miserable in a Tower."

Alida said crossly, "You know as well as I that she is blocking her *laran*; and you know why. You told me the story of her mother's death, when Valentine was born. She is not the first young girl whose *laran* was shocked open by a rapport she could not avoid and was not mature enough to endure—a traumatic birth, too close at hand to be shielded, or a death of someone she loved." Certainly, Rohana thought, that described Melora's desert death in childbirth. Alida continued, "But she cannot avoid it forever; some day it will return in full force; and she should be trained within a tower against that day. Of course her parentage—that Dry Town father of hers—is against her—but they might be persuaded to over-look it. Certainly not at Arilinn. They are so particu-lar about Comyn parentage, but Rian is to go there. I am sure one of the lesser Towers would have Jaelle. Margwenn at Thendara perhaps, or Leominda at Neskaya. Should I try to make such arrangements? I would be happy to try—"

"I am sure you would, Alida," said Rohana, wea-rily, "but this time your skills at arranging things are not needed; I promised Jaelle that if she spent a year here, I would make no further objection if she wanted to take Oath as a Renunciate."

Alida's mouth fell open; her eyes, very large and blue, stared at Rohana with an unbelieving gaze. "I know you said so when she was a child," she said, "but are you really going to hold to that? Even if she has *laran*?"

"I promised," Rohana said, "and my word is good. I do not lie even to children."

"But—" Alida looked more innocent and confused than ever, "The Council—they will not be pleased, Rohana. There are so few living Aillard women."

'I think I can persuade the Council," Rohana said.

Alida sighed. She said, "You will soon have oppor-tunity. They have sent word to summon Gabriel for the season, and since you still call yourself Aillard and not Ardais, and sit in Council as Aillard, it con-cerns you, too. But now that Jaelle is of age—and since you are pregnant—I was so sure—"

"You were so sure that you told them that Melora's daughter would be ready to take her Council seat this season, did you not, Alida," Rohana said softly. "Well, you will just have to tell them you were lying or fantasizing, will you not?"

Alida's blue eyes flamed with indignation.

'Lying? How dare you? How could I imagine that you would allow Melora's daughter to elude her duty by such an unlawful commitment?"

"Not unlawful," Rohana said. "The Charter of the Renunciates allows that any freeborn woman may seek Oath among them. It is true there have been times when I thought Comyn daughters were born less free than any small-holder's child; I had never thought you would agree with me, Sister-in-law."

"You are making a fool of me, Rohana!"

"No, my dear, you are doing that admirably for yourself. When you informed Council that Melora's daughter was ready for Council, you made a commitment you had no right to make and meddled in something which was really none of your business. I did not bid you speak of this to the Council, and you will simply have to get out of your own lies for yourself." Rohana lay back against her pillow and closed her eyes; but Kindra felt that behind the carefully impassive face Rohana was smiling.

"Rohana," implored Alida, "You cannot do this, the Council will not allow it."

Rohana sat up sharply. "Do you really think they can stop me?"

"Surely there is some other way—"

"Oh, yes, certainly," Rohana said wearily, "I could petition to take the Oath myself."

Alida cried out "You would not! You are joking!"

"Not a bit of it," Rohana said, "but it is true, I probably would not. But to get freedom for Jaelle, I might well tell the Council how unfit a guardian Gabriel is for any young girl; I might well testify to how he has humiliated and insulted me before my whole household, and petition to dissolve my marriage, to have him confined as a lunatic, and to forfeit his Council position and his place as Head and Warden of Ardais. If Kyril were not worse than his father, I would certainly do so."

"Oh, Rohana!" Alida was sobbing now, "For the honor of the Comyn—this would be a scandal to the Seven Domains—you would not drag the honor of Ardais in the mud so, would you?"

"I am tired of hearing you babble about the honor of Ardais," Rohana said, "What have you done to preserve it? It suits you well to have Gabriel incompetent to manage his own affairs while it means that *you* can manage them with no chance he will be able to forbid you. Did it occur to you that if Gabriel goes on much longer like this, he will drink himself to death or cause a scandal we cannot keep safe inside these walls? He is my husband, and I loved him once; for his own good he should be subject to someone who can restrain him from killing himself once and for all. I cannot"

"Do you think I want him to die?" Alida asked.

"You are certainly doing nothing to prevent it, and it seems to me that you are fighting all I can do to prevent it," Rohana said. "Can't you admit, Alida, that I am doing the best for the Domain and even for Gabriel? As much as you dislike me—"

"Please don't say that," Alida interrupted. "I don't dislike you; I admire and respect you—"

Rohana sighed and closed her eyes. She said without trying to answer Alida, "The representatives from Council, are they here?"

"They are awaiting audience with Gabriel—or with you if he cannot meet with them."

Rohana said wearily "Perhaps they had better see him, so they will not think I am merely trying to avoid—"

Alida protested, "But such a disgrace for them actually to *see* him like this!"

"I did not bid him drink himself into a stupor or excite himself into a seizure," Rohana said. "They must see him, Alida, or they will believe—as I think Kyril believes—that I am trying to take over the rule of the Domain for my own purposes. Send for the hall-steward."

Still protesting, Alida went, and Kindra, who had stood silently in the shadow of the bed-curtains, advanced to her side and said, "Are you able to deal with all this, Rohana?"

"It must be dealt with one way or another," said Rohana, "and there is none to do it if I do not. But you should not be—no one should be subjected to my family."

Kindra said, "You should not be subjected to your family," and felt a wave of tenderness for Rohana. *If I could only safeguard her against all this aggravation.*

Rohana lay silent with her eyes closed, hoarding her strength. After a considerable time, there was a soft rap on the door, and Rohana sat up, saying "Let them in; I must speak with them."

Three young men came into the room and bowed low to Rohana. All three bore proudly the flaming red heads of Comyn; the leader bowed to Lady Rohana and said "My lady of Ardais, I am sorry for the illness of your lord; it is all too obvious that he will not be fit to attend Council this season. Will you, as usual, take his Council seat?"

"As you can see, this year I cannot," said Lady Rohana, "My health will forbid it for this season. If my child is born healthy and strong, I might come toward the end of the season."

"What, then, of your ward—the daughter of Melora

Aillard?" asked the young man. "May we speak with her and ask if she is ready to be sworn to Council as Heir to Aillard?"

"That you must arrange with Jaelle herself," said Rohana, and when they had gone away, she sent again for Jaelle, who came sullenly to her.

"Jaelle, the representatives of Council are here; you must go South with them to Comyn Council and tell them for yourself that you renounce your rights, through Melora, to Comyn Council."

Jaelle protested "You promised me that I could take Oath—"

"And so you shall, if that is what you wish," Rohana said, "but I cannot renounce your rights for you; you must do that for yourself."

"But how—"

"They will ask you to present yourself before the Council, and they will ask you if you are ready to take your place in Council." Kindra said, "And then you must answer 'No.' That is all there is to it." She added "If you are old enough to swear Oath as a Renunciate, you are old enough to renounce Council privilege."

"But what do I do then?"

"Whatever you wish," said Kindra. "If you choose, you can go at once to the Guild House and await my coming to take Oath if you will."

Jaelle said sulkily, "I had thought we would go south together."

"Well, we cannot," Kindra said curtly. "For the moment at least, my duty lies here, and yours in Thendara, at Council."

"Oh, very well," Jaelle said angrily. "If it means more to you than coming to witness me take the Oath." She slammed out of the room angrily, and

Rohana heard her talking in the hall to the young men sent from Council.

"Will she ever forgive me, Kindra?"

"Oh, certainly; there is nothing wrong with her but that she is sixteen years old," Kindra said. "She is angrier now with me than with you. Give her a year or two. It would be even less than a year if she were involved in the running of a Domain, but even so, she will forgive you. She will even forgive me my loyalty to you. Some day."

Only one more confrontation remained for the day; at sunset, Kyril asked admission to the room and came in quietly, kissing his mother's hand in a respectful manner.

"I am sorry to see you sick, Mother. When he heard, Father was eager to get up and attend you, but his steward would not let him out of bed."

"I am glad there is a sensible man to look after him," Rohana said. "What do you want, Kyril? Surely you did not come to wish me health."

"Why should you think not, Mother? You have worn yourself out caring for my father's responsibilities; why do you not let him look after his own—"

"This again, Kyril?"

"You are making my father a nonentity and a laughingstock before all of the Domains."

"No, my dear, the gods did that. I save him the pressure of decisions he is unfit to carry, and I try to keep his honor intact before others." After a moment she said, "Would it be better if the crops went unplanted, the stud-books unkept, the resin-tree harvest ungathered? Are you able to take over that work? I would gladly yield all this to you if you could handle it."

"You mock my ignorance, Mother? That was not

my doing either. Now perhaps, if I am to go to Nevarsin, I may learn to manage such things."

"The gods grant it, Kyril," she said. He knelt for her blessing. She gave it fervently, laying her hands on his curly head.

Then he rose and stared down at her, frowning. "Is it true what Jaelle says—that she is to become a Free Amazon?"

"The laws allow it for any freeborn woman, Kyril. It is her choice."

"Then that is a vicious law and should not be allowed," Kyril said. "She should marry if anyone can be found who would overlook her parentage."

"This saves us the trouble of finding some such husband for her," Rohana said. "Leave it, Kyril; there is nothing you can do about it."

Kyril said angrily "I tried—" and broke off; but it was obvious to Rohana what he meant. A deep blush spread over his face.

She said scathingly, "And you tried to make her see what she might be missing if she refused marriage? You cannot forgive her that she did not fall directly into your arms? For shame, Kyril; this was a breach of hospitality—she is my fosterling. You should have respected her, under this roof, as your own sister! But she goes south to Thendara tonight, so no harm is done." After a moment she said, "Kyril, we part tonight; you go to Nevarsin; let us at least part without hostility. Wish me well, and go to say farewell to your father in peace."

Kyril flung himself to his knees and kissed his mother's hand again. He said, subdued, "I owe you gratitude for caring for Tessa; I was worried about her. Are you sending me away because of that scene this morning—because I made my father look a fool?"

"No, my dear," Rohana assured him gently, "It is high time you were sent away to be prepared for your place in life and in the Domain. You should have gone years ago. Now go and say farewell to your father and refrain from quarreling with him if you can; you set out at daybreak."

"And Rian is to go to a Tower?" Kyril said. "I am glad; he will make a good *laranzu*, and he at least will not contend with me for Heirship to the Domain."

"Surely you never thought he would, Kyril," Rohana said, as she put her arms around his neck and hugged him in farewell. "Goodbye, my dear son; learn well, and make the most of every opportunity. When you come back—"

"When I come back, the Domain will not be in need of woman's rule," said Kyril, "and you, Mother, can rest and confine yourself to a woman's work."

"I shall be glad of that," Rohana said softly, and when Kyril had gone, she sighed and said to Kindra, "And yet he was the dearest and sweetest of little boys. How could I have gone so wrong in his upbringing, that he turned out like this?"

"You were not the only force in his upbringing," Kindra said. "The world will go as it will, Rohana, not as you or I will have it. And I fear that is true of our children, too. Yours and mine, my Lady."

IV

It was very quiet at Ardais when the young people had departed. Kindra welcomed the quiet for Rohana's sake; Dom Gabriel was on his feet again, more or less, looking shaky and weak, but with the aid of his

stewards even managing to make some show of su-
pervising the replanting of the resin-trees.

Although no longer confined to bed, Rohana felt
unable to be much out of doors or to ride; she
allowed the steward to assist Gabriel with the replanting and took such minor exercise as she required, walking in the courtyards. Kindra felt this
confining but did not wish to leave Rohana, nor to
affront Dom Gabriel by coming into his presence
unasked. As for Jaelle, Kindra missed her but felt
that the absence of her sharp and critical presence
made life easier for everyone, especially Rohana.

The only remaining young person besides Glorie, the
girl Tessa, kept a very low profile in Kyril's absence, ap-
pearing but rarely in the hall; Rohana was just as well
pleased that the girl was content to take her meals in
her own room and did not grudge the extra service.
There was no reason Gabriel should be reminded of
his humiliation at his elder son's hands. Sometimes
at Rohana's invitation the girl joined the women at
their sewing in the conservatory; as far as Kindra
could judge she was a harmless shallow little thing,
with nothing much to say for—or of—herself. She
did not seem to miss Kyril and made no effort to
regain *Dom* Gabriel's interest.

For the most part of a tenday, life at Ardais went
on in this quiet way. One morning Kindra wakened
to the sound of a great windstorm which roared and
wailed around the corners of the building so as to
drown out most human conversation. Looking from
a window she saw nothing but acres of tossing leaves,
trees bending like live things almost to the ground,
snapping off short into broken stakes. In her near-
forty years, Kindra had seen no weather even remotely like this; no one ventured out except to tend

the animals, for any except the strongest farm workers would be blown off their feet. Kindra stepped out on a balcony and had to hold fast to the railing lest she be slammed back against the stone wall. The very air seemed to crackle with weird energy, although there was no thunder. Rohana looked troubled and refused to approach the balcony.

"Is it the wind that frightens you?" Kindra asked. "I have never known anything like it; I am a strong woman but I was very nearly blown off my feet. You could have a bad fall—which could be dangerous for you just now."

"Do you think I would care?" Rohana asked. "I am so sick of being inactive, of doing nothing! I don't care what happens—" Then she broke off and looked guilty. "But this far along in pregnancy, my child is strong enough that I can feel his struggle to live; I cannot endanger that life." Kindra was appalled; she had had no idea that any such thoughts had been crossing Rohana's mind. She felt deeply troubled for her.

"Not the wind," Rohana went on, "but the energy in the air; it can ignite fires when the resin-trees are so dry. We had too little snow last winter. Unless it begins to rain before the wind dies, we must send out a fire-watch at first light.

Kindra had never heard of such a thing; though she knew lightning was the major cause of forest-fire, this strange storm without visible lightning or thunder was new to her.

The sun was not visible; in the swirling wind, clouds of leaves, snow from the crags, and loose gravel occluded and hid the sun; a mysterious yellow twilight gradually took over the sky, which toward nightfall turned an eerie greenish color. There was no visible sunset; the light simply faded toward darkness until it was gone. In the darkness the wind went on howling like some chorus of demented demons. Whatever lights, torches, or candles were lighted were blown out almost at once by the drafts in the corridors; it was difficult to light fires in the main fireplaces, for the suction of the high winds in the chimneys blew back and tried to extinguish them. Elorie wrapped Valentine in blankets and brought him down from his nursery to join the others in the great hall before the fitful and smoking fire which seemed perpetually on the very edge of going out. He was fretful until *Dom* Gabriel, to Kindra's astonishment, took the child on his lap before the smoky hearth and croaked old military ballads in a quavering voice to distract the child.

Elorie said "It must be terrible to be out in this, Papa, do you think Rian and Kyril are safe by now in Nevarsin or wherever they have gone?"

"Oh, yes, for sure they will be in Nevarsin by now," Gabriel said, counting on his fingers. "What the devil ails the fire, Rohana?"

"The wind in the chimney keeps putting it out," Rohana said. "I will do my best to spell it to burn." She reached into the bosom of her dress and drew out her matrix, unwrapping the stone and gazing into it. Slowly the fire on the hearth flared up with a stronger blue light, and for a little time it burned with an almost steady light. Rohana had enclosed a candle in a windproof glass so that it, too, burned strong and clean; against the unholy clamor of the wind the burning hearth fire gave a curious illusion that all was normal. But after a time the suction of the wind pulled the fire raggedly back toward the chimney, and it began to beat uneasily in long rag-

ged flames; behind them the tapestries on the walls
bellied out like great sails with flapping sounds. It
was, Rohana thought, as if every one of the hundreds of people who had lived and died here were
flowing outside in the great screaming winds, howling and shrieking like a chorus of banshees. Yet it
was only wind. The servants began to bring in the
dinner; Rohana directed that it should be brought to
the fire and set up on small tables and benches
there.

"You have done well," she said to the cook. "Are
the fires in the kitchen burning properly?"

"We have an enclosed stove," said the main cook.
"And so we managed to roast a little meat for you
and the master, my Lady; but there is no bread, for
the oven will not draw. Your fire here is the only
good fire in the house; we can boil a kettle here for
tea, perhaps."

Dom Gabriel said in his rusty voice, "Shall we have
some hot mulled wine?"

"Yes, tonight I think so," said Rohana. In this
weather, whatever would content him was good. He
drank, and fed a few sips to the child in his lap.
Valentine coughed and spluttered but enjoyed the
attention, and when Elorie protested, Rohana shook
her head. "It will make him sleepy, and he will sleep
the better," she said. "Let him be for this once." She
carved up the fowl and they ate before the fire,
balancing the plates on their laps.

But in spite of Rohana's best efforts, the fire was
beginning to sink and burn with a bewitched light,
pale and fitfully. When the scant meal had been
eaten, such as it was, Rohana let the fire sink and
die; it was simply too much effort to maintain anything like a natural flame.

"Take *Dom* Gabriel to his chamber, Hallar," she ordered the steward. Her voice could hardly be heard over the wild clanging outside and in; the roar of wind, the banging of branches and shutters against the house.

As the man eased *Dom* Gabriel to his feet, Valentine clung to Rohana and said, "It sounds like the whole castle will blow down. Do I have to sleep alone in the nursery with the wind howling like this? Can I have a light?"

"A light will not burn tonight, *chiyu*," Elorie said, picking him up. "You shall sleep in my room in the trundle bed."

Dom Gabriel said grumpily, "Why not put him in the cradle and be done with it? He's a big boy now, aren't you, Val? Not a mollycoddle, are you, boy? You don't need a light and a nurse, do you, big fellow?"

"Yes, I do," Val said shakily, clinging to Elorie's skirt, and Elorie held him close.

"It's better than letting him be frightened to death alone, Papa."

"Ah, well—at least he is not my son," *Dom* Gabriel growled. "It's nothing to me if he turns out to be no kind of man."

Rohana thought, *Better no kind of man at all than a man like you,* but she was no longer sure that Gabriel could read the thought; there had been a time when it would have been instantly clear to him. In any case it did not matter. She wished Gabriel a good night aloud, and with her arm through Kindra's started through the dark and wailing hallways toward her own room.

Her women were clustered in the corner of her room, moaning in terror, their wails almost drowned out by the shrieking gale; as she came into the chamber, a shutter tore loose and slammed around the room, smashed into sticks of kindling and flailing everywhere. One of the slats struck Kindra and she could not keep back a cry of pain; the women took up the cries. Kindra said sharply, "It's only a stick of wood!"

"But it's cut your forehead, Kindra," Rohana said, and dipped a towel into a jar of water that stood on her dresser, sponging away the blood that trickled down her forehead. The women struggled to haul the shutter closed again. The banging sounded like some clawed thing trying to fight its way in, but something on the shutter itself had broken, so that the shutter would not fasten, and the wind was raging in the room.

"You cannot sleep in here like this," Kindra said, for the room was filled with the choking burden of dust, snow, and dead leaves borne on the howling gale, and the door into the corridor had come loose and was battering to and fro. "I am glad I will not be the one to sweep all these rooms tomorrow."

"Jaelle's room is sheltered," Rohana said, and led Kindra down the hall toward it, turning into the small room enclosed in a sheltered corner of the building, with relief. It was quieter here, and the women could hear their own voices more easily. As Kindra helped Rohana into her night things, she knew Rohana was still tense, straining to hear the wind, to know the worst.

"I am as foolish as Valentine," Rohana said, "afraid to be alone where a candle will not burn and I cannot be sure the walls will not fall around me."

"I'll stay with you," Kindra said, and slid into bed beside her. The women clung together in the dark, listening to the banging of shutters, fighting of branches against the walls and shattering of the few glass windows in the building.

After one such outburst of noise, Rohana, tense in the darkness, muttered "Gabriel will be beside himself with despair; we have so few windows and glass is so expensive and hard to have fitted. For years now he has been trying to make the place weather-tight, but a storm like this . . ." and she fell silent. "Even a few months ago, I would have gone to him and tried to calm him, but now he would mock me—or there might be someone with him who would mock me—I would even be grateful if that girl Tessa would go to him and comfort him—" her voice drifted into silence.

"Hush," Kindra said, "You must sleep."

"Yes, I must—after all this there will be work for everyone tomorrow," Rohana said, closing her eyes and snuggling against Kindra. A faraway battering sound made her wonder what other structure had come loose, fighting wildly against the storm. Then there was a sudden swashing sound, a rushing against the shutters.

"Rain," Rohana said. "With this wind it is being thrown against the walls like waves. But at least now we need not fear fire before daylight."

The sound was like a river in full flood, but Rohana had relaxed. Kindra held her close, troubled for her, knowing that it was as if the weight of the whole domain rested on this single body, which seemed so frail and was so surprisingly strong. *And all the weight is on her; now, when it sounds as if the whole world is breaking down into wind and chaos, she bears it all on her shoulders—or in her body like the weight of her child.* Kindra held Rohana close, wishing that she could ease the burden for her friend; *It is too much for one woman to carry. I have always thought that the wives of rich men were idle, letting their men determine what they might do; but she is as powerful and self-determined as any Renunciate. The Domain could not be better managed by five strong men!* she thought, holding Rohana tenderly in her arms, *yet she is not strong, she is a frail woman and not even in good health.*

Gradually the distant sound of the roaring wind seemed merged into a song, a lullaby on which she cradled and rocked the woman in her arms. And at last, knowing Rohana slept, she slept, too, in spite of the great howl of the wind.

IV

Rohana woke to silence; sometime before sunrise the wind had died. She was still nestled in Kindra's arms and for a moment she felt a little self-conscious; *I went to sleep clinging to her like a child.*

It reminded her a little of the days when she had still believed that Gabriel was strong and had all things under his control. She had felt so secure then; and she had been sure that whatever was beyond her strength, she could turn to Gabriel for his help. Now, for these many years, not only could Gabriel not help her, he was not even strong enough to carry his own burdens and she must look after his welfare as if he were one of the children. She thanked the Gods that she had always been strong enough to look after herself and Gabriel, too, but it had been sweet to feel Gabriel's strength and enjoy his protection—and his love. It had been so long since there had been any strength on which she could lean.

Love. She had all but forgotten that there had truly been a time when she did love Gabriel—and when, in truth, he had loved her. She had clung to that long after his love for her was gone, even after her own love had died out, starved into death by lack of response; that illusion that if only she could cling to her own love, his might one day return.

Was love always an illusion, then? She supposed that Gabriel did love her in his own way—a fondness, born of habit, provided she demanded nothing, asked nothing of him. She still cared for him, remembering what once he had been. *I love my own memory of the illusion that once was Gabriel's love,* she thought, and began to turn over in bed, knowing she should rouse the servants; there would be much to set to rights after the great storm,

Then she froze as far above her in the great tower, a bell began to toll with insistent regularity, in groups of three; clang/CLANG/clang, clang/CLANG/clang. She sat upright, her breath coming swiftly. Beside her, Kindra murmured "What is it?"

"It is the fire-watch bell," Rohana said, "Somewhere on the estate, a fire has been sighted; probably during the great wind, a fire was ignited and smoldered unseen, too sheltered to be put out by the rain. It is not the danger signal yet." She put her feet to the floor and sat up, steadying herself with her hands as the room seemed to swing in slow circles round her.

She managed to get up, thrusting around with her feet for her slippers, her bare toes avoiding the cold stone floor. Kindra got up and found her robe, then followed Rohana toward the hall. The floor lay thick

with dust, dead leaves, little knots of foliage, gravel
in little piles. *What a cleaning project for someone!* The
fire-watch bell continued its slow pattern of tolling.

The great hall was filled with people gathered for
the sound of the bell; obligatory gathering, for the
purpose of dealing with the single greatest danger in
the mountains, or, for that matter, anywhere in the
Domains; fire. Little Valentine, like all children made
wild by the break in routine, was running about,
shouting; Rohana made a step or two to capture him
but could not; she sat down and said firmly "Come
here, Val."

He came to a halt an apprehensive few steps from
her; she reached out, grabbed his shirt-tail, and beckoned to Elorie.

"Find Nurse Morna, and tell her that her only
responsibility for this day is to keep Val safely above
stairs, out of danger and out from under people's
feet."

"I could look after him, Mother." Elorie offered.

"I am sure you can; but I have other things for
you to do today. You must be my deputy, Lori.
First—" Rohana found a seat on a bench and established herself; one of the women brought her a cup
of tea while the old nurse was found and Val, yelling
with rage at missing all the excitement, was carried
away.

"Now," she directed Elorie, trying to recall everything that must be done, "Go to the head cook and
tell her that if the ovens can be lighted, we must
have at least a dozen loaves and as many nut-cakes.
Then if anyone has been butchering, we must have
at least three chervine hams roasted for the workmen, and she must kill three fowl and put them over
to make soup. And you must go to the west cellar

and bring up the barrels there—get two of the stewards to carry them, you cannot even lift one barrel—and a couple of women to help unpack the barrels; they will have a hundred each of clay bowls and mugs. And at least four dozen pairs of blankets and so forth—and three or four sacks of beans and dried mushrooms, and barley and so forth, for the camp, —and have Hallert harness up the big cart to take the men up to the ridge."

Elorie hurried away to the kitchens, and Rohana beckoned to one of the stewards.

"One of you must stay close to the Master today," she said, addressing herself to Hallard "You or Darren; try to see that he does not become too excited." There was no way she could prevent him from drinking, when law and custom demanded for every man on the fire lines his fill of wine or beer; but if Gabriel collapsed on the fire-lines as he had done before, or had a seizure, she could only arrange that it did not disrupt the serious business of firefighting.

"I will look after the master," promised Hallert; he had been with the family since *Dom* Gabriel's father died.

"Thank you," Rohana said fervently. Outside they heard the old cart rumbling up to the door, and the men and the younger, more able-bodied women went to climb in. Rohana was about to join them when Lady Alida stepped in front of her.

"You know a ride in that jolting cart would be really dangerous now," she scolded in a low voice.

Rohana sighed. She knew this already; she felt heavy and sick, constantly and painfully aware of the weight of pregnancy, frantic with fear for her child, but conscious of divided duty and loyalty.

"What other choice is there, Alida? Can we let the Ridge burn?"

Kindra said "If you will trust me, Rohana—this would not be the first fire-camp I have managed."

Rohana felt an overpowering sense of warmth and gratitude. Kindra was there, yes, able and trustworthy and fully capable of doing what she, Rohana, was not strong enough to do.

"Oh, could you, Kindra? I would be so grateful," she said with overpowering warmth, "I will leave it all in your hands, then."

"Indeed I will," Kindra said, taking Rohana's hands in hers and putting her firmly back into a chair, "Everything will be all right, you'll see; we have got at it quickly and it will not get out of hand."

Alida scowled; "They will not obey an Amazon," she pointed out to Rohana. "She is not an Ardais."

"Then they must obey her as they would obey me—" Rohana said "*Or you.* You must see to it, Alida; it is that, or I must go no matter what."

Alida, she knew, might otherwise sabotage Kindra's efforts out of pure spite; she did not know Kindra well enough to trust her simply for the good of the Domain. "Promise me, Alida; for the good of the Domain. Gabriel really is not strong enough to do this, and—just now—neither am I. Do not try to tell me that you could boss a gang of fire-fighters."

"No; certainly not. How would I have learned such a skill?" Alida said haughtily.

"The same way I did," Rohana said, "but fortunately for Ardais's safety this day, Kindra n'ha Mhari is willing to take over. *If* you will back her up."

Alida stared angrily into Rohana's eyes, and Rohana knew it was alien to her—to submit to the authority of the strange Amazon. But at last Alida said "For

the good of the Domain. I promise." Rohana heard
what she did not quite dare to say aloud;

Some day, Rohana, you will pay for all this.

"No doubt I will," she said aloud, "When that day
comes, Alida, call me to account; for now, I do what
I must, no more. Promise me, on the honor of
Ardais."

"I promise," Alida said, and added to Kindra;
"*Mestra*, anyone who does not obey you as myself,
shall be dealt with as a traitor."

Kindra said solemnly "Thank you, Lady." She clam-
bered up into the cart over the tongue, stepping up
agilely between the animals, and took her place at
the front of the workers; the driver clucked to his
beasts and the cart lumbered out of the yard. Alida,
standing beside Rohana, said with a reproachful look
"How is it that you could not see reason when I bade
you, but for that Amazon you immediately saw sense
in what I was saying—"

Rohana said, more gently than she intended "Because I have known Kindra a long time, and I know
how efficient she is; whatever she does will be as well
done as I could do myself."

She went into the house, and set herself to confer-
ring with the cooks; in another hour or two, the
smaller cart, laden with food and with field-ovens,
went up toward a flat spot short of the actual fire-
camp, from which the men would be fed and cared
for during the emergency.

And then there was really nothing to do, except
somehow to occupy her time, sewing on baby-clothes,
a neglected pastime—in all of her previous pregnan-
cies she would have had a full layette for the pro-
spective newcomer at least a month before this. Her
women, the few who had not gone to the fire-lines

because of age or inexperience, were all pleased to
see her finally making provision for the coming child
and more than glad to help her at it; by noon there
was a basketful of stuff assembled, small blankets,
diapers, even quite a number of pretty little embroidered dresses and petticoats salvaged from the other
children. Rohana's mind, no matter how she dissim-
ulated, had not been entirely on what she was doing,
and she broke off to say "Oh—I was afraid of this."
She hurried clumsily to the courtyard; it was not the
small cart, as she had thought from the sound, but a
wheelbarrow, into which his steward had loaded the
unconscious *Dom* Gabriel, as the only available vehi-
cle, and trundled him down from the ridge; Rohana
thanked the man, and with Alida's help she set herself to applying restoratives and getting the sick man
to his bed; she showed him, with soothing words, the
baby-clothes and blankets she had gotten together
for the baby, knowing it would please him to think
of the child; after all, he was the one who had wanted
it.

At last Gabriel dropped off to sleep and Rohana
went to her own room and to bed. She slept but ill,
tossing and turning; twice she dreamed that she had
gone into labor on the very fire-lines and woke crying
out in fear. It would be more than a few days, she
knew, perhaps a full moon; babies tended to be born
more readily at the full of the largest moon, Liriel,
and Liriel was just beginning to show her narrowest
new crescent in the evening sky.

She was in no hurry; she dreaded the thought,
with the household in such disorder . . . the boys
away, and not yet recovered from the great storm.
Also, though she had not counted her time very accu-
rately, it seemed too soon; she felt her child was not

yet ready to be born strong and healthy. But the constant dreams—she knew this from experience—meant that the unborn child's *laran* was intruding on her own. If she must have a child, she wanted one who was vigorous and strong, not a feeble premature one who would need a lot of care. Which reminded her that unless she wanted to breast-feed it herself—she didn't—she must consult the steward or estate midwife about another pregnant woman who would be having a child at about the same time and could breast-feed her child with her own. If I am to go to Council, I cannot be troubled with feeding a babe; it must be sent out to a nurse. So she determined to make inquiries about a healthy wet-nurse so that she could do her duty to Comyn Council without harm or neglect even to this unwanted son coming so late in her life.

Forgive me, child, for not wanting you. It is not you I do not want; it is the trouble of any child at my age. She wondered if anyone would understand this. Other women she talked to seemed only to feel that she was exceptionally blessed, having a child after the regular age to hope for such things was past. But did they really feel that way, or was it only that this was what women were supposed to feel? Kindra had spoken of other women seeming always content with their lot. *Am I simply, like Jaelle, constantly rebellious and questioning? I had thought myself wholly resigned—are then the Renunciates really as dangerous to the institutions of contented, happily married women as Gabriel—and Alida—think they are?*

Certainly Kindra was the only person who had even *seemed* to understand how she felt. *And truly that could be dangerous*, she thought, without bothering to ask herself why.

Toward afternoon of the next day they could still smell the smoke; Gabriel was up and around, but looking exhausted and weary. Most of the day Gabriel was content to lie on a balcony overlooking the Ridge where they could smell and see the smoke and the distant fire; but he was too languid and weary to worry. Rohana did enough of that for both, and found that much of her worry was about Kindra; would the woman expose herself to peril, or have enough sense to safeguard herself from the worst dangers?

VI

The sun was still invisible but the sky was darkening and night was evidently falling. Rohana jerked erect as if pricked painfully with a needle; somewhere within her mind, a signal had flared into brilliance, a warning. But with whose *laran* had she unknowingly made contact? A pattern of fire, fear. . . .

There was no one on the fire-line with sufficient *laran* to reach her this closely except Alida; Alida, who was herself a *leronis* and who had spent, like Rohana, several years in a Tower in training. But the general lack of sympathy between herself and Alida would prevent casual or accidental communication of this sort; this time it was obvious that Alida for some reason had deliberately reached out for her.

Warned by that silent signal, Rohana withdrew her mind from what was happening around her and concentrated on the matrix jewel inside her dress.

What is it? Alida, is it you?

You must come, Rohana. The wind is rising again; we

must have rain or at least keep the wind from raising a firestorm which it will be likely to do.

Sudden dread clutched at Rohana, a warning of clear danger; at this stage in her pregnancy it was not safe to use *laran* except in the simplest and most minimal way. Yet if the alternative should be a firestorm which could ravage the entire Domain of Ardais and threaten every life in the countryside, what alternative did she have?

I cannot come out to the fire-lines; I cannot ride now, and I should not leave Gabriel. You will have to return here and we will do the best we can.

A silent sense of acquiescence; and the contact was withdrawn. Rohana sat silently with her eyes closed. Gabriel, with too little *laran* to know precisely what was happening, but too sensitive to let everything pass unaware, turned to her and asked gently, "Is something amiss, Rohana?"

"*Laran* signal from the fire-lines," she murmured, glad of an opportunity to speak of what she felt. "We desperately need rain, and there has been no opportunity to gather a *laran* circle together. Alida is returning, and she and I will try to do what we can—at least to keep the wind from rising again."

He lay without moving, except for his eyes, too exhausted and languid to have much to say. At last he murmured, "It is at times like this, Rohana, that I regret I have done so little to learn use of my *laran*. I am not wholly without it."

"I know that," she said soothingly, "but your health was never really strong enough to let you make full use of the talent."

"Still, I wish I had been able to do more," he insisted. "I would not now be so completely useless to the Domain. With fire approaching, I feel so helpless—more helpless than any woman—since it is you women who must do what you can to save the Domain and I am here useless, or worse than useless, just another body to be protected. Perhaps we were too quick to send the boys away, Rohana; both of them have some *laran*."

"It would have done no good to keep them here, Gabriel. I could not work in a laran circle with my own sons."

"No? Why not, pray?"

"There are many reasons; for one reason and another it is not done." Rohana did not want to go into the many reasons why parents and their grown children were barred from working together in matrix circles. "There is no reason to trouble yourself about it now, my dear," she said peacefully. "Alida and I will do what we can; no one alive can do more. And try not to be concerned or your fears and worries will jam the circle." Vaguely she wondered if she ought to make sure that he was drunk or drugged before they began whatever it was that they would have to do. Now she was conscious at the edge of her mind of a horse being ridden breakneck—Alida was usually a careful if not an overcautious rider; now she was afraid and racing for Castle Ardais at an almost dangerous speed. Rohana felt a burst of fear; if it could so override Alida's caution, the danger must be great indeed. She resisted the temptation to look back at the advancing fire through Alida's eyes; that could only exaggerate her own fears, and now she must be calm and confident.

Now she could hear the rider's hoofbeats in the courtyard below the balcony where she sat. She laid her work aside, scornfully looking at the embroidery and being grateful that she had something more to give her Domain and people. How must Gabriel feel at a time like this? Well, she knew how he felt; helpless, he had said, *helpless as a woman.* But I am a woman and I am not helpless; I suppose that is just Gabriel; he associates helplessness with women in spite of the fact that I, a woman, am the strongest person in his life.

Alida was dismounting in the court, and to Rohana's relief, Kindra was with her.

"Let us make ready quickly," she said, and the women went up to the conservatory. Rohana and Alida seated themselves in two chairs facing one another, knee to knee.

"Can I do nothing to help?" Kindra asked, concerned.

"Not much, I fear, but your good will can do us no harm," Rohana said.

Alida added, with instinctive tact, for once knowing how Rohana felt, "Sit here with us and make sure we are not disturbed; that no one should break in on us."

Alida had her matrix in her hand. "Do not look at the stone," she warned Kindra with a quick gesture. "You are untrained; it could make you seriously disoriented or ill."

Helpless, like the rest of us, but, unlike us, not knowing it.

Rohana, knowing that she was delaying, swiftly thrust the field of her concentrated attention within the stone, moved upward and outward to survey, as if from a great height, the fire raging on the ridge above the Castle. With her enormously expanded senses she could see the air currents that fed the fire . . . she seemed to ride upon them, hungry to feed the swirling updraft of the fires. For an instant the exhilaration of it swept over her, all but carrying her to become part of it, but conscious of the link with Alida keeping her earthbound, she controlled herself, searching for remedies to the inexorable strength of the fire.

If there were enough moisture in these clouds to bring heavy rains—

But there was not; the clouds were there, heavy laden with enough moisture for rain—but *not* enough to drown the threatening firestorm. She felt Alida reaching out, making swift strides through the overworld. It was as if hands clasped theirs, wings beat beneath them as they flew.

How can we help you, sisters?

Rain; it is fire we face; give us clouds for rain.

The faceless voices—Rohana sensed they were from Tramontana Tower—swiftly grasped them, displaying the mountains below as if on a giant picture; only a few scant clouds, and when pushed toward Ardais, not sufficient at this season for anything but raising more wind from the imposed motion, so that the best they could do was worse than no help at all.

The voices from Tramontana were gone, and Rohana, with a sense of helplessness knew there was nothing to do with the fire but let it burn as it wished, down the ridge toward the Castle, where it would be arrested by the stretch of deeply plowed fields and by the stone of the Castle itself.

She opened her eyes and lay back exhaustedly against the cushions of her chair.

"I have never felt so helpless," Alida said.

"It is not your fault, Alida, it is only that sometimes there is nothing that can be done." She was suddenly seized by a wave of weakness, a gnawing pain reminding her that matrix work this late in

pregnancy could bring on premature labor. With
great bitterness she thought that she had risked her
last child—and without even the justification of ac-
complishing what she had tried to do, the saving of
Ardais. Bent over, gasping with pain, she said, "Alida,
warn them, the fire will come this way, they may
have to fight at the very house doors . . ." and felt a
wave of blackness sweep over her. When she woke,
she was lying on her own bed in her own room, and
Kindra was beside her.

"The fire—"

"Lady Alida is gathering them together with soaked
blankets and rugs; I knew not how strong she was in
a crisis," Kindra said.

Rohana said flippantly, "I have not wanted to give
her time to develop her strength; but now I am glad
she has it." She started to rise, but was checked by
pain, and Kindra held her back.

"Your women will be with you in a few minutes;
Dom Gabriel became troubled and had to be taken
to his rooms and put to bed, too," Kindra said.

Rohana lay quietly, feeling the powerful forces
working within her body. It was out of her hands
now, inevitable, and she felt the usual resistless terror. Now she could not escape. She clung to Kindra's
hands almost feverishly, but the Renunciate made no
sign of leaving her though her clothes were smoke-
stained and still reeked of the fire-lines.

The women came and examined her; none of
them could say whether or not she was actually in
labor; they would simply have to wait and see. Rohana,
knowing that nothing she could do or say could do
anything one way or the other, tried to rest quietly,
ate and drank the food they brought her, tried to
sleep. Far away she heard voices and cries; but there

was no way even the worst of fires could cross the wide band of plowed lands around the castle—thanks to all the gods that it was not late in harvest when these lands would be covered with dry plants which would burn—and at last the very stone of the castle would resist fire. She was grateful that Gabriel had been carried to his bed; close-quarters fighting at the kitchen doors would agitate him beyond bearing. She hoped Alida had given orders for a sleeping-draught for him, at least.

That abortive attempt to link with Alida and use *laran* against the fire—had been her only failure ever in use of *laran*. She hated to fail, though she knew that even a fully trained Tower Circle could have done no better. The very cooks fighting with soaked rugs had done better; one of them had stepped on a live coal and burned through his shoe sole, but had not been seriously hurt. All was well, the castle had suffered no harm; only she felt this intangible sense of utter failure. *Everyone sooner or later finds something he or she cannot do,* she told herself, but she did not believe it; she was not allowed ever to fail at anything.

She lay fitfully slipping in and out of sleep; when she woke again, she knew it was late morning of the next day; the sun was shining through a smoky sky, and she knew she had escaped the consequences of her rashness; she was not in labor, not yet: this child would not be born today, at least.

Kindra came when Rohana's women came to look after her, and Rohana stretched out her hands in welcome.

"How can I ever thank you? You have done so much for me—for all of us."

"No," Kindra chided, "I did only what was neces-

sary; I could hardly have denied that kind of help no
matter where I guested. But she smiled and bent to
embrace Rohana. "I am glad nothing worse was to
be faced. And this morning you look well!"

"I am very fortunate," Rohana said and meant it
with all her heart. 'And not the least of my fortune is
to have such a friend as you, Kindra."

Kindra lowered her eyes, but she smiled.

"Sit here beside me; I have been told by these
women that I must stay in bed and do no more than
a flowering cabbage, lest I excite my naughty baby to
trying again to be born before his time; I am so
bored!" Rohana exclaimed. "I was not born to be a
vegetable! And these women think I should take for
my model a nice contented cow!"

Kindra could not help laughing a little at the image. "You, a vegetable, never! But perhaps you could
pretend to be placid, perhaps like a floating cloud—"

"When I was a young girl, I had a cousin who
traveled southward to the sea; he told me of sea
animals who are graceful in the water, but when they
try to go on land they are so heavy that their bodies
cannot support their weight, and they can only crawl
and flop about." Rohana, trying heavily to tug herself upright and turn over in bed, showed Kindra
what she meant. "See, I am like one of these beached
fish-creatures. I think this must be a very big baby; I
was not as heavy as this even a tenday before Rian
was born, and he was the largest of my children.

Kindra sat on her bed and patted her hand com-
fortingly. She said, "I seem to remember that older
women with later children always feel heavier and
more fretful; you forget how hard the last one was.
Probably just as well, or who would ever venture to
have a second child, let alone a third."

"I am certainly less patient than I was at nineteen when Kyril was born; I had been out on a nutting party, gathering nuts till it was too dark to see," Rohana said, "and when I woke in the night, I thought only that I had eaten too many nuts, or the stew I had eaten for supper had upset my stomach. It went on an hour before even Gabriel thought to call the midwife . . . and he was not inexperienced; his first wife had borne him a child. The midwife laughed at me, saying it would be noon at least before anything happened—but Kyril was born an hour before dawn. Even my mother did not believe how quickly it was over!"

"Then you are one of the lucky ones who gives birth easily?" Kindra asked.

Rohana grimaced. "Only that one time; Rian took two days to get himself born after he started signaling he was ready—and he has always been late for everything since, from dinner to birthday-parties. As for Elorie—I will never tell anyone much about her birth lest young girls hearing should be frightened. But I hope this one is not so bad as that." She shivered, and Kindra squeezed her hand.

"Perhaps you'll be luckier this time, then."

A serving woman appeared with Rohana's breakfast on a carved wooden tray.

"Lady Alida said you would not be getting up today, Mistress."

"For once," Rohana said, "I am grateful for Lady Alida's wish to show that she can manage everything as well as I do. Let us see her opinion of what a pregnant mother should eat; a little toast with honey, perhaps? Or did she have sense enough to consult the midwife?" She uncovered the tray; porridge and honey, with a lavish jug of cream, a dish of boiled eggs and one of cut-up fresh fruit. Evidently Alida *had* consulted the midwife—or Gabriel, who knew that pregnancy never affected her appetite. Thinking of Gabriel made her ask "What of the Master? I heard he was sick again last night—"

The woman said "Aye; Lady Alida ordered him a sleeping-draught; he was abed late this morning, and he's roaming about downstairs with his eyes swollen, growling as if he were spoiling for a fight."

Oh, dear. Well, at present she could not get up and deal with it. Perhaps Alida would have the sense to offer Gabriel some remedy for the after-effects of her sleeping-draughts. Rohana applied herself to her breakfast with an appetite only slightly diminished by the thought of Gabriel roaming around looking for something to grumble, complain, or storm about. She was safe and insulated here.

"You said I was like an Amazon, but not nearly enough," she said to Kindra, spooning up the last of the eggs in her dish. "You are braver than that, I suppose. You would not hide away to avoid an unpleasantness. Yet I wish I could stay here in this bed till the baby is safely born—Gabriel could not complain at me then."

"We have a saying; take care what you wish for, you might get it," Kindra said, accepting a slice of fruit. "But if you do wish to stay abed, would anyone stop you?"

"Only my own sense of what needs to be done," Rohana said. "I could not justify more than two days, say, abed, considering how well I feel. Then it is all to be faced again. Gabriel grows no better, and his drinking, I fear, is the last step in his disintegration."

Kindra asked, as the women took away the tray,

"How came you to marry Lord Ardais, Rohana? Was it a family match? For he seems not entirely such a man as I would have expected you to wed."

"I could defend myself and say so," said Rohana, "for surely my parents were more eager for the match than I. Yet it is not entirely true. Once I liked Gabriel well—no; I loved him." She added quickly, "It is only fair to say he was much different then; his sickness was something which passed across him now and then like a shadow—a look now and again of absent-mindedness; forgetfulness—he would not remember a promise or a conversation. And then he had not begun drinking so heavily; I thought at that time that the drinking was only an attempt to keep his pace among some roistering companions, not a fault within himself."

"I still feel you were designed by nature for something other than domestic cares," said Kindra.

Rohana smiled; Kindra thought the mischievous smile was at odds with the heavy body and swollen features.

"Kindra, is that a polite way of saying that I am not sufficiently dignified for a pregnant, middle-aged mother of three children who are already men and women?"

After a moment Kindra realized that a very real insecurity lay behind the flippant words. She hastened to reassure her.

"No indeed. I meant only—you seem too large of mind to be confined to domestic trivialities. You should have been a *leronis*, a wise-woman, a—I have a friend in the Guild House who is a magistrate, and you could fill that position at least as well as she."

"In short," Rohana said, "an Amazon."

"I cannot help feeling so," said Kindra defensively. "I still wish it were possible."

Rohana took her hand. She said, "Ever since I journeyed with you, I have wished it might have been so. Had I been given a real choice, I might have remained in the Tower as a *leronis*; Melora and I both wished for it. You know what befell Melora—and in a sense, when I wedded as my family desired, I felt that I was comforting them for what Melora could not . . ." her voice trailed off into silence. She sought Kindra's hand and said softly, "I think sometimes that Melora meant more to me than anyone in my life; this is why Jaelle is so dear to me."

There are times when I feel you understand me almost as she did. . . . The women were silent, then Kindra leaned forward and put her arm round Rohana. They embraced in silence; then, abruptly, the door swung open and *Dom* Gabriel stood in the doorway.

"Rohana!" he bawled, "What the devil is this? First I catch your slut of a daughter in the hay with a groom, and now I find you—" he broke off, staring in consternation.

"Now do I begin to understand why you have avoided my bed these many months," he said deliberately, "but if you had to console yourself, could you not find a man—instead of a woman in breeches?"

Rohana felt as if she had been kicked, hard, under the solar plexus; she could not catch her breath. Kindra would have moved away from her, but Rohana clung to her wrists.

She said, "Gabriel, I have suspected for many years that you are not only sick, but demented; now I am sure of it." She added, hearing her voice bite like acid, "Leave my room until you can conduct yourself

decently to our guest, or I will have the stewards
drag you out!"

His eyes, red-rimmed, narrowed and Rohana, wide
open, could read in his mind speculations of such
obscenity that she thought her heart would stop. She
felt sick and slimed over with his thoughts; she wanted
to scream, to hurl her porridge bowl at him, to
shriek foul language that she herself only half
understood.

Kindra broke the deadlock; she rose from the
edge of the bed, leaving Rohana against the pillows,
and said swiftly to the chamber-woman, "Your mistress is ill; attend her. Send for the midwife!" Rohana
let her eyes fall shut; her hand released Kindra's and
she collapsed, half fainting, as the woman scurried
away.

Dom Gabriel snarled, "One word from me, and three-
dozen women on this estate do just exactly as they
please! Does no one hear me?"

The midwife, coming in in time to hear this—in fact
Kindra suspected she had been in the next room
waiting for such a summons—lifted her head where
she bent over Rohana attentively, to say "Lord Ardais,
in this chamber alone you may not give orders; I beg
you, go and give orders where you may be obeyed.
May I summon your gentlemen?"

"Rohana's not as sick as all that; time I made a few
things really clear to her, what I will an' won't put up
with," Dom Gabriel grumbled. "Going to throw me
out of my own wife's bedroom? Then throw that
damned she-male in britches out, too!"

"My lord, I beg you, if you *will* stay here, be
silent," demanded the midwife. Rohana heard all
this as if from very far away, through wind and
water, very distant. She struggled to sit up, hearing

another sound; the distant sound—or did she hear it only through her *laran*—wild, hysterical sobbing; then Elorie, weeping, burst into the room. She ran and flung herself down at the edge of Rohana's bed. The midwife said "You must not disturb your mother, mistress Lori—but Rohana struggled upright.

"Elorie, darling, what is it?"

"Papa—" she sobbed, stumbling over the word, "He called me—he—" Her face was red with sobbing, her cheek bleeding with a long cut, one eye already blackened and swollen.

"Gabriel," Rohana said firmly, "what is this? I thought we agreed you would never strike the children when you were not sober."

Gabriel hung his head and looked wretched.

"Am I to sit by and watch her play the slut with any stable-boy—"

'No!" wailed Elorie, "I didn't, and Papa is *crazy* if he *really* thought so!"

"So then what were you up to with that young—"

"Mother," Elorie sobbed, "It was Shann. You know Shann; we played together when we were four years old! I scolded him because he had not properly curried my pony, and I took the currycomb in my own hand to show him what I wanted! Then when we finished, we were looking in one of the loose-boxes—"

'Watching the stallion, an' makin' all kinds of lewd filthy jokes about it," *Dom* Gabriel snarled, "I *heard!*"

"Oh, Gabriel; the children are farm-bred; you cannot expect that they will never speak of such things," Rohana said. "What a tempest over nothing! Elorie—?" she looked at her daughter, and Elorie wiped her eyes and said "Well, we were talking of Greyfoot's foal, true—but Shann meant no harm, and when

Papa began to strike him with the crop, I tried to grab it—Mama, is he really *crazy?*"

"Of course he is, darling, I thought you knew that," said Rohana wearily. "You should know better than to provoke him this way. I wish you could learn to be sensible and discreet enough not to set him off."

"I didn't do anything wrong," Elorie protested.

"I know that," Rohana said wearily, "but you know your father; you know what will upset him."

Kindra interrupted, "Elorie, your mother is not well either; can't you see that? If you must have a tantrum like an eight-year-old, can't you find your old nurse or someone like that to have it in front of, and not trouble your mother? If there is more of this, she could go into premature labor, and that would be dangerous for her and for your little sister or brother."

Elorie mopped at her eyes and snuffled. "I don't see why she wants to have a baby anyhow at her age; other ladies don't," she grumbled.

Gabriel's steward had entered the room. He said in a soft self-deprecating voice, "By your leave, sir," and gave Gabriel his arm. Gabriel shook him off and walked to the bedside.

"You going to let them throw me out of here, Lady?"

"Gabriel, I beg you," Rohana said in a stifled voice, "Truly, I am too ill to deal with all this now. Tomorrow when I am better, we will talk—that I promise you. But please now go away."

"Whatever you say, my love," he mumbled and went, turning back to say, "You too, Elorie; don't you pester your mother," and the door closed.

Rohana had the sense that she wanted to cry and

cry until she melted into one vast lake of tears. She held painfully to composure though her heart was pounding. She held out her arms to Elorie, who was crying harder than ever.

"Mother, don't be sick, don't die," the girl begged, and Rohana could feel the frail shoulders trembling in her arms.

"Don't be foolish, love; but I must have rest," she said, "That is all I need; your father has upset me terribly. Please run along now."

The midwife rose from the foot of the bed and said "I want it quiet in here," and Elorie, still sobbing and wiping her face, hurried out.

Rohana still clung to Kindra's hand; when all the other women had gone away, she whispered to Kindra, "Don't leave me. I could not blame you if you refused to remain here another minute; but I beg you not to leave me alone with—" she broke off, choking. "But why should you stay? I should never have exposed you to such—such unspeakable accusations—it is my fault. . . ."

Kindra squeezed her hand. She said "There is no honor in contending with a madman or a drunkard. I have heard worse. And—I asked you this once before in a somewhat different form—does it really offend you so much? Is it such an unspeakable accusation as all that?"

Shocked and startled—of all things this was the last she had expected to hear—Rohana said "Oh. That. Oh, I see. No; I loved Melora and I swore an oath to her, but it was the way Gabriel said it; as if it was the filthiest thing he could think of to say—about you *or* about me—"

"To the lewd of mind, all things are filthy," Kindra said. "He did not spare his own daughter, I noticed, and on flimsier evidence yet. The truth is that I really love you, Rohana, and I feel no shame about it, according to custom or not. I would not have spoken of this while you are sick and busy with other things; but he has brought it out; I feel no evil in loving a woman, and if he were an example of loving a man, I would feel disgust for any woman who chose men instead."

Rohana said in a low voice "I can certainly understand that. I said to you once—in the Dry Towns—that in the Domains, when two young men swear the oath of *bredin*, that they will be friends all their lives, and that not even a wife or children shall ever part them, there is nothing but honor for them; but if two maidens swear such an oath, no one takes it seriously, or at best, take it to mean only—*I shall love you until some man comes between us*. Why should it be so different?"

"I would say—and I do not know if you would agree—" Kindra said, "that it is because men never take seriously anything women choose to do unless it concerns a man. But that is why I am a Renunciate and you are not. But I would willingly swear an oath with you, Rohana."

And if you were a Renunciate I could love you without caring what people said; my primary vows and commitments are to my sisters.

It was not the first time Rohana had suspected Kindra had more than a little *laran*. She was touched and overwhelmed by the thought that Kindra loved her; she had thought before this that the Renunciate was the only person who understood her; but it seemed that Gabriel's accusation had fouled a thing she thought wholly innocent. *No, she does not understand this about me, I love her, but not like this,* and almost without realizing it, she withdrew her hand from Kindra's.

The Amazon looked sad; but as she had said, this was why she was a Renunciate and Rohana was not. She had not expected Rohana—certainly not in her present state of turmoil—to understand. She said gently, "Hush, you mustn't worry about anything now; there will be time enough to talk about all this when you are stronger."

Rohana was almost relieved at the sense of exhaustion and weariness that swept over her. She reached up her arms and hugged Kindra childishly, grateful for her kindliness and strength.

"You're so good to me," she whispered. "The best of friends."

Kindra thought, *I would have spared her that scene with Dom Gabriel. Yet it is what he is and it is what she must face sooner or later.*

She kissed Rohana again on the forehead and silently went out of the room.

If we are fortunate, it will not send her into premature labor.

VI

Rohana woke from a nightmare of going into labor alone, unprepared and in the desert outside the Dry Towns. Waking, she realized with enormous relief that she was not in labor, and the child in her body was quiescent, with only the routine dreaming movements. All the same she knew from experience—after all she had already been through this three times— that such dreams were a warning. Labor was near, though not imminent. She rose sluggishly and dressed in an old unlaced house gown. She was not able to face the thought of breakfasting in the Great Hall, but Alida would be only too pleased to deputize for her. She sent for some fruit and tea; when she had finished, one of her women appeared at the door.

"My lady, the Master asks to see you."

At least he had not pushed his way in unannounced. Rohana sighed.

"Drunk, I suppose."

'No, *Domna*; he looks ill, but sober."

"Very well, let him come in." She could not, after all, avoid his presence indefinitely here at Ardais.

But when this child is born, I shall go to Thendara for Council, or to my sister Sabrina, or home to Valeron. . . .

Gabriel looked small, almost shrunken inside his untidy old farmerish clothes. His face held the crimson discoloration of the habitual drunkard, but he seemed wholly sober. His hands were shaking; he tried to conceal them within his sleeves, but although he had carefully shaved himself, his face bore many small telltale cuts.

"My dear," she said impulsively, "You should have your man shave you when you are not well."

"Oh, well, you know, me dear, a fellow don't like to ask—"

"Nonsense; it's the man's duty," she said sharply, and heard the harsh note in her voice. "You shouldn't need to ask; I'll have a word with him."

"No, no, me dear, let it go. I didn't come for that. I am glad to see you lookin' so well, now. The little feller in there—he's quiet still?"

"I don't think it will be today, and perhaps not tomorrow," she said, "but it will be soon. We are fortunate—with the fire—"

And that terrible scene yesterday—she forebore to say that it aloud, but he heard it anyhow and awkwardly put an arm round her waist. He did not for once smell of wine and she managed not to pull away when he kissed her cheek. All the same she could sense, at the touch, the confusion and fuddlement in him, and it repelled her.

"I knew I'd need to be sober if you were in labor," he said and reached in the old way for *rapport*; instinctively she flinched and he did not press for it but said aloud, "I know yer angry with me. You should be; I was filthy drunk. I shouldn't a been so rude; no matter what *she* is, I know *you*, Rohana. Forgive me?"

Have I not always forgiven you? she asked, not in words, but she shrank from the thought of the long hours of labor when by custom they must share the birth in full rapport, telepathically entwined. *Trapped together in their minds.* . . . She *could not* endure it. He had been so different when Kyril was born, and during Rian's birth, which had been prolonged and very difficult, she had clung to his strength as to a great rock in a flood that was drowning her; his hands, his voice and touch holding her above the flood, pulling her back from the very borders of death. This would be the fourth time that they had gone down together into the inexorable tides of birth.

Yet how could she endure it after these intervening years of struggle and humiliation, after his foul accusations? He meant well; she was touched at the dreadful effort it must have taken to present himself here, sober and shaven after a profound drinking bout; *his poor shaking hands, his poor cut face,* she thought with a wave of habitual tenderness; but she clung fiercely to her pride and anger; if he wished to

revive his view of himself as strong supportive father, let him go to Tessa when her child showed
signs of being born! Then she remembered: he had
not fathered Tessa's child, but he must have had
reason to think so: Disgraceful! He should not think
that with one day's sobriety and attentiveness he
could wipe out a decade of neglect, abuse, and
humiliation.

Yet there was no alternative; by iron-bound custom, the father endured childbirth with the mother,
and she would be given no choice. Somehow she
must steel herself to endure the hours of birth in his
presence, and thank the gods if he did not present
himself drunk.

Rohana asked deliberately and was shocked at the
cruelty in her own voice, "Have you visited Tessa
this morning? She would, I am sure, be relieved to
see you well and sober."

His face twisted, half in anger and half in humiliation.

"Oh, Kyril's girl—if you like, me dear, I'll send her
away. We could have her married off to somebody
decent—"

"No," she said deliberately, "Alida told me there is
no doubt it is an Ardais child and she, too, has a right
to her father's roof. She is not offensive to me."

"You're better than I deserve," he muttered, "I
ought never to ha' brought her here."

"It doesn't matter," she said. "Gabriel, I am very
weary; I want to rest; and so should you. Thank you
for coming—" *And thank you for being sober and gentle;
I couldn't bear another scene. . . .*

He kissed her clumsily on the cheek and murmured a formal prayer for her health, then went
quietly away; and Rohana stood staring at the closed

door behind him, in something very like horror. At
least when he was a drunken beast she could protect
herself by despising him; but how could she protect
herself against this well-meaning mood and humility?

Not today and not tomorrow, she had told Gabriel;
and as the day and the next day wore on toward
sunset, Rohana, dragging around from hall to conservatory, from conservatory to kitchen, telling herself she was making certain all would go well while
she was laid up abed, felt weary to the point of
sickness. In vain she reminded herself of what she
had told other women in her state; the last tenday is
longer than all the other months together. She could
settle to nothing; not to a book, not to a piece of
fancy-work nor to plain sewing, not to her harp or
her *rryl;* she took up one thing after another restlessly, and felt as if she had been pregnant forever
and would be so for the rest of her life, if not for all
eternity.

As the afternoon of the third day dragged wearily
toward sunset Rohana watched the sun sink toward
night with distaste; another day over and another
night to come, during which once again she would
not sleep, but lie restless in the dark, tossing and
turning and hearing the clock strike the dark hours
. . . she could not remember when she had truly
slept.

She had set all in order with kitchens and estate—
she had even brought the stud-book records up to
date and made notes of some of the sales agreed
upon at the last horse-fair; two of their good breed-
ing mares to be sold into the lowlands, one more to
the Kilghard Hills—the Master of MacAran would
travel here to fetch them, but the payment had

already been received. They needed another saddle horse—Elorie was outgrowing her pony, but there was no saddle horse on the estate which was right for her. She had thought of Rian's horse—but it was a big, ugly raw-boned gelding, no ride for a girl . . . at least not if the girl was Elorie who was very concerned about beauty and elegance in riding-clothes and mount. Why Elorie should be so concerned with outward appearances Rohana did not know; somehow she had failed to educate her about what was important; but it could not be remedied in the next few days.

"It is a pity," she grumbled to Kindra, "that the Guild Houses do not educate girls as the *cristoforos* at Nevarsin do boys; I am sure that a year in a House of Renunciates would do Elorie all the good in the world."

"It might," said Kindra. "We must consider it. But alas, most of their fathers would fear we were teaching them what they should not know; and I fear much of what we teach would not please their fathers nor even many of their mothers."

"Well, there should be some place where girls should be taught—if only in charity, to keep down madness among their mothers—but you would not know," Rohana said. "You left your daughters, you said, when they were still little children."

"And ever since," said Kindra, "I have been raising other women's half-grown daughters—which in one way is simpler, since they are not my own and if they make preposterous she-donkeys out of themselves, it is no blow to *my* pride or self-respect. And sooner or later they do grow up to be a credit to us. Lori will too, you will see."

"That's not much comfort to me now," Rohana

said. "I look at her and feel I have raised a simpering idiot who cares about nothing but the color of the ribbons on her ball-dress—or whether she should arrange her hair in curls or braids for any particular occasion."

Kindra asked gently "Did you never so?"

"Never; I was a *leronis* at her age, and too busy for such things." Rohana said crossly. She went out into the courtyard, her long gown trailing, and toward the stables.

"Where are you going?" Kindra asked.

"Nowhere. I don't know. I'm tired of being in the house. I'll think of something." Her voice was absent-minded and irritable. Inside the stable, she went and offered a lump of sugar to her favorite mare. "Sorry, little one, I cannot ride today," she muttered, fondling the horse's nose. She passed down through the line of horses, caressing here, offering a tidbit there, drawing back and closely examining others.

When Kindra came up inquiringly, she said, "I should make ready for the horse fair, it is only a handful of tendays away . . . this year we should put up a pavilion for anyone for whom the sun is too hot, so that we can talk business out of the sun's rays."

It seemed fantastic to Kindra that at this point Rohana should be thinking about the horse fair, but no doubt it was habit—many years of thinking first and always about the management of the Domain.

Rohana wandered out to where two men were repairing saddle tack and said, "Hitch the small cart."

Kindra demanded, "What now? Surely you cannot go from home— "

"Only to the top of the Ridge," Rohana said. "I

must know whether the fire damaged too much, and how the replanting is coming along."

"You mustn't really. No, Rohana, it's impossible. Suppose you went into labor on the way—"

"Don't worry so," Rohana said, "I'm sure I will not. And if I did, at least it would be over!"

There was really no more Kindra could say. In spite of her extreme courtesy, Kindra was abruptly reminded that her friend was a lady of the Comyn, and the Head of a great Domain; further she was Kindra's hostess. It was really not for Kindra to say what Rohana could and could not do. She watched, feeling helpless. This really was not wise; in the Guild House they would have forbidden a woman—at this stage of pregnancy and after more than one false alarm of labor—to stir beyond the garden!

The cart was hitched, and Rohana climbed into it. "Come with me, Kindra; this is our gentlest horse. She could probably take the cart to the Ridge herself. Elorie drove her when she was only seven; she used to carry the children and their nurses everywhere before that." Kindra, unwilling to let Rohana drive off alone, climbed in and took the reins. Rohana did not protest.

And it was true that the old mare plodded along very gently. Along the Ridge, the earth was still scorched with the impact of fire; but already, along the rim of the hill where a long line of evergreens sheltered the field a little, a group of men were setting out a wavering line of resin-tree seedlings.

Along the Ridge, stark against the sky, there was a small stone hut, evidently a shelter for workmen caught by bad weather or for travelers. Rohana alighted from the cart and turned her steps toward the shelter; Kindra followed helplessly.

"What are you doing, Rohana?"

"The shelter must be checked, the law requires that it be kept stocked and in good order, and Gabriel would come up here a hundred times and never think to stick his nose inside." She disappeared into the darkness and Kindra followed.

"Disgraceful," Rohana exploded, "the mattresses are rat-eaten, the blankets have been stolen, the pots broken. I will send someone up here tonight to restock the place; if I could lay my hands on the criminal who tore this place up—I would rip him asunder! To do a thing like that—it is not only inconsiderate, but a traveler who destroys a place like that should be hanged! For he condemns anyone who comes here in bad weather to possible death from cold and exposure!" She staggered slightly and sat down unexpectedly on the bench. Kindra had not expected to see her so angry; she had not betrayed anger like this even when Gabriel brought Tessa home. But Rohana was still agitated as she shook her fist at the damaged supplies in the travel-shelter; Kindra came and held her upright, and she could feel Rohana actually trembling, see the beating of the blue pulse in her temples.

"I beg you, don't excite yourself; I am sure there is someone, do let me go and call one of the men to go down and give the orders for you," Kindra said, trying to speak in a soothing tone of voice.

"And look, someone has dumped a load of fresh hay in here; how annoying! For warmth, I suppose, but the danger of fire at this season seems to me too strong: They should not have done that." Rohana was walking around agitatedly, scowling; she stopped and sat down unexpectedly on the bench again, with a surprised look on her face.

"What is it, Rohana?" asked Kindra, but before Rohana could reply, she knew the answer.

"Is the baby coming?"

Rohana blinked and looked startled.

"Why—yes, I think so; I didn't really notice, but—yes," she said, and Kindra groaned.

"Oh, no! You cannot possibly be jolted all the way back in that cart!"

"No," said Rohana, almost smiling, "Here I am and here I must stay, I suppose, till it is over. Don't look like that, Kindra, I am certainly neither the first nor the last woman to give birth in a barn; you can send the men down for the midwife and one or two of my women—the ones I had chosen to help me."

"Shall I ride down myself?"

"No, please—" Rohana's voice suddenly wavered "Don't leave me, Kindra, stay with me."

Annoyed as Kindra was at this sudden development, she was touched and could not draw away from Rohana. "Of course I'll stay with you," she said in a soothing tone. "But now let me go out and send the cart down for your women and the midwife."

Reluctantly Rohana let go of her hand, and Kindra went out to where the cart waited. She said to the man on the seat, "You must go down quickly; the Lady is in labor and cannot be moved. Go down and fetch the estate midwife, and her women, and clean blankets, and everything she will need here; and *Dom* Gabriel and Lady Alida, of course," she added as an afterthought. She was not sure Rohana wanted either of them, but she could not take the responsibility of keeping them away.

"I'll go at once," said the man. "Truth to tell, *mestra*, I wondered about that when I saw her come

up here. Something about the look on her face—
when my own wife is near her time, she gets restless
like this."

"I wish you'd warned *me*," Kindra muttered, but
not aloud.

VII

Rohana rested on the load of fresh hay, vaguely
musing on the lucky coincidence that had brought it
here fresh when everything else in the shelter had
been damaged or destroyed. With the automatic confidence of a trained *leronis* who had been a monitor,
she ran her trained senses through her body, keeping pace with what was happening. Labor, for having started so recently, was progressing very rapidly;
the contractions were already coming at intervals of a
couple of minutes apart. All seemed well with the
baby, who was already in the deep pre-birth trance
of some babies; the alternative was a state of agita-
tion mingling terror and rage at the process, and
Rohana was just as grateful she need not—as was
often the case and had been the case with Rian at
least—spend all her own strength in calming the
baby's terror. She had heard a lot of debate among
the *laranzu'in* in Arilinn and elsewhere about which
state was better for the child's ultimate welfare; but
Rohana was not sure that any of them knew any
more than she did about it, and at the moment she
found it easier for her own sake that this baby was
one of the tranced ones. She would not have imposed a trance on a wide-awake and angry one, as
some of the women who debated the two viewpoints

considered to be best, just for her own convenience; but she found herself whispering to the child: *Just sleep, rest, little one; let me get on with this and you can wake up when it's over.*

The intensity of the contractions was by now very painful, but Rohana was so relieved that the waiting was over that she did not care how quickly it went; although she hoped she could hold out until the midwife got here; she did not really want to give birth alone. The unwitnessed birth of a child, no matter how regular the circumstances or how certain the parentage, invariably left, for the child's whole lifetime, his ancestry open to question except from the most charitable. Rohana lay back and tried to relax, knowing that, even though it was going well and quickly, there was a long way to go.

It seemed a long time—she lay alone. There was considerably less light in the shelter when she heard the heavy crunching of cart wheels, and Annina, the estate midwife of Ardais, rushed into the shelter, bearing a lantern, an armful of blankets, and what seemed like a cartful of other impedimenta. She immediately took charge.

"Marga and Yllana, lift her there—careful—spread out those blankets and the sheet on the hay—now ease her down. There ye are, my lady, all comfy, aren't we?"

It was a considerable improvement over lying on the prickly hay, and when they slipped her into a warm nightgown, it felt good. The midwife managed to get a small fire lighted at the far end in a small enclosed stove, and Rohana smelled the comforting smell of herbs for tea. She hoped the water would boil soon; she wanted a cup.

Alida knelt beside her.

"Rohana! Oh, we were all so worried about you, dearest! You should never have gone up to the Ridge, it was unforgivable of that Amazon to take you up there, but you should have had better sense than to listen to her. But now at least you're safe and warm—it looks like snow tonight—"

Rohana had reached a stage where she could not focus on Alida's chatter.

"Go away, Alida," she said, trying to get the words out between the careful breaths that were all that allowed her to stay at least mentally on top of the pain. "I have work to do. Don't blame Kindra. It was my doing entirely. She didn't want to come—without her I'd have come alone, and she knew it, so she came along." She stopped and concentrated on her breathing again, reached for Kindra's hand and held it, squeezing it in a bone-crushing grip. It felt good to focus on Kindra's strength, which in her heightened, wide-open state was as palpable as the heat from the stove or the swish of the rain outside the shutters.

Thrusting into the comfort of Kindra's touch was a familiar, unwanted touch, a sullen glow of suspicion in it as Gabriel's eyes rested on her hand in Kindra's.

"You gave us all a scare, me dear," Gabriel said, and to Rohana the tenderness in his voice was smooth and false. "But ye're safe now. Shall we send away all these people so you and I can get on wi' our work? Annina, o'course, can stay, that's her business but none o' these others—right, love?"

With a painful shock, Rohana surfaced from the carefully held focus on the contractions. One of them got a head start on her, and galloped across her consciousness so that it took all her effort to keep from screaming aloud.

She took a great breath, bracing herself against the next.

"No!" she cried out, "No! Go away, Gabriel! I won't have you here!" And with her last strength, a great blast of voiceless rejection, "Go *away!*"

"Oh, you mustn't talk like that," Alida crooned at her. "Gabriel, she doesn't know what she's *saying!* Never mind, Rohana, he's not angry at you, are you, Gabriel? Of course not, at a time like this—"

"O' course not," said Gabriel, and held a cup of wine, from which he had already taken a sip, to her lips. "Here, love, drink some o' this, now, it'll make you feel better—"

With dull amazement she remembered that this ritual had actually been welcomed at Kyril's birth and Rian's. Now it filled her with such disgust she thought she would vomit. *Serve him right if I did, all over his best shirt,* she thought and did not know whether to cry or giggle or weep. She thrust the wine back at him, spilling it all over his hand.

"No; I want some tea, Annina. Tea, do you hear? Gabriel, get out of here; out, out, OUT!" She was screaming now and knew she sounded hysterical; the blast of revulsion, purely automatic and without thought, reached Gabriel and Alida and Alida looked pale and rushed outside; Rohana heard her vomiting just outside the shelter.

Well, she got the message, Rohana thought; *I wish Gabriel were half that sensitive; it would save me a lot of trouble.* For Gabriel was still kneeling beside her smiling stupidly.

"Never mind, me dear. I know she don' know what she's sayin'" he confided in the midwife, "I wouldn't leave her for a thing like that—"

"If you don't—" she said, trying to aim her fury and revulsion at him alone, "I will—"

I will faint, I will die, I will vomit all over him, I will get up and run screaming out of here and have my child in the deep woods alone and after dark where we will be eaten by banshees. . . .

She saw with definite satisfaction that Gabriel turned a dirty-white color and rushed outside. This would be a tale creating scandal through the Domain and the Kilghard Hills; but she felt she absolutely *could* not bear his presence. Her fingers tightened on Kindra's, and the other woman gently patted her hand.

Well, that's over, she thought, without any sense of triumph, simply that now she could breathe freely without the oppression of Gabriel's presence, *now let's get this over with. . . .*

IX

The night wore on, endlessly; the lantern burned low and was refilled; Rohana seemed to float outside her body, conscious only of Kindra's presence like a lifeline.

Why do I want to survive this anyhow? Gabriel will never forgive me. I have lived long enough; my older children no longer need me; better to die than to make the decision to walk away from Ardais and Gabriel forever, yet if I live I cannot return to the kind of life I have been living these last few years. Nor will I ever again agree to bear a child for Gabriel's pride of fatherhood or for the Domain. . . .

That reminded her of the phrase in the Renunciate

Oath; *never to bear a child for any man's pride, position, clan or heritage . . .*

I should never have returned to Gabriel; when I returned from the Dry Towns, I should have stayed with the Free Amazons; Kindra at least would have welcomed me . . . and I should not be here fighting for the life of a child who should have never been conceived, a child I do not want. . . .

Then she realized sharply; *it is not only the child's life for which I am fighting; it is mine. My own life. But what good is my life to me now?* That was the question she could not answer. *Why should I live to nurse a drunkard? My own son is a worse monster than his father, so it is no good saying I am keeping the Domain for Kyril. And whoever comes after Kyril, for all I know, may be worse yet. Why not let the Domain collapse now, as it would do if I died, as it would have done a dozen years ago if I had not married Gabriel. The Domains will survive, as they survived without the Aldarans. Or it will go to the Terrans who are so eager to claim it . . . to map it, to know all about it.*

My life is over anyhow. . . .

Then, opening her eyes for a moment between pains, she looked directly into Kindra's encouraging gaze; and thought;

Even now, if I live, this need not be the end of my life; but for certain if I die, there will be nothing more; and I will never know what might have happened.

She began to listen again to the insistent suggestions of the midwife, to her murmured instructions. No, she would not die; she would fight to live, fight for the life of this child. Outside the shutters the light was growing and the wind had dropped so that she could hear the hissing of the snow.

Later, she knew that Gabriel had stood outside the

shelter all night in the snow, lest he should be summoned, believing that she would die, praying that he
could speak to her before she died, that she might
speak a word of forgiveness. That was much later;
for now she did not want to know.

She was conscious only of endless pain and struggle, effort which seemed to demand more fight than
it would have been to die.

More and more seemed to be demanded of her;

"I can't"—she whispered, and without words the
challenge came; *You must. . . .*

And then at the very end of endurance there was
a moment of surcease, of rest; and she knew (*from
experience*) that she should now feel relieved and triumphant; and she heard the midwife cry out in
triumph:

"A boy! A son for Ardais!"

Not for me? Rohana found herself wondering and
wished she could fall asleep; but there was Gabriel,
his face flushed (and, all the Gods at once be thanked,
still sober) his shaking hands gently holding the boy—
bending to kiss her carefully and clumsily, holding
the small wrinkled infant wrapped in an old baby
blanket she had knitted for Elorie twelve years ago.
She thought Elorie had taken it long since for swad-
dling her dolls.

"Won't you look at our son, Rohana? A third son.
Aren't you glad now that I wanted this, now that it's
all over?"

"Over for you," she said. "For me it is only beginning, Gabriel, fifteen years or more of trouble. Must
I bring this one up, too, to fear and despise his
father?"

He said shakily "No. I swear it, Rohana, by whatever
Gods you wish. This night—this night I knew if I

had lost you, I would have lost the only good thing ever to come into my life."

Yes, but you have sworn before this, too . . . so many oaths, she thought, but did not bother to speak aloud. She took the blanketed baby into her arms, holding him close, and snuggled him against her bare breasts; almost at once, with the singleminded obsession she remembered from her other confinements, struggling to undo the blanket, to count every precious finger and toe, memorizing them, then to count them again in case she had missed one, to run her hands lovingly over the softness of the little round head. She remembered the old story she had been told in Arilinn—that for the first hour after their birth, babies remembered their past lives, before the veil of forgetfulness was lowered again. He was awake, looking at her with watery blue eyes.

Gabriel said "He's a pretty child, Rohana. But, boy, if you ever give your mother this much trouble again, I'll box your little ears—"

"Oh, fie, Gabriel, what a way to greet the poor babe—threatening to beat him," she murmured, not really listening, focused on the child. She murmured to him, carefully edging the words with the strongest touch she dared of telepathic rapport;

"Hello, my darling; I'm your mother. You will meet your father later . . . he was holding you but I'm afraid you didn't notice him."

Just as well, she thought, but tried to shield the thought: he was not old enough to face hostility.

"You have two brothers—I'm afraid they won't be much good to you . . . and a sister; she at least will love you; she loves all babies. I have decided to name you Keith . . . I hope you like the name. It is a very old name in my family, but as far as I know, not used in Gabriel's. . . ."

She could not think of anything else to tell him, so she returned to smoothing his little body with her hands memorizing him, feeling such a flood of helpless love she felt she could not endure it. *To think I didn't want you!* It was like the monitor's touch she had learned so long ago. . . .

Over and over his tiny body went her loving hands, as if she could enfold him forever in her tenderest love, and keep him forever safe. But already she knew the truth, and knew the very instant when her youngest and last child slipped away from the touch and left her holding a lifeless bundle of chilling flesh. She flung herself into Kindra's arms and wept, hardly knowing it when they lifted her into the cart and carried her through the falling snow down to Ardais and into her own room and her own bed, still holding the little blanketed bundle, trying to soothe him and search out where her lonely baby had gone, alone into the snowstorm . . . when they took him from her, she let him go without protest and heard Gabriel weeping, too. But why should he cry? He had not really known the child as she had even in that single hour of his life.

"No, my lord," said the midwife firmly. "It would have happened even had the child been born here in her own bed, on her own cushions. It was nothing she did, certainly nothing *mestra* Kindra did, nothing anyone could have known or prevented. His heart was not formed to beat properly."

Rohana was still crying; she knew she would never stop crying again until she died. . . .

She cried for two days; toward the end of the

second day Elorie came in, crying too, and Rohana hugged her fiercely, thinking, *this then is my baby, the youngest child I shall ever have.*

"Do you mind if he is buried in your doll blanket, Elorie? I had no time to make him one of his own; it was what he wore while he lived, the only thing I could give him. . . ."

Elorie said, subdued (*her eyes were red; had she been crying, too? What had she to cry about?*) "No, I don't mind; let him have it. I'm so sorry, Mother, I'm really so sorry."

Yes, she is: she wanted another baby to play with. I'm sorry she didn't get it. When she had gone, Rohana lay in her somnolent daze, not wanting to move—it hurt too much—or to do anything except lie there and remember the few minutes she had held the living child in her arms, vainly needing time to stop so that she could hold on to them and to him. But already the fleeting moments were fading from her mind and Keith was only a fading dream. He had gone where the dead go, and she could not follow.

Life goes on, she thought drearily. *I don't know why it has to, but it does.* Now she was remembering the nebulous half-plans she had made before the birth; *when this is over, I shall go South, away from here.* Painfully she realized that, sincerely as she mourned, deeply as her body and soul hungered for the child who had gone from her, now she was free to make plans which did not involve being tied to a frail newborn for at least a year. This realization was slow and guilty; as if by realizing that freedom was welcome, she had somehow created the situation and was guilty of desiring it.

I did not want this child; now when I do not have him, I

ought to rejoice, she thought; but her grief was too new, too raw, too real to accept that yet. Nevertheless, she was beginning to accept that when the shock of birth and loss faded, she would indeed be grateful; that her state at the moment was a purely physical state of shock.

Accepting this, the next time one of her women came tiptoeing in to ask if she wanted anything, she made the fierce effort of dragging herself upright in bed and said, "Yes; I want to be washed and I want some soup."

The women brought the things, and with Kindra's help she managed to wash herself and to eat some soup. She realized that Kindra had not left her for more than a few seconds since the birth and that she had taken this for granted; now she was aware of it and grateful again, now that she could look a little outside the circle of anguished pain and preoccupation of the last couple of days. It was like surfacing from a very deep dive, clearing her lungs and mind of water at last. . . .

She said "As soon as I am better, I must travel South. Perhaps for the Council; but in any case I cannot stay here. Shall I travel with you, then, Kindra? You will not be sorry, I think, to get away from here."

"I will not," Kindra confessed, "Not of course that you have failed in any way in hospitality. . . ."

Rohana laughed dryly. "The hospitality of this place I think is cursed," she said. "I swear I shall never impose it on any other."

Kindra smiled at her.

"I have said before this that you have the spirit that would make you a notable Free Amazon, Rohana. I wish you might return with me to the Guild House and there take Oath as one of us. . . ."

Rohana said through a dry mouth, "I am trying to decide if there is any way in which I can in honor do exactly that, Kindra. It is clear to me that I am not needed nor wanted here."

Kindra's eyes glowed. She said softly, "I have prayed for days that you would see how right that would be. If you are not wanted by anyone here, you would be so welcome there." She added, almost in a whisper "More than this . . . I would swear an oath to you."

"And I to you," Rohana whispered, almost inaudibly; but Kindra heard and impulsively kissed her. Rohana remembered that moment—now it seemed a lifetime ago—when Gabriel had burst into her room with unspeakable accusations; now she did not care what he said or what he thought.

Who would *not* prefer Kindra's affection and her company, to his? And if he chose to make of that choice something evil or perverted, that was only evidence of his own foul mind.

But I must not detain Kindra selfishly here; she has work and duties of her own, which she has generously sacrificed to stay with me while I needed her so much. She tried to say what she felt for Kindra; but the woman said only, "There is nothing that cannot wait until you are able to travel, and then we will go together."

"Together." Rohana repeated it like a pledge. Oh, to be free of the burden and weight of the Domain, of knowing that the welfare of every soul from Scaravel to Nevarsin was in her keeping; of managing everything from the planting to the stud-books—well, now Alida would manage all that, and be glad of the chance.

She began to think for the first time in many years of what things she would take with her, if she were going south not only for the handful of tendays of Council season, but for an indefinite stay—perhaps forever, whether to her family's Domains in Valeron— surely there would be some place to go—or to a Guild House where she would no longer be Lady Rohana of Aillard and Ardais, but simply Rohana, daughter of Lhane. She would have no regrets about laying down the larger identity; she had borne it too long. There were not many possessions; her cloth- ing, (and little enough of that, for most of what she had would not be suitable for a Renunciate; a few riding suits and some changes of under-linen) her matrix stone, locks of the children's hair . . . no; not that, no keepsakes; she must put the Rohana who had been Lady of Ardais wholly behind her. The Lady of Ardais will disappear forever; will anyone ever know or care what has become of me? Surely it would never occur to anyone to seek within a Guild House. . . .

And I who for years have sat in Council, dealing the laws of this land, who will sit in my place, who will speak for Ardais? Will there be anyone to speak for my people? Will they be left to Gabriel's whim or Kyril's selfishness? Or Alida's cold self-interested pride?

That is nothing to me; for eighteen years I have borne that burden which is not even mine, simply because Gabriel would not or could not—it matters not which. Now he must do his destined work or it will go undone; he can no longer shift this burden, unwanted, to my shoulders, *I have served long enough, I will serve no more.*

That afternoon she felt stronger, and when Gabriel came to see her, she told the women to let him in. He was still, to her mild surprise, sober; this had been his longest sober stretch in years. Well, she no longer cared whether he were drunk or sober; what he did was now nothing to her. But she wondered numbly why he had never attempted this when it had mattered so much to her, when she had wrung herself inside out trying to keep him sober enough and strong enough to deal even with the smallest matters of the estate, when this sobriety would have meant so much to her; when she had loved him.

His hands were shaking, but he was beginning to look a little more like the handsome young Dom Gabriel she had married eighteen years ago. His eyes were clearing; she had not remembered how blue they were.

"You look better, Rohana."

"Thank you, my dear; I am better. Physically at least."

"Too bad," he said bluntly, "I was kind of looking forward to havin' a little feller around again. Somebody else to think about." He added with great bitterness, "Somebody to try an' stay sober for. You don' care any more, do you?"

The directness of that made her flinch; but this new sober Gabriel deserved honesty.

"No, Gabriel, I'm afraid I don't. I'm sorry; I wish I did." She added after a moment, "Elorie cares, my dear. Her father means a great deal to her."

He said broodingly "I suppose it makes no sense to try. Sooner or later . . ."

Sooner or later he would begin having seizures again, and only drink would ease the pain and formless fears. And there was no reason to care. It was too late to begin again. If the child had lived . . .

perhaps there might have been some reason to try again to rebuild a life together. They might have done so with a child to begin again. Even so, it was probably too late for Gabriel. He could not endure the pangs of returning to sobriety, to a decency he would only see as deprivation. With the child they would have had a reason to try. Now there was no reason and she was free; the pain she felt was only the pain of a closing door.

She could not help thinking of Gabriel looking at her and Kindra, accusing her of the unthinkable. Now when he knew she had gone away with Kindra, nothing would ever convince him he had been mistaken; perhaps, she thought with a pain, he had not been mistaken. Maybe she had failed with Gabriel because at the heart of her innermost self what she wanted was not anything Gabriel could provide. Perhaps what she had really wanted all along was the womanly tenderness and strength which Kindra could give her. So Gabriel, in his drunken accusations, had spoken more truly than he realized.

Was it that? And if it is so, is it my fault? Or if it is my fault, is it a crime? Was I ever consulted about whether I wanted a husband at all, much less whether it was Gabriel I wanted? I certainly never considered marrying anyone else, nor in eighteen years of the gatherings of the Comyn, of men of my own station and caste, have I ever looked on any single one of them with desire or a longing that fate had cast me into his arms and not Gabriel's. Unhappily married women look elsewhere—I am not so naive that I do not know that. But if it is simply that I married the wrong man, then why, in Evanda's name—who is Goddess of Love both lawful and profane—why do I not dream of some handsome young man of Comyn kindred? Why then do all my dreams of freedom center upon a woman—upon a Free Amazon—upon Kindra, in fact? Why?

I was given to Gabriel, and I have done my duty—and his—without looking back, for eighteen years. After all this time, am I not entitled to some freedom and happiness for myself? Why must I give what remains of my life as well as what I have already given?

Gabriel had turned away and was moving aimlessly around her room in the way which always made her fidget; she always wondered what he wanted of her. Whatever it was, she had never had it to give. She wondered if he knew the decision she was making. There had been a time when he always knew what she was thinking. Well, if he did, she need not explain herself. And if he did not, he deserved no explanation. She would do what she must; she would take her freedom. No one could expect more of her than she had already given. The women of her own Domain, the Aillard, would understand; and if they did not—well, at least she would have her freedom.

The words of the Renunciate Oath, which Kindra had explained so many years ago, were ringing in her mind;

From this day forth I renounce allegiance to any family, clan, household, warden, or liege lord, and take oath that I owe allegiance only to the laws of the land as a free citizen must: to the kingdom, the crown, and the Gods.

No longer a symbol of a great Domain; but simply and solely herself. I have lived all these years by what I owed to others; never by what I owed myself.

She watched Gabriel leave her room and go down toward the Great Hall. As she surmised, he was heading straight for a drink. It would be madness to try again.

And what would they say in Council, when it was known that Lady Rohana, head of the Domain of Aillard, and by default, holding the Domain of Ardais, in Gabriel's place, had been lost to the Guild House?

The Renunciates held their charter by suffrage. Kindra had explained to her once that the Renunciates were not allowed to seek recruits, but only to accept such women as sought them out.

It does not matter if a few craftsmen's wives or farmers's daughters, battered wives or exploited children, run away to the Guild-house. But if the Guild House should reach out to take the Head of two Domains, will they still be tolerated? Or will the Council seek redress from the Guild House? Could their charter survive if they seduced from her sworn duty, say, the Keeper of Arilinn? Ludicrous as the picture was of Leonie Hastur fleeing the Tower in her crimson veils and taking the vows of a Renunciate, still it must be faced as a possibility. If she, Rohana, could be tempted from her clear duty, was any woman in the Domains above suspicion? Would this then mean the destruction of the Comyn? And was it worth preserving at such a price—that women should all be enslaved and without choice?

No, there was no question of that. She was free to do as she would; but then she must decide to live for herself without taking thought for the duty she owed to everyone else. Should she sacrifice Domain, family, the well-being of every man and woman in the Domain in order that she might do whatever she wished and live for herself alone? To Kindra, the price was too much to pay; she had chosen the duty to herself; but then, Kindra had never owed a duty to anyone, nor chosen that duty; Kindra had been given in marriage, no doubt without inner consent;

while she, Rohana, had long enjoyed the privileges of a Comyn lady; and should she enjoy them while they exacted of her nothing, and refuse the burden when it grew heavy? And if she chose to take her own way and live her own life, would the Council not revenge themselves upon the Guild House—even withdraw once and for all the tolerance extended to the Guild Houses and withdraw the Charter given to the Renunciates? *That could destroy Kindra, too. . . .*

No; with all my prestige I will fight for that right—none shall touch the rights of the Guild House while I live. And I am Comyn; who could deny me even should I demand for myself what any small-holder's daughter can have . . . my freedom?

Gabriel was in the Great Hall. Rohana, still shaky on her feet, followed him down and saw him fill a glass from a decanter on a sideboard. She sighed; she need only remain silent, and there would be no need for confrontation or choice. Would he even know she was gone—or care? Would he not be relieved, even, to know himself alone with his bottle, to find in it the death he was certainly seeking? Had she any responsibility then to him? He drained it quickly, raised his hand to the steward demanding the decanter be refilled.

Rohana said, "No. No more."

She stood before the steward, bracing herself weakly with both hands.

"Listen to me, Hallert," she said. "From this moment forth, when you give the Master more drink than enough for his thirst, it is not his anger you will face; it is mine. Do you understand? *Mine.* The Master needs to be well and strong for the days that are coming soon at Ardais." She saw Gabriel scowl and said urgently, "I will help you, but you must work with me. Kyril is not ready for the Domain, Gabriel. You must somehow stay strong so that he cannot take it from—from us—which he would be all too ready to do."

For a moment an old determination flickered in his eyes. It would be enough for now; there would be struggle ahead, and he would fight her about this again, but somehow she would preserve the domain for Gabriel; and perhaps by the time Kyril reached maturity, he would have improved and matured enough to be trusted with the Domain. And if not— well, they would face that when the time came. At least it would not—now—come this year or next.

"You're right," Gabriel said. "That young upstart— not ready for the Domain. We'll keep it for a while yet."

Rohana suddenly realized that without any conscious act she had made her decision; she had acted almost without thinking. And therefore there could be for her no other choice; this was her allotted destiny, the road she would walk whether she would, or no. The world would go as it would, not as she would have it.

She was filled with a great and terrible sense of loss; she had lost everything else long ago, and now she knew that without any deliberate choice or renunciation she had lost Kindra, too, and all the hopes she had had for another life.

She said to the steward, "Bring the Master some cider or apple juice; he is thirsty." The man scurried away and Rohana sighed, looking in her mind into Kindra's stricken face when she knew of the decision which had been already made, flinching from the long and lonesome road she must tread alone. Kindra was freedom and—yes—love, but this love and freedom could not be hers. She was not even free enough to seek freedom.

Oathbreaker

Marion Zimmer Bradley

In the cool of the evening, Fiora of Arilinn moved silently through the Keeper's Garden, the Garden of Fragrance. Here she had come to be alone, to enjoy the drifting scents of the herbs and flowers planted by some long-ago Keeper. She wondered who that Keeper had been, the Keeper who before recorded time had created this peaceful place, her very own retreat. Had she, too, been blind? Or, perhaps he— for Fiora knew that in ancient times some men, too, had been Keeper—even in Arilinn. Some day, perhaps, when work was not so pressing, she might undertake Timesearch and try to discover something of that long-ago Keeper.

Fiora smiled, almost wistfully. When work was not so pressing—that was like saying, when oranges and apples grew on the ice walls of Nevarsin! The life of a Keeper, certainly of a Keeper of Arilinn, was too crowded to allow for the indulgence of purely intellectual curiosity. There were novices to be trained, young people to be tested for *laran*, and, if possible,

claimed for a period of service in Arilinn or one of
the few remaining Towers. And there was much
other Tower work, complicated by the unending service in the Relays. From this last, however, Fiora was
exempt; a Keeper had more important work to do.

For this moment Fiora was at liberty to enjoy the
privacy of this special garden, her own particular
domain. But not for long; she heard the sound of
the garden gate, and even before her mind reached
out to touch him, she know who it was from the
fumbling step and the faint scent of kirian which
hung always about him; Rian Ardais, the aging technician she had known since childhood.

He was drunk again with kirian. Fiora sighed;
she hated seeing him this way, but how could she
forbid it, even though she knew he would sooner or
later destroy himself? She remembered that Janine,
the old Keeper who had trained her when she was
new-come to Arilinn, had mentioned Rian's contin-
ual intoxication:

"It is the lesser of two evils," "It is not for me to
refuse him whatever it is that he needs to keep his
balance. He never allows it to affect his work; in relay
and circle he is always perfectly sober." Janine had said
no more, yet Fiora had heard the unspoken words
clearly, how can I stop him or deny him that surcease, when the alternative would be that he could
no longer tolerate his work here at all?

"*Domna* Fiora," the old man said unsteadily, "I
would not intrude upon you in this condition without necessity. You have earned leisure, and—"

"Never mind," she said. She had seen the old man
once, before the illness which had deprived her of
her sight. She still saw him as handsome and erect,

though she knew he had grown skeletal and his old hands trembled. Except, of course, working in the lattices, when they were always perfectly steady. How strange that was, that he should retain the ability to remain steady within a matrix lattice, when he could not so much as shave without cutting himself.

"What is the matter, Rian?"

"There is a messenger in the outer courtyard," he said, "from Ardais. Young Dyan is needed at home, and if it is possible, I must go, too."

"Impossible," Fiora said, "You may go, of course; you have certainly earned a holiday. But you know very well why Dyan cannot." She was shocked that he should even ask; the strictest of laws stated that for the four months after a novice had been accepted at Arilinn, nothing might intrude on his training. Drunk or not, Rian should have been able to handle that without appealing to a Keeper. "Send the messenger away and tell them Dyan is in isolation."

Then she realized that the old man was shaking. Fiora reached out with the awareness which served her better than sight. She should have known. He would not not have interrupted her here without need, after all, and it was really far more urgent than she had believed. She sighed, realizing how hard he had tried to keep any hint of his distress from reaching her, and came all the way back from the peace of the garden.

"Tell me," she said aloud.

He spoke, carefully disciplining his thoughts so that Fiora need not pick up anything but the spoken word if she chose.

"A death."

"Lord Kyril?" But that was small loss to any, thought Fiora. Even in the isolation of Arilinn, the young

Keeper had heard about the Lord of Ardais, about his dissolute life, his fits of madness. So many of the Ardais clan were dangerously unstable. Kyril mad; Rian himself, though he tried his best, addicted to the intoxication of kirian. It was to soon to know about young Dyan, though she had hopes for him.

"Yet even for a death in the family Dyan may not be released so soon." Although, if it were Kyril, Dyan would be Heir to Ardais and there would be no question of allowing him to take oath at Arilinn in service to the Towers.

"It is not Kyril," Rian's voice was shaking, and though he tried to keep rein on his thoughts she heard it clearly, would that it had been no more than that! "It is worse than that. The Gods witness I love my brother and never once envied him heirship to our house; I was content to make my life here."

Yes, Fiora thought, so content that you cannot get through a tenday without making yourself drunk with kirian or some other drug. But who was she to mock the man's defenses? She had her own. She only said, again, "Tell me."

Yet he hesitated. She could feel him thinking; Fiora was Keeper, sworn virgin, such things should not be spoken before her.

At last he said, and she could feel the desperation in his voice, "It is *Dom* Kyril's wife, the Lady Valentina. She has been an invalid for years and his youngest daughter—Dyan of course is the eldest, his son by his first wife—his daughter Elorie has been acting as his hostess. Some of Kyril's parties are—dissolute," he said, carefully choosing the most neutral word he could.

So Fiora had heard. She nodded for him to go on.

"The Lady Valentina was reluctant for Elorie to appear at these parties," Rian said, "but Kyril would not have it otherwise. So *Domna* Valentina appeared, despite her illness, to protect the girl's character. And Kyril, in a drunken rage—or worse—struck her."

He paused, but Fiora already knew the worst.

"He killed her."

It was indeed worse than Fiora had believed. Kyril had always been a dissolute man—the roster of his bastards was said, and not altogether in jest, to equal the legendary conquests of Dom Hilario, a notorious lecher of folk-tale and fable—and there were tales that he had more than once paid heavily to hush up a brutal beating. Fiora was too innocent to be aware of the sexual implications of this, and would have believed it meant no more than ordinary drunken brutality. But murder, and of a lawful wife *di catenas*—that was something else, and probably could not be hushed up at all.

Still Fiora hesitated. "You are Regent of Ardais till Dyan is of age," she said after a moment's thought, "and I am hesitant to interrupt his training. We know he has not the Ardais Gift, but he is potentially a powerful telepath. An untrained telepath is a menace to himself and everyone around him," she added, quoting one of the oldest Arilinn maxims of training. "I know this is a serious crisis in Ardais and perhaps in all the Comyn, *Dom* Rian; it may well demand Council action. But must it involve Dyan? You are *Dom* Kyril's brother and Regent. And you may go as soon as you wish; I will give you leave at once. But why must Dyan accompany you? It is not even as if the Lady Valentina were his mother; she was no more than his stepmother. I think you should go at once and that Dyan should remain here."

Rian twisted his hands. Fiora could sense the man's desperation; she did not need sight for that. Once again she was aware peripherally of the strong smell of the drug that clung to him, blocking out the scents from the garden, and felt with irritation that he had profaned her favorite retreat; she wondered if she would ever walk in it again without the overpowering scent of drug and misery which she could feel on the evening breeze. Silence; the blind woman was tense with the pain of the man who faced her.

Rian was not, Fiora thought, really an old man; it was sorrow and perhaps the side effects of the drugs which made him seem so. He should have been in the heartiest stage of his middle years; he was no more than a year Dom Kyril's junior. Yet he seemed decrepit, and she had seen him so in the eyes of everyone at Arilinn. He still stood silent before her, and after a moment she heard the small sound of the stifled sob.

"Rian, what is it? Is there something else?"

He did not speak, but the Keeper, open in empathy to the misery of the man before her, was overwhelmed with his despair. In that moment she knew why Rian drugged himself, why he seemed an old man when he was younger than Kyril, as she heard his first stammering, shamed word.

"I am—I have always been afraid of Kyril. I dare not, I have never been able to face his—his anger, his brutality. Ever since I was a young man, I have tried never to face him at all. Dyan is not afraid of his father. I dare not go home, especially not now, unless Dyan is with me."

Fiora tried hard to conceal her shock and pity, realizing it was not untouched with a contempt of which she knew she should be ashamed. Rian's weaknesses were not of his own choosing. Yet she knew nothing would even be the same again between them. She was Keeper; she had won through to that high office by achievement, hard work, and an austerity which would have broken nine women out of ten. She was Rian's superior, but the man was her elder, and she had always liked and even admired him. The liking remained unchanged, but she was shocked and distressed by the change in her own feelings. Nevertheless, the young Keeper made her voice gentle, without judgment.

"Well, then, Rian, it seems there is no help for it. I will speak with Dyan. If it can be done without totally wrecking all his training so far, I will give him leave to go with you to Ardais. Send him to me"— she hesitated,—"but not here." She would not have her garden further spoiled for her. "I will await him, an hour from now, in the fireside room."

Dyan Ardais at this time of his life—he was about nineteen, she thought—was still as slight as a boy. Fiora, who of course could not see him, had seen him often enough in the eyes of the others in the circle at Arilinn. He was a darkly handsome young man, dark hair coarsely curling about his face, which was narrow and finely made. He had also eyes of the colorless steely gray which, Fiora knew, often marked the strongest telepaths. If Dyan was a telepath, though, he had learned to barrier his thoughts perfectly, even from her.

In the training which had made her Keeper, she had learned to be impervious to all men; and Dyan was no exception. But though Fiora was innocent, she was a Keeper and a telepath and in the course of the early training, when Dyan had first come here, she had learned many things about him, and one was this; he would forever be impervious to her or to any woman. That did not matter to Fiora; he was neither the first nor the last lover of men to make a place and a reputation for himself in the Towers. What troubled her was that a boy so young—Fiora herself was not past twenty, but a Keeper's training made one age rapidly in both body and mind—should be so braced, so impassive and invulnerable. At his age, a novice in a Tower should be open to his Keeper. Was it some early warning sign of the Ardais instability, which might later show itself in becoming, like Rian, addicted to some drug? Or—in fairness, she remembered what she knew of Dom Kyril—was it only the effect of growing up in the presence of a madman? As far as she knew, and she would have known, Dyan used kirian only for the necessary work in the Towers and for training. And though some Ardais drank far too much, she had noticed that he drank only moderately and at dinner. He had, as far as she knew, no glaring character flaws; some Keepers might have considered his homosexuality a flaw, but it did not trouble Fiora as long as it created no trouble within the circle, and so far she had not heard of any dissension that it had caused; the others in the circle were tolerant and seemed to like him. He seemed a quiet, inoffensive youngster, yet something about him, something subliminal which she could not yet quite identify, still troubled her; why should a youth of Dyan's age be opaque when to his Keeper he should have been transparent?

Dyan bowed and said, in the musical voice which was, to Fiora, one of his most attractive qualities, "My uncle said you wanted to speak to me, Domna."

"Has he told you anything about what it is?"

"He said to me that there was trouble at home, and that I was needed there. No more than that . . . no; he said, too, that it was important enough that I should have to go home even though I have not yet passed my first period of probation here." He paused, expectantly.

Fiora asked, "Do you want to go home, Dyan?" And for the first time she sensed a trace of emotion in his voice.

"Why? Has my work here been unsatisfactory? I have—have tried very hard—"

She said quickly "It is nothing like that, Dyan. Nothing would please me more than that you should complete your training with us here, and perhaps work with us for a time, perhaps many years; although, as you are Heir to Ardais, you cannot spend a lifetime here. But, as Rian has told you, there is trouble at home which he feels he is not competent to meet alone. He has asked us as a favor that you be allowed to go with him. This is very unusual at this stage in your training, and I need to assess whether it will do any damage to interrupt your training at this point." She added forthrightly "If you are here only because you are unhappy at home, as you can see, your dedication to Arilinn is certainly in question."

She could feel that he smiled. He said "It is true that I have no great love for living at Ardais. I do not know how much you know about my father, Lady, but I assure you, a desire to escape the chaos of life at Ardais is a healthy sign of a sane mind. That I find pleasure in my work here—is that a bad thing?"

"Of course not," she said, "and I have no particular fault to find with you at this point. Who has been training you?"

"Rian, for the most part. He has told me that he thinks I will make a technician. And Domna Angelica has said she believes I have mastered the work of a monitor. She said she thought I was ready for the monitor's Oath."

"That I will certainly authorize," Fiora said, "and it is even your right to take it at my hands if you desire. Even so, you must have realized while we were talking that you have not answered my question, Dyan. Do you want to go home?"

He sighed, and that heavy sigh answered her question. Fiora was not a maternal woman, but for a moment she felt she would have liked to shelter the youth in her arms; a fleeting sensation, and one, she knew, which would have distressed Dyan as much as herself. Recalling herself to the duty of questioning, not only in words, she reached out to him; she could feel the tension in his shoulders, the weight of the lines in his face, telling her better than sight what the answer would have been to her question.

"I do not. But if I am needed, how can I refuse? Rian means well, but he is not—" he paused, and she felt him searching for truthful words which would not reflect on his kinsman, "not worldly."

She did not challenge the polite evasion of what she had really asked him; though she felt, with some distress, that he should have been willing to be more honest with his Keeper.

"Dyan, you are a responsible young man; what do you think? Will it harm your training? I shall leave it to you."

The sigh he gave seemed drawn up from his very

depths. He said "I thank you, *Domna*, for asking that question. The only answer that I can give is that if the Domain demands my presence, I must not think of anything else."

Again, without really knowing why, Fiora felt an enormous pity for the young man before her. "Spoken like an honorable man, Dyan."

She could sense the very stoop of Dyan's shoulders, as if he bore the weight of a world on them. No, not a world. Only a Domain. She said gently "Then it remains only to give you the monitor's Oath, Dyan; you must not leave here without that. Then you are free to do as your conscience bids you."

She took leave of them a few hours later at the front gates of Arilinn. Rian already in his saddle, stooped and looking older than his years; Dyan standing beside his horse, his handsome face drawn with tension which Fiora could sense, without sight, from her distance of several feet. He bent over her hand respectfully and she could feel the lines drawn in his face.

"Farewell, Lady. I hope to return to you soon."

"I wish you a pleasant journey."

"That is impossible," Dyan said with a faint tinge of amusement. "The journey to Ardais lies through some of the worst mountains in the Domains, including the Pass of Scaravel."

"Then I wish you a *safe* journey: and I shall hope that you may be able to return soon and that when you arrive at your home you find the problems less serious than you have foreseen," she said, and they mounted and rode away. As he went, Fiora felt enormous anger. *No,* she thought, *I should never have let him go!*

The kinsmen rode in silence for some time. At last Dyan said "You knew that Fiora had insisted that I take the monitor's Oath before I left the Tower. Is such haste usual, uncle?"

Rian sighed and said "Indeed, it is customary to give the Oath even to children at the first moment they are old enough to understand its meaning."

"Then it was not a personal statement that Fiora did not trust me—that she was in such haste to bind my Oath?" Dyan asked.

Rian frowned and said "Of course not. It is customary."

"Indeed."

"You can hardly have any qualms of conscience about taking the Oath of a monitor," exclaimed Rian, recalling the words of the Oath ... *to enter no mind save to help or heal, and never to force the conscience of any.*

"Perhaps not," Dyan said after a moment, "Yet I cannot help but feel as if I had ceded some right over my own conscience. I thought not that I needed any to keep my conscience, nor an Oath to bind me to ethical use of *laran.*"

"The Oath is needed most by those most reluctant to take it," said Rian, "those who feel they need it not should surely have no qualms about it."

He felt that Dyan wanted to say more. But he didn't.

The journey took four days, at the best speed they could make over the mountains. When they came in sight of Castle Ardais, Dyan noticed that the crimson and gray pennant was flying which announced that the Head of the domain was in residence.

"He is here," Dyan said. "Perhaps I wished that he had fled us. The Domain is in mourning; this is arrogance."

"More likely," Rian said, "he feels himself so justified that it would not occur to him to flee justice."

Dyan said sighing "I remember him as he was *before*—when I was a little child. I loved him; now I can hardly remember when he was not a brute. I remember hiding in a cupboard from him when he was drunk and roaring all over the castle, threatening us all . . . I think it the saddest of all that Elorie will remember nothing but this and has no memory of a father to love; because despite everything, Rian, never doubt this; I love my father well, whatever he has done."

"I never thought to doubt that, lad," Rian said gently. "Once I loved him, too."

Almost on the threshold, Elorie appeared, pale as death; it looked to the men as if she had neither slept nor eaten since her mother's death. She flung herself, weeping, into Dyan's arms.

"Oh, my brother! You have heard—my mother—"

"Hush, little sister," Dyan said, stroking her hair. "I came as soon as I heard. I loved her, too. Where is our father?"

"He has barricaded himself in the Tower room and will let no one near him, not even his body-servants. For a full day afterward, he was drunk and shouting and roaring all over the castle, offering to fight anyone—" Elorie shivered, and Dyan, remembering similar episodes when he himself was very young, patted her as if she were a little girl. "Then he hid himself in the Tower room and would not come out. I had to arrange everything for—for Mother—"

"I am sorry, little sister; I am here now, and you need not be frightened of anything. You must go and rest now, and sleep. Tell your nurse to put you to bed, and give you a sleeping draught; I will take care of everything, as befits Warden of the Domain," said Dyan. "And as soon as your mother is buried, you cannot stay here alone with Father, not now."

"But where can I go?" she asked.

"I will find a place to send you; perhaps you could be fostered at Armida or even in one of the Towers; you are Comyn and nobly born," Dyan said, "but now you must sleep and eat and rest; you must look seemly and lady-like when your mother is laid to rest. You do not want to look as if you dwelt under siege here—even," he added shrewdly, "if that is what you feel like."

"But what of Father? Will you let him hide there in the Tower saying evil things of how Mother drove him to kill her?"

Dyan said quietly "You must just leave father to me, Lori, child."

And at her look of relief he stroked her hair again and said to Rian, "Ring for her nurse now, will you, and tell her to take Lori away to her rooms and look after her properly."

"Oh," Elorie sighed, and he could see that she was near to collapse, "I am so weary, so glad you are home, brother. Now you are here, everything will be all right."

When Elorie had been taken to her own rooms, Dyan went into the Great Hall, and called the *coridom*.

"Lord Dyan, how good to see you," the man said, and curiously repeated what Elorie had said; "Now you are here, everything will be all right." It was like a weight on him; Dyan thought, with smothered rage, they should be seeking to make things easy for him, instead of all waiting until the burden could be put on his shoulders. He was not ready for the weight of the Domain; could he not even complete his education? He should have known when he was summoned, a year earlier than he had been promised from Nevarsin, that he might assume the place of Warden of the Domain, when his father was ill with the autumn fever; they had feared he might die and had lost no time in naming Dyan as Warden. *It was the fever that did it,* Dyan thought; *some injury to his brain. Before that he had been drunken and dissolute, but sane, and only rarely cruel.*

There had never been any question, he thought dispassionately, of naming Rian as Kyril's successor. Not even the most optimistic of Ardais kindred had believed Rian fit for that office; they were all ready to dump it on the shoulders of a boy of nineteen.

The *coridom* began telling how the ill-fated feast had begun; but Dyan waved him to silence.

"None of that matters; how came he to strike down my stepmother?"

"I am not sure he knew he struck down any; he was drunk."

"Then, in the name of all the Gods," Dyan shouted in frustration, "when all of you know he has these rages when he is drunk, why do you not keep him away from drink?"

"Lord Dyan, if you who are his son, or the Lady who was his wife, cannot forbid it, how are we who are but servants to do so?"

224 Marion Zimmer Bradley

Dyan supposed there was some justice to the question. But now it was too late to leave such things to servants or chance.

"There's no help for it; the man's mad, he must be watched over, perhaps locked up so he'll do no harm to himself or others," Dyan said.

"And what of the Domain, with my Lady dead and you all away in the Tower?" asked the *coridom*.

Dyan sighed heavily and said "Leave that to me. Now I will go and see my father."

Dom Kyril had barricaded himself inside the topmost room of the north tower, and Dyan struggled in vain with the heavy door. Finally he shouted and kicked at the door, and at last a quavering voice came from inside.

"Who is there?"

"It is Dyan, father. Your son."

"Oh, no," the voice said. "You can't get me that way. My son Dyan is in Arilinn. If he were here, none of this would be happening; he'd make sure my rebellious servants did my will."

"Father, I journeyed last night from Arilinn." Dyan said, feeling his heart sink at the crafty madness—real or feigned?—in his father's voice. *If I had been here, it is true, this would not have happened; I'd have had him chained first.*

"Damn you, Father, open this door or I'll kick it in!" Dyan backed up the threat with a mighty kick that rattled the hinges.

"I'll open, I'll open," said the voice petulantly. "No need to go breaking things."

There was a creak in the mighty lock, and after a moment a small crack widened and Dyan saw his father's face.

Once *Dom* Kyril had been handsome, with the good looks of all the Ardais men. Now his eyes were bloodshot, his face puffy and swollen, the features blurred with drink and indecision, his clothes filthy and disheveled. He looked with hostile grimaces at Dyan and muttered "What are you doing here, then? You were so anxious to go off to the Tower and get away, now what are you doing back?"

So that would be his defense? Pretending to ignore what had happened and putting Dyan on the defensive?

"I went with your leave, Father. Was I to think the Domain could not be trusted with its ruler? Come, Father, don't pretend to be madder or drunker than you are."

Dom Kyril's bloodshot eyes grimaced closed; he said "Dyan, is it you? Really you? Why is everybody angry with me? What did I do this time? I need a drink, boy, and they won't bring me wine—"

Dyan was not surprised; but now he understood his father's ravings. A long-term drunkard, abruptly deprived of all drink—by this stage no doubt he was seeing things crawling out of the walls at him.

He could understand the servants; but at this point if they were to have any rational discourse, his father must have at least enough of the poison to give him the simulacrum of sanity. His brain had grown unused to functioning without drink; Dyan could see the shaking hands, the uneven gait.

He should never have been allowed to come to this point. No doubt they found it simpler to abandon the man to drink himself to death, rather than contend with him for his own good. *If I had been here*, Dyan thought painfully, looking at the wreck of the father he once had loved. *But as he says, I was eager to get away from the problem, and so it is as much my fault as his. I am no better than Rian.*

"I'll get you a drink, Father," he said.

He went down to the foot of the stairs and found wine and told the *coridom* to bring food. His father drank with haste and eagerness, slopping the wine on his shirtfront, and after, when the shakes had subsided, Dyan managed to persuade him to drink some soup.

The shivering and trembling slowly stopped. Now, when he had had a drink, Dyan thought, his father seemed more sober than when his system was free of the drink. It was true that he could no longer function normally without it.

"Now let us talk sensibly," said Dyan, when the man who faced him had been restored at least to a semblance of the man he had once known. "Do you know what you have done?"

"They were angry with me," *Dom* Kyril said, "Elorie and her mother—damn all puling womenfolk—I shut her up, that's all," he said craftily, "Never was a woman didn't deserve a lick or two. Won't hurt them. Does them good, and they like it really. Has she been bawling to you because I hit her?"

But Dyan heard the craftiness in his father's voice; he was still pretending to be drunker than he was, and madder.

"You wretch, you killed her," he exploded, "Your own wife!"

"Well," murmured the drunken man, staring at his knuckles, "I didn't go for to do it, I di'n mean any harm."

"All the same—no, Father, look at me, listen to

me—" Dyan insisted. "All the same, you are no longer fit to rule the Domain, and after this—"

"Dyan—" His father tugged at his arm, "I was drunk; I di'n know what I was doing. Don't let them hang me!"

Dyan brushed off his grip with distaste. "There's no question of that," he said. "The question is what's to be done with you so you won't kill the next person who crosses your path. I think the best thing for you to do is to turn the Domain over, formally, to me or to Rian, and confine yourself to these rooms except when you're in your senses."

"So that's what this is all about," his father said furiously. "Trying again to get the Domain away from me? I thought as much. Never, hear me? It's my Domain and my rule and I should give it over to an upstart boy?"

"Father, I beg you; no one shall harm you, but when you are incapacitated, I can care for the Domain safely in your place."

"Never!"

"Or if you do not trust me, give it over to Rian and I will stand by him faithfully—"

"Rian!" His father made an inexpressible sound of contempt. "Oh, no, I know what you're up to. Look at me, Gods—" he spread his hands and began, drunkenly, to weep. "My brother, my children—all my enemies, trying to get the Domain out of my hands—lock me up—"

Dyan never knew when he had made the decision he made now, but perhaps at first it was only a desire to silence the drunken whining. He reached out with the new strength of his *laran*—it was the first time he had used it since training began at Arilinn—and gripped his father with the force of it.

The words trailed off into incoherence; Dyan gripped harder and harder, knowing what he must do if this was ever to be settled and the Domain of Ardais free of a madman's rule.

When he stopped he was white and shaking, stopping himself with force before he killed the man. He knew, shamed, that this was what he had wanted. His father was slumped on the floor, having slid, during that monstrous battle, from his chair.

Dom Kyril mumbled "Of course . . . only rational thing to do. Call the wardens an' we'll have it done."

Silently, without a word, Dyan went and summoned the *coridom*. All he said was "Summon the Wardens of the Domain; he is rational now and ready to do what must be done."

Within the hour they came; the council of old men of the Domain, who had been notified of the emergency days ago; by whose counsel and agreement the Ruler of Ardais held his power.

"Kinsmen," Dyan said, facing them; he had gone to his room and changed into a sober suit of the formal colors of the Domain. He had also summoned his father's body-servant and had him washed and shaved and made presentable. "You know what sorry urgency brings us all here. Even before the Lady of Ardais is laid to rest, the Domain must be made secure."

"Has he agreed to turn the Domain over to you? We tried to persuade him, but—has he agreed to this of his own free will?"

"Of his free will," said Dyan. *Even if he had not, what other choice have we?* he wondered, but did not speak the question aloud.

"Then," said the oldest of them, "we are ready to witness it."

And so they all stood by as Kyril Ardais, calm now and evidently in his right mind, went through the brief ceremony where he formally and irrevocably laid down the wardenship of the Domain in favor of his eldest son Dyan-Valentine.

When it was over and the Council of Ardais had given Dyan their allegiance, Dyan relaxed the stern grip he had kept on his father's mind through the ceremony. The man slid to the floor, whining incoherently and retching. Dyan told himself; this had had to be done, there was no other way; but it left a bad taste in his mouth. This he knew to be a misuse of his *laran*. They should have kept him at Arilinn. . . .

What was the alternative? he asked himself grimly. Put his father into the hands of healers—for a year perhaps—until he came entirely to himself? No time for that. No, he had done what he must: No man can keep another's conscience. No, nor any woman either, he thought, scalded by the memory of Fiora and the monitor's Oath. This was, no doubt, why he had been reluctant to take it. Well, he could not cede the right to do what his own conscience bade him, not for many oaths. But it should never have happened. He would not even see Elorie; she was among those who had forced him to this.

Fiora of Arilinn had been informed of the arrival of the men from Ardais; she sensed some tension in each of them not consonant with only settling family affairs. Rian seemed calm; yet, reading in his mind what had befallen, she was angry, No, Rian was not on the surface the kind of man to rule a Domain; yet it was not right, either, that he should have been passed over. Given the responsibility, he might have grown into it; now he would always accept his own weakness and unfitness. It was wrong that he should be allowed to hide here, forever unable to grow to his own strength, forever immature. Her hands went out to him, impulsively. "Welcome back, my old friend," she said, clasping his hands. "I had feared you were lost to us." Feared? She had *hoped* he would achieve the strength to take his brother's place; but in the test he had not done it.

And turning her attention to Dyan, she realized that he seemed weary, but calm, and the barrier had dropped; he was not opaque to her; he had arrived at some inner strength, achieved some unknown potential.

"Dyan, I am glad to see you again," she said, truthfully if inaccurately, and she touched his hand lightly; and at the touch he was transparent to her, he no longer even wished to hide what he had done, or why; and in that moment she was shocked. She said "Dyan, I am sorry to see what has happened to you."

"I have done what I must, and if you know what I have done, you know why. Hypocrites, all; none of them had the courage to do what must be done. I did; and now you, too, will censure me?"

"Censure you? No. I am the Keeper of Arilinn, but not the keeper of any man's conscience," she said, knowing it was not true; she had sought to bind his conscience, and had failed. "I say only that now you may not return to us, and you know why. Recall the words of the monitor's Oath; *to enter no mind save to help or heal and never to force the conscience of any. . . .*"

"Lady, if you know how I forced my father's assent, you know well why I did so, and what alternatives I had." Dyan said, his face carefully impassive, denying her touch. Fiora bent her head.

This was wrong, what she must do. Now they could have no control over him, no link to right whatever wrong had been done; he was forever beyond even a Keeper's help or touch.

"I do not judge you. I only say that having violated that Oath you have no place here." But where, then, she thought wildly, could he go, having stepped beyond her judgment, gone further than he had ever wanted to go. Already his life was to be led outside the laws laid down for them all. Must he be an outlaw before he was out of his teens? Desperately, she realized that he had put himself outside even her help. She said slowly "Will you take my blessing, Dyan?"

"Willingly, Lady." His voice shook, and she thought, with deep pity, *he is only a boy, he needs our help more now than ever. Damn our laws and rules! He had the courage to break them; he did what he must. I wish I dared as much.*

She said, slowly, holding out her fingertips to him, "You have courage. If you always act in accordance with your own conscience, even when it violates the standards of others, I do not censure you. Yet if you will let me counsel you, I would say you have embarked on a dangerous path. Perhaps it is right for you; I cannot say."

"I have come to a place in my life, Lady, where I cannot think of right or otherwise, but only of necessity."

"Then may all the Gods walk with you, Dyan, for you will need their aid more than any of us." Her voice broke, and he looked down at her—she felt it—with pain and pity. *For the first time and maybe the last in his life he is reaching out for help and I am bound by my own oaths and laws not to help him.* She said quietly, "You may send Elorie here when you will."

Dyan bent over Fiora's hand and touched his lips to the corpse-pale fingers; he said "If there are any Gods, Lady, I ask their help and understanding; but why came they not to my aid when I needed it most?" He straightened, with a bleak smile, and Fiora knew he had barricaded himself again; he was forever beyond their reach. Then he rode away from Arilinn without looking back.

Blood Hunt

by Linda Frankel and Paula Crunk

Sherdra was glad to see the last of the sun. Setting, it cast great ruddy splotches into the darkening forest as the young catman, his rusty-gray fur mottled with crusted stains, came limping wearily through the icy brambles. Perhaps the night's familiar shadows could veil him, offer a secure place to hide from his would-be murderers; although the best he had done so far was to keep barely beyond their sight. Behind him, he could hear the faraway ravenous howling of hounds still on his track. It had been more than a tenday since Sherdra—last surviving warrior of the clan of Firebearers, so far as he knew— had fled the last rout of his people at the place the humans called Corresanti. He had thought some days before that the human Guardsman had given up the chase. But he had called hunting-brothers to join him, it seemed; and they had come companioned by hounds. Why should anyone so fervently seek the life of one so fallen in *gyar*? Perhaps some human had discovered he was hunting-brother to his mar-

233

tyred leader. Sherdra hoped no one had guessed
what he bore: emblem of rank as well as of power.

He dropped to his knees by a narrow, cold stream,
lapping greedily at the water. Suddenly he stiffened.
His thin lips drew back into a soundless snarl. Someone was coming through these woods, along the creek
bank. Sherdra leaped for the relative safety of the
trees. Drawing his clawsword, he fought back a spinning nausea. Grimly he waited, preparing himself
for what seemed inevitable.

"Oh—proud Brother Francis rode out one day,
over the hills to Edelweiss," a voice rang out, star-
tling in the forest's stillness. Sherdra understood barely
one word. But as he peered through the branches,
he smiled, after his fashion. No; not a Comyn Guardsman; rather, a shabby, gaudy peddler-man, singing
away lustily—and most foolishly, Sherdra thought.
He tensed his muscles to pounce.

The man was riding a sleek gray gelding, red
ribbons plaited in its flowing mane and tail; a less
showy pack animal followed placidly behind. . . .

"A ghost wind turned him all awry, and set him on
the path to vice . . ."

Sherdra licked his dry lips. Either animal would
make a fair meal for a starving warrior. But now the
man had ceased his screeching yodel, and was approaching more slowly, as if uneasy. A change in
strategy seemed dictated. As swiftly and as quietly as
he might, Sherdra began to climb a tree conveniently
placed for his purpose.

Come closer, little bird, Sherdra whispered silently,
sending his will through the purple jewel, *Soulseye,*
along the mindpaths as his hunting-brother had taught
him. *Come, fly into my net.* . . . Sherdra inched higher
upon the shaggy tree limb that overhung the narrow

path. Thank the Goddess that the peddler's horse, undoubtedly more astute than its idiot master, had not yet scented him.

His nails slipped on the ice-slicked branch; giddy, he almost lost his balance. His mind was darkening again. Desperately he fought to clear it. The howling of the devil-dogs, flame-eyed, was echoing and re-echoing within the tortured confines of his skull. *Why doesn't that fool hear them? Dare I take this risk?* Almost he could see the face of his old grandam, her green eyes aglow with hearthfire, hear her soft, throaty voice: *The wise hunter knows which prey to let pass by. . . .*

His sight cleared abruptly; and he saw he had no choice. The peddler had drawn rein, almost beneath him. His horse was snorting nervously. The man murmured to it, stroking its neck; but his eyes were looking keenly all about him. Sherdra could almost smell his rising suspicion, and fear. Taking a deep, steadying breath, Sherdra launched himself into space—

—Down, savage-hard against the man's back, claws raking, reaching for the deathhold on the tender-fleshed neck—the terrified horse plunged sharply, tumbling both rider and assailant onto the ground. Screaming, the man pulled free of Sherdra's grasp, rolling away several yards, heaving up, gasping, to his feet.

He seemed incapable of further flight, a trembling rabbithorn transfixed by the hunter's stare—pale hairless face, pale frightened eyes blinking rapidly under a tousled cap of pale hair. Sherdra threw back his head and howled—recklessly, uncaring—for the sheer joy of this capture.

"Ask death-passage of your Goddess, bare-skin,"

the catman snarled, unsheathing his sword—and sprang again.

"No—" the man dodged his leap, whirling beyond his reach with a firedancer's grace: one with which Sherdra would hardly have credited a mere human with.

"I pray you; stop," the peddler said, retreating, holding out his empty hands toward Sherdra. "Surely we can discuss this matter reasonably if all you want are my goods. Talk-talk?"

Sherdra, panting sharply, furious at himself for having missed such an easy snatch, stalked his prey more carefully.

"Then I am sorry for you, poor beast," the man said, reaching inside his cloak. Dodging the wide sweep of the clawsword, he swung around and behind Sherdra's back.

Sherdra leapt about, turning, twisting in midair; lashing out with his free hand, talons raking down the peddler's face. The man cried out sharply, and retreated again, this time stumbling.

"Coward. Castrate. That is all you deserve," Sherdra spat, wishing his true strength were not so drained that he must dishonor his sword on this— Grimly, he pursued, ignoring the fires that were beginning to snake down his right side where the old wound still festered. He would put an end to this—he must.

But this time the peddler stood firm. Indeed, his reflexes were excellent. He wielded his own sword with the cool grace that only comes with long practise. His sword? A common peddler with a sword? And such a sword: the jewels in its hilt shone blood-red with the last rays of the sun as Sherdra was driven back remorselessly, step by step. Who was this man? How in the name of the Goddess—

He dodged to avoid a swift, slashing stroke, but

too late: the peddler's blade sliced along Sherdra's right shoulder.

Typically, Sherdra would have recovered quickly from his surprise and dealt well enough with this hawk featured out with sparrow's colors. But his thoughts were whirling, colliding with each other. His eyes were dimming; he avoided another onslaught chiefly by instinct. In this fog of pain and confusion, he couldn't hope to stand against the human. *Flame-eyed wolves, leaping upon him in the darkness—*

No! It must not be! To yield to such a one as this. Desperate, he aimed a savage blow at the peddler's head. This was deftly parried; Sherdra was knocked breathless to his knees. The human might have delivered the death-blow then. Instead he stepped back, bowing with an irony lost on the catman who stared at him through a red haze. . . .

His last strength slipped away. The sword dropped from Sherdra's numbed fingers. So. So. It must be so. Defeat and death. They must be one and the same as *gyar* demanded. *Grandmother, you were right; I should not have—* "Oh, Ashyr," he whispered to his twin, his sister, who had been far away from him for a long time, "You must make a passing-song, for me. . . ."

Do the moons shine upon the Last Hunting-Ranges? That they might, but the Goddess could scarcely have brought these vile human features to taunt him for an eternity. There would be scant divine justice in that, for all his lacks. Damn! Why hadn't the fool simply killed him when the time was ripe?

The fellow bared his teeth. It was no hostile gesture since he had taken strips of cloth from his own ragged garments to bind Sherdra's wounds. An im-

age of being bathed by strange hands revolted all his
senses. A look of—*concern?* flashed in his companion's eyes. Sherdra cringed at the touch of a naked,
near furless limb, But when the hand lifted, much
faintness and fiery throbbing went with it. No, this
could be no mere peddler. The touch of healing . . .
this was some Comyn trick to take him alive. Sherdra
cursed his helpless state, using all the obscenities of
five clans. If he had known others, these would have
spewed forth readily in a string of eloquent snarls.

"Now look here. I admit that I'm no beauty, but
that's no cause to get upset."

Incomprehensible jargon, but the tone seemed ami-
able enough. His Comyn captor could afford gener-
osity. Sherdra resolved to remain unmoved by any
overtures. He shielded his thoughts against any in-
trusions. His enemies would learn nothing.

The man was offering him something to drink.
Sherdra spat it out and swiped weakly at the ugly
face still hovering over him. The human jerked his
head back, just in time.

The peddler said something else, his tone remark-
ably cooled. The white-rimmed alien eyes were unpleasantly intent upon Sherdra. He covered his face
with his hands, not out of fear but in dismay that the
man should have so little respect. Instead there was
this nauseating pretense of kindness.

"If I had half the sense I was born with—" The
human shook his head, and rose to his feet. Sherdra
burrowed his head under his arm and forced himself to relax totally, feigning sleep. Finally the man
made a windy noise, and went away.

The moons—two of them, anyway—were casting
their dim, obscured light through the long, narrow
entrance of a small mountain cave. Sherdra was re-

pulsed by the thought of those naked hands lifting him, carrying him here. He had been laid against the back cave wall and wrapped in blankets of a peculiar and unsettling smell. However, a warrior cannot be foolish-proud in adversity. Thank the Goddess; his captor must be a unique breed of idiot. For he had not been shamefully bound; nor stripped of *Soulseye*, as he had been stripped of all his other weapons.

Cautiously he uncovered his head, looked furtively about. His black-tufted ears twitched. That grating, hissing roar outside could only be a wintry wind, warning of the approach of an early blizzard. Sherdra wondered how long he had lain helpless here, at the dubious mercy of an enemy. But the simple succession of lights and darks concerned him as little as they did any of his people. He worried more about how he would manage when he escaped from this unlooked-for shelter and his odious host.

And for the first time in many lights, he allowed his thoughts to dwell upon Ashyr, who had left him without a word. Well; she had been wise to flee, before the final disaster. He could not remember when that had happened. Doubtless she had found sanctuary among their northern kinsfolk. Doubtless.

A campfire smoldered red-yellow between him and the cave entrance. Sherdra relished its warmth but did not like the sight of the tall, rangy figure bent over it, cooking something, apparently. An oddly flavored but tantalizing scent reached Sherdra's nostrils. Hunger was clawing again at his innards.

The human was muttering to himself. What, singing again? No, more like cursing. He was complaining of the loss of his pack-animal who had evidently bolted off and disappeared into the woods, when Sherdra had jumped him.

"Small wonder we never prosper, Pícaro," said the
fellow to his horse, secured near the fire, who stopped
munching winter-feed a moment and favored his
master with a somber brown stare as if he understood and sympathized.

Sherdra would rather not have understood. But a
part of his mind was beginning to sift out some sense
from what the alien said. It was because of this
talent—to comprehend quickly the tongue and mind-
speech of utter strangers—that Sherdra had been
chosen by the Clanmothers to be their voice to distant and very foreign tribes. He had, on occasion,
even spoken with some of the human Dry Town
traders with whom some of his folk did business. But
he had never imagined he would grasp the devious
and unstable Comyn mind. . . .

He considered a swift leap upon the man's back.
But his muscles seemed to have the consistency of
water. Water . . . yes, he did crave that. He wished
he could not smell what the peddler was cooking.

Sternly, he reproved the rising clamor of his bod-
ily needs. Spirit must never yield to the claims of
ignorant flesh, particularly in the presence of enemies. So the Great Cat would have counseled him
anyway: Myor, who had been his hunting-brother. . . .

*Ah, Myor, why did you not listen to us, when Ashyr and
I brought you the counsel of the Clanmothers, to turn aside
from the path they had foreseen as leading only to a dishonorable and terrible end for us all? Ashyr spoke truly.*
"His spirit has sickened, Sherdra. He is very mad.
He has been snared by the evil thing that lives in that
great unnatural witchstone he fondles so lovingly,
uses—he thinks—to bring down darkness and mortal
terror upon the human folk. Their sorcerers will
retaliate. I scent the burning of living flesh, not

many days off. Sherdra, we must bind him, bring
him away for healing; or else kill him, if only to save
for him what *gyar* he has not already forfeited."

*And I said, looking into his laughing, triumphant, pos-
sessing eyes, I can do nothing to my brother. When did you
leave us, Ashyr; then, or many days later? I felt you no
more within the watch circle at the Caves—it is well you
valued most your own freedom. By now you are surely safe.
Goddess, let this be—*

No; no; he must not dwell on this. To do so
brought down upon him the memory of Myor, burning, burning, as the huge matrix crystal exploded
into flame, set at the will of the human witch-lords;
burning and screaming, screaming to me for help—

*And I, fallen whimpering to the ground, paralyzed, terror-
struck by the visions they set upon us: the visions of devil-
spawned wolves. . . .*

No. He would not think of that. He could not risk
further madness. The howling in his mind had qui-
eted; so let it be.

*Well, here he comes again. He sees that I am awake and
is eager to satisfy his curiosity concerning me, and to draw
out my secrets. I marvel at his ignorance. I wish I were not
so weak. Still; still; shall we play a game, little bareskin?
The wager is trifling: only a life.*

"Had a nice sleep?" the man inquired caustially,
holding his drawn dagger where the catman might
see it easily. The catman seemed to shiver then; he
looked wide-eyed all around him. His gaze encountered the human's own and shyly slid away. He made
a feeble effort to rise, then subsided, mewling
plaintively.

The peddler considered a long moment. Sympa-
thizing with the animal that had sought to slay him

might prove dangerous. But he seemed fairly helpless yet; besides, he was in need, and the empath felt this.

He approached warily. *Stranger, my name is Coryn.* "Coryn," the man said aloud, pointing emphatically to himself. "And you?" The catman gave no sign he understood, only shrank back a bit more within his blankets.

Coryn thought, *Of course; we are too alien to share speech, even with the mind.* He had heard tales of telepaths related by blood but forced to speak only with the language of the headblind between themselves because of the mere emotional distance separating them. *So I might as well be talking to a mute. I wonder, does he even know how to use that starstone he carries? It is hardly insulated properly. . . .*

"I do not mean to hurt you," he said. "If I did, would I go to all this trouble? No; for I took a Healer's Oath at Nevarsin, not to withhold what help I could give, even to creatures such as you. 'All sentient creatures, no matter what their outward form or inward shape of mind, are equal in the eyes of the Creating Power—' Is that the way it goes . . . please; let me help you." He knelt by the catman's side, laid his free hand against the other's brow, monitoring for remaining injury. The alien pulled away roughly, hissing. The spittle flew in Coryn's face.

Coryn sat back on his heels. Somehow he controlled the impulse to jerk the catman up, smash him across the mouth.

"I should not look for gratitude from your kind, I suppose." Coryn rose stiffly and wearily, drained. He had ministered efficiently enough to his own wounds; these were healing, but his renewed effort on behalf of this—animal—had set them all to throbbing once again.

The alien, more alert now, was looking him up and down. A short, rumbling hum burst from his throat. Coryn's gaze, hostile, curious, met the unblinking golden eyes. "So you can smile, too, after your fashion? Are you satisfied with the damage you wrought?"

The catman made an odd, fluttering gesture with one paw. Coryn inexplicably felt further insulted. Then the catman closed his eyes, settling back against the rocky wall, as if dismissing his intrusive host.

Sighing, Coryn started to turn away; then thought better of this. The creature was still weak and weary, true, but the memory of their initial encounter was yet fresh in Coryn's mind.

"Somehow I dislike tying you up; but I do not want puss pouncing on me unawares, either—" He touched the alien lightly on the shoulder. The only response was a slight drawing away, as if he stank. *The poor beast should eat soon,* he thought. *I do not relish having to hand feed a bound and angry captive. And that storm brewing outside is like to keep us reluctant companions here for several days. . . .*

"Look at me," he said roughly, almost shouting, "or I'll shake you out of that devil's hide! Look—" He stamped his foot, feeling vaguely ridiculous.

The catman yawned hugely; but one yellow eye did slit open.

Coryn reached back in his memory for something he'd heard an old trader—a self-avowed (if highly unlikely) former captive of the catfolk—describe. Slowly he made the signs for *peace* and *truce*. He repeated these, without apparent effect.

"Very well, then. Let me entertain you some more."

He produced a short but ample enough length of rope from a commodious pocket of his peddler's cloak. He shook it in the catman's direction, then pantomimed tying of hands and feet. He threw the rope down, then again sketched the truce-symbol in the air. Puss could not have looked more bored.

"Pr' ya *hoom*," the creature rumbled. "Ska dahasa *tush*— "

Coryn recognized the mockery, if not the words. "I suppose I do resemble the poor tongueless fool I saw at Festival Fair, trying to mime his wants from a crowd of provincial idiots," he said ruefully. "Bearer of Burdens, you know *I* am an idiot! I've told him now what I must do, which means more bites and scratches for clever Coryn, I should guess.

"I hate to do this, but—" He looped the rope around his right hand, reached again for his knife. The alien growled softly, and pulled himself up into a half-crouch. "Don't fight me again," the man murmured.

A sudden searing image assailed his mind: an emaciated catman, bound in chains in a dark place, howling and dancing. . . . *A witless raver, his long fur matted with his own excrement, bound as the People would do to no other, but this one is very ill and can hurt with mind, as well as claw. The old she tending him so coldly was his other. . . . Do not* (unintelligible) *put this . . . shame upon me. . . .*

Coryn stood shock-still. *I hear you,* he said by the mindtouch. *The meaning, only a little; but the feeling—ah, cannot you try to understand me, too?*

He eagerly probed, without response from the barriered alien mind. But the catman rose, slowly. Coryn tensed.

With a quick, fluid gesture, slender furred hands

shaped the truce-sign. Coryn saw how incomplete and inept his own gesture had been.

Nodding, the man repeated the gesture. Amber eyes, seemingly less hard, met his own briefly; then the alien sat back down, trembling faintly.

"Perhaps we can learn to talk together, after all," the young man said. "But for this moment, I'll leave you in peace. Some food then, perhaps?"

Coryn limped to the campfire. He was very cold. He lifted the steaming pot of tea from the coals and poured fragrant liquid into a drinking bowl. Sipping slowly, enjoying the warmth of the bowl against chilled fingers, he let odd thoughts surface along the drowsy currents of his mind.

I've never seen a catman before. Until recently, I thought such folk were the stuff of scare stories my old aunt used to tell me, to frighten me into proper behavior. . . .

Still he is a beautiful savage—and with laran to spare; incredible! I wonder if he got those hurts at Corresanti. . . . There was some gossip flowing around the inn at Vandemyr— where I could be right now, as content as a poor man might be, curled up beside the charming Illona, in her wide bed, by the fire—talk to which I paid little heed, as usual—some catfolk meddling with an illegal matrix, or something equally far-fetched, and terrorizing the entire Alton Domain, until they were routed by Damon Ridenow—of all people! Now that must be a tale! Well, I have been gone from these parts for over a year; I wonder. . . . But now I must see to my guest's wants.

He poured another bowl of tea, took a panful of stew, and brought these to the catman, offering them with a tentative smile. "I hope you like your food cooked."

The alien sniffed at the food suspiciously; then turned his face away. Coryn might have cursed, him-

self; but he had learned many painful lessons in patience at the monastery. "Look—" he took a sip of
tea, a bite of the thick stew—"if this is poison, we can
make a death-song together. I'm not that bad a cook."

Still the catman ignored him, staring stonily at a
spot apparently just behind Coryn's backbone. Coryn
bit his lip. The sensible thing was, of course, to lay
the food, a skin of water, where his unwilling guest
might reach it, then withdraw. But it was all he could
do now not to bend over, gasping, with a knifelike
nausea he knew was not his own. So keenly could he
feel the catman's dizziness, the bite of his ravenous
hunger.

"Poor, proud fool—you can't know you are making me a bit uncomfortable. I doubt if you have been
schooled in the proper courtesies of a telepath; and I
was never totally successful, in screening out pain.
The one little drawback of my Ridenow genes, I
suppose."

Coryn took a deep breath. He realized that the
catman's concept of "truce" did not extend to accepting sustenance from an enemy.

*Father would say my compassion outruns my common
sense, as usual. I should have left this one to die in the first
place. He would probably be correct. But I cannot choose
not to help—*

*Firebearer, or whatever your name is, listen: I promised
not to hurt you. I meant that; on my honor, there is no
trickery here. You must eat, to bring back your strength. . . .*

Naturally his fine speech was ineffective. As he
had done once or twice when he cared for a sick one
who would not eat, he projected images of peace,
peace and healing—the rich strong broth warming
chilled bones, bringing new life to the blood, bring-

ing healing and peace . . . peace. . . . He reached out
his hand again, to touch, to soothe.

*Ah, little bird, you are cold; come shelter against my
heart.*

Yes, he was very cold. He leaned closer, looking
into the shining amber eyes, very wise, very beautiful, beckoning. Someone was singing, in a rough,
nearly incomprehensible, but not unpleasant voice,
of home. He *was* at home; safe and warm; his mother
cradling him against her breasts, stroking his fur—
his *fur*? His father was not angry at him, not any
more, never any more. A cold iron barrier was melt-
ing, giving way; the catman—*Sherdra*—was glowing
with lines of gentle, welcoming fire. He stroked the
other's hand, so velvet warm, so—

He recoiled, barely in time, flashing his knife between them. The gleaming claws were nearly at his
throat. Yellow eyes blazed lightnings as the catman
drew back slowly, slowly.

"Zandru! What did you do to me?"

The alien made a soft, puzzled sound. It seemed
very tamed, very quiet, hunched over as if despon-
dent, weary unto death; seeming only a gray-furred,
befanged beast, its hollow eyes blinking up at Coryn
as if in simple ignorance.

Coryn backed off, rubbing his head. Could he
have imagined— Then he laughed aloud. The catman's ears pricked forward at the strange sound; he
turned his head to one side, almost coyly.

*I thought we had declared a truce. But I congratulate
you, vai laranzu, on your superb technique.* Coryn knew
his sarcasm was lost on the catman, but he no longer
cared. *The question is, what do I do with you now—Sherdra?
What chains will keep your claws from my throat—and
from my mind?*

Then keep your—paws—off my mind, Comyn.

Panting, Sherdra heaved himself to his feet. Coryn drew his sword, dropped into a defensive stance.

Amusement bubbled up from beneath the black tide of Sherdra's anger.

What, are you still afraid of me? You who are strong and reasonably whole, while I. . . . The game is yours, for the moment; you should take advantage of it. Afraid of a few—bites and scratches? I should expect no more, from one who gives his word so lightly.

You accuse me of breaking my word? You miserable, treacherous, lying savage—I only sought to help you, to heal, even after you had hurt me. You prove now I was right in my first impulse, to slit your throat and leave you for the carrion-birds—

Sherdra said aloud, "Then come, little bird, try to correct your mistake!" He clapped his hands together, as one does when accepting a challenge.

Coryn took a step forward. Sherdra braced himself against the cave wall, and brandished his claws. *Why do you hesitate? For one who has dared to do what even an outborn, clanless loptail would not—seek rapport with a Firebearer when a truce-of-forebearance is spoken between them—it should not be hard to strike an unarmed enemy. Come on, Comyn; you are starting to bore me.*

But Coryn, smiling tightly, was lowering his sword. "Why should I waste the energy? I can wait you out. Since you will take nothing from my hands, it will not be long before starvation and pain will render you as helpless as—a sick kitten. . . ." *Think better of it, Sherdra, before you attempt any more suicidal attacks on me. I am your only hope of survival; in your place, I would be more polite.*

I did not give you leave to speak my name.

"Now look here—"

Enough. You have fouled me enough with your filthy touch. I will listen/be open to you no more.

The alien barriers went up again, stony-hard.

Coryn said a few words under his breath, that might have shocked his former mentors at the monastery. "You'd better sit down, before you fall down—No? All right, have it your way."

With an air of deliberate insult, he turned his back on the catman, and returned to the fire. "It will be a pleasure, when you come begging," he flung over his shoulder.

This last was lost on Sherdra, who in the past few moments had been attending to something else. A nightmare vision lunged through the doors of his perception; his sister, Ashyr, surrounded by the wolves. *No! I had thought you safe!* He gave a little wail of protest; the human looked up from tending the fire, and laughed. "So you are learning the price of your pride, after all? Have you discovered you are hungry?"

Incredulously, Coryn realized then that Sherdra was crying, though not in any manner he would normally recognize. The catman stumbled forward, hands outstretched, groping as if nearly blind. Before Coryn could reach him, he collapsed.

So once again, blood kin calls for help, in vain. . . . Sherdra felt the man's hands grab his own roughly, pulling his talons back from his own throat. And then there was nothing, nothing but the merciful obliterating dark.

When she saw the narrow mountain trail blocked ahead of her by a huge, impassable rockslide, the woman knew she had no chance. She had been a fool to let them run her this way.

A doubly-damned fool, to have ventured out of the safe hiding place she'd found some days before, in her struggle northward toward the border of her kinsfolk's hunting-ranges, and a hoped-for sanctuary. Exhausted and sick in spirit, she had meant to rest only as long as she had dared, then press on. But even though she had known the woods were infested by the human hunters and their hounds, early this morning Ashyr had crept out uncaring from her shelter, compelled by the sharp perception of her brother Sherdra somewhere to the south, harried and desperate. *So he has finally left the deathplace of our clan and followed after me. That, at least, has some meaning.* He had not responded to her call, and Ashyr had no witchstone to help her track him. But knowing he was in need, she had continued resolutely on, moving as quietly as any ghost through the forest that fairly reeked of her enemies' smells.

She had found fresh traces of Sherdra's passage, on a high ridge sloping down to a pocket-valley. She had even broken into a little run, calling out heedlessly, "Sherdra!" even knowing he must be yet some distance away. The shock she had felt as she had heard the human hunters shout at her from a covering shadow, heard hounds burst into a triumphant howl, still tingled along every nerve as she stood now helplessly contemplating her death. She had used every means she knew to evade the pursuing dogs and their masters, but without success. She wondered if Sherdra would ever know in what manner she had helped him. *They must have been on his spoor, but I shall be their prey.*

Now they were surging up the trail behind her, the lean, black wolfish hounds, having outrun their masters in their lust for the kill. As yet, they were out of sight; but she knew they were only a few yards distant. With the practiced eye of a born climber, Ashyr surveyed the sheer cliff wall to her right, saw there was no sure grip her one good hand could fasten on to draw her up and away from the death pursuing her. She ran to the edge of the trail and looked down. Why did she bother? It was as she had seen before. Some mad demon-hag had clawed out a slick-sided chasm whose depths, shrouded in mists, made her mind reel.

"Goddess!" Ashyr cried aloud, acknowledging she would not escape.

She should jump. She was too weary to fear death, much. But there was no greater shame to a Firebearer woman, Guardian of the Sacred Flame, than to be torn to pieces by the animals of the not-men.

She should jump; but even as she tensed her trembling muscles to leap, the new life stirred within her womb. *My children. They deserve a better choice than this.* She should have thought of them before she had so rashly endangered herself—and them. Sherdra would have cuffed her hard for her lack of foresight; she bore a far more precious gift to a decimated and defeated people than his.

Perhaps she could make a stand, even hide, there among the tumbled rocks. Ashyr whirled about, and raced for the rockslide.

And the first of the hounds appeared, scrambling around a rocky corner. Barking fiercely, it launched itself full at its quarry. Ashyr neatly sidestepped it, dealing it a savage blow. The dark head, cleaved to the bone, spouted blood. Whimpering, it fell back, tried to crawl away.

Ashyr's talons fastened hard upon its body. With a triumphant scream, she pitched the hound from the cliff.

But she had delayed too long. Now the pack were all around her, snarling and feinting at her, cutting off the only possible route to escape. Ashry's sword flashed, drinking blood from another wolfish throat. Another dog sprang at her; she kicked it deftly aside, jumped backward to avoid another charge. Barely in time, she caught herself. At her back was only emptiness. She swayed on the edge of the chasm.

The surviving hounds inexplicably drew back, muttering as if between themselves. For a delirious moment, Ashyr imagined them discussing the situation. She smiled into their flame-bright, hollow eyes, showing them her teeth. Now, as if warned by the fate of their comrades, they advanced on her slowly, bristling, but in a hideous silence.

She would like to take a few more with her, Ashyr decided. She danced a few steps on the edge of the cliff, daring them to come try a fall with her. The leader of the pack growled bitterly. Then he stopped, and held his place. So did the other hounds, despite their obvious bloodthirst. Ringed in, Ashyr wondered what Master had trained them so well.

Harsh human shouts, the uneven trampling of horses' hoofs, broke the unnatural silence. Ashyr saw human riders coming up. In their forefront was a tall thin one in green and black, his scanty headfur the all too familiar and accursed color of an apish witchlord. She saw the sword glimmering in his left hand; she also spied a looped rope in his right. So they meant to capture her, after all?

Shouting at her, the Guardsman spurred his horse forward. Ashyr's eyes widened at such foolishness. She winced in near-sympathy as the human lord's horse stumbled over a surprised dog. Cursing, the man beat the hounds out of his way. But his horse slipped again, sideways, on a patch of ice. The human was nearly thrown. He fought to right himself, jabbing a finger at her, screeching something to his fellows just behind him.

All this is very amusing; but now I must leave, Ashyr thought, pitying the hounds, their hard work spoiled by the clumsiness of their masters.

Two men had dismounted; they rushed toward her. Ashyr flicked them a scornful glance; then turned to confront the emptiness. "Forgive me, children," she whispered to the daughter and the son who must now remain unborn. "Goddess, receive us kindly—"

Later, the Guardsman swore that the woman laughed as she plunged from the cliff.

By true nightfall, the men had found a place beneath a stony overhang, which offered a reasonable shelter from the rising wind now spitting ice and snow into their faces. The Guardsman from Thendara—their leader and employer—had, incredibly, tried to argue them all into taking up the trail again. It seemed that the creature they had tracked to its death was not the one Dom Julian had wanted. He wanted a male, not a female. "But what difference did it make, anyway?" the exhausted men grumbled among themselves. Old Dakstar said it truly: One dead cat is very like another. And Dom Julian had promised them all, when he had hired them for this hunt seven days ago, that it should take no longer than three, to either run the beast to earth or conclude it had escaped them. Fortunately, Kraigan, their tracker, who seemed to know something of the ways of the Comyn, had persuaded the stonefaced young lord that the weather warranted at least finding a haven for the night.

"Else we would be out riding in the bitter cold, this monent," young Carlo said to Dakstar, piling more scraps of wood on the fire. "What does he want, a trophy for his castle walls? If that is the case, I will return to that gorge, and climb down. And bring him back her teeth and claws—even her fluggy tail."

"Lad, do not be silly—"

"He promised to release us when this hunt was over. To my mind, it is. Do you know, he even said we would go all the way back to where we started, at Vandemyr, just to pick up the 'proper' trail? Dakstar, Dakstar; I should not have come, not for all the copper he promised us. My Alissa will be worrying about me; and her time is so near—"

"Shush!" The older man peered nervously over his shoulder at Dom Julian, who stood a good way apart from them on a rocky knoll, staring, it appeared, into nothingness. Dakstar thought again that the Guardsman resembled more a carved figure of a man than a living being. He appeared oblivious to anything they might say; and yet—"Shush, Carlo. He's a fine pair of ears on him. And these Comyn can look right through a man's skull as if it were made of clear glass, and see every thought inside."

"He is not much of a Comyn, for that matter, only the nephew of a minor lord; I heard him admit that to Kraigan," Carlo retorted, brown eyes flashing. "And surely if he looked within your empty skull, it's little enough he'd find there."

A brief, hot quarrel broke out between them. This was silenced by Terenz who, returning from tending the horses, inquired coolly why dinner had not been started. Julian, perfectly aware of everything that had passed between Dakstar and Carlo, smothered a chuckle. Terenz did not have Carlo's gift for invective, but his size, and a certain look that settled on his face when he was displeased, usually won him prompt attention.

Julian shivered and drew his cloak of fine, dense fur around him. He considered his companions in their threadbare, patched garments and briefly felt sorry that he had harried them so on this long and seemingly profitless trail. He knew they longed to be safe and warm in their homes. Julian would have rather been at home himself. But he had a duty to perform.

Oh, Alaric— It was hard to believe even now he could not look up and see his bredu smiling whimsically at him, hear the deep voice chiding him for his latest obsession. *Julian, Julian; give it up, go home, make your peace with your uncle, wed the pretty Lindir maiden he has chosen as bride for you. There's surer comfort there than what you now pursue. You will not find me again on this cold, cold vengeance-trail, dearest, if you killed a thousand catmen.*

I only mean to kill the one, Alaric; only the one who took you from me—I will be comforted then.

He was jolted out of his dark reverie by the sound of booted feet crunching toward him. Kraigan, the tracker, was approaching, head down. Julian thought he must have been off burying his dead hounds. The only strong emotion Julian had seen in the odd little man was when Kraigan had acknowledged there was no chance of retrieving the body of the dog that the catwoman had flung from the cliff. He had burst into noisy tears and then stamped off, consigning all catfolk to Zandru's tenth hell.

"Well, it is the luck of the trail as you have so often said," Julian had spat after him. "Did you expect her to stand there and be savaged?" Kraigan had probably thought him strange, that he could feel any sympathy for the plight of the hunted. But he was not out to rid the world of catfolk; just this one.

Kraigan paused a few feet from him and lifted his face to the wind, almost as if scenting it. "That is quite a blow coming, *Dom* Julian! Zandru's pumping his icy bellows, hard—" His honey-colored eyes, so incongruous in his dark withered face, looked slyly sideways at the young Guardsman.

"I have already heard your—weather report," Julian replied stiffly. "And all this means is that we are forced to hole up here another day while the catman gets further and further away—"

"It would be hard enough to pick up his trail in fair weather, providing he's anywhere in the area. My dogs need rest, and mending, in any case—"

Polite deference had never been Kraigan's strength, and when Dom Julian did not respond except to shrug his shoulders, the tracker added, "If you'll pardon me for saying so, I wonder why you didn't bring your fellow Guardsmen and Comyn kin with you, since this particular beastie's so important."

"They were all riding home or to their weddings, after the last battle." Julian would not share with Kraigan his more bitter reflections: *And I, of course, was expected to return to my rightful duty—pulling drunks off the streets of Thendara. The murder of one's bredu is very regrettable, naturally, but does not warrant a wild, reckless chase after the animal who—maybe—was responsible for his death and who—maybe—wielded the powers of a matrix. War games are over for the summer. Why provoke further trouble? Or so my kinsmen might have said, had I bothered to stay and persuade them after they first refused to come with me—*

He realized dimly he was not being fair to his

kinsmen. It had not happened exactly that way. But the first few days after Alaric's death were misted as with blood, all but drowned in grief and rage. The first clear recent memory he had was of stumbling into the tavern at Vandemyr, compelled by his body's need for warmth and food. Alaric was dead; and he had lost the trail of his friend's murderer, somewhere in these foresaken mountains.

The innkeeper—a buxomly pretty woman Alaric might have admired—had seen his trouble, though she could not guess its cause. Quickly she had brought him hot food and drink and murmured something about a pleasant room upstairs, where the *vai dom* might rest in privacy.

"Thank you, but no," he had managed to reply. "I still have a few hours of daylight left and cannot waste the time when I might—" He glanced across the room, where a few fellows were loitering by the fire; he said "no" again to the woman, who was pleading, "But sir, you look dreadful." He looked again, more sharply, at the crowd of village rustics; and laughed. "Excuse me, mestra." He had recognized one of the men; maybe his luck had turned at last.

Approached with Julian's improbable plan, Kraigan had first refused, incredulous that anyone should be interested in having any more to do with one of the "murthering beasties," whatever the provocation. Julian persisted in his pleas, knowing that Kraigan, a professional tracker sometimes employed by the local nobility on similar bloodhunts, had the skills and knowledge he required. Once he had even observed Kraigan firsthand, working with his hounds as if they shared one mind, tracking down the poor fugi-

tive with admirable success. That Kraigan chose to
deny his *laran* and remain unmarked among his
peasant, headblind kindred, was nothing to Julian
then, except as this gift might serve the Guardsman's
ends. Finally, having seen Julian's coppers, the
man became quite agreeable. He had observed that
if there was any chance of finding a particular
fugitive catman, his superbly-trained hounds might
succeed.

"They have tracked such creatures before, and
recently. As a matter of fact, I have a piece of fresh
skin in my gear, to refresh their memories of what
they will follow," Kraigan had laughed.

Julian had not wished to know where Kraigan had
procured this useful article. It was enough he had
found help at last to carry through his desire for
vengeance. Indeed Kraigan had been very helpful,
rounding up provisions as if by some swift sorcery, en-
listing the other men at the tavern—his nephew
Terenz and some distant cousins, Julian gathered—to
join the hunt. They had seemed eager enough to be
in on the kill of one of the animals that had preyed
on their distant neighbors to the south. Julian had
not been enchanted with the quality of these men,
nor their strength of purpose. But he was in no
position to be choosy.

Julian had allowed himself, mainly because of
Kraigan's insistence, only a few hours of rest; within
a short while, they had all been on the trail. And
within a day or two, the hounds had struck a cattish
spoor; and then, this very morning, Carlo had shouted
with a devastated surprise as he spied the black-
furred, erect creature running, as it were, at their
sides, through the trees—Julian remembered the
freezing-hot rush of joy that had struck flame to his

ashy heart as he had imagined fortune had blessed
him at last. Instead, at trail's end, there was only that
miserable woman, probably caught innocently enough
in the hunter's nets; and she, even she, had escaped
him— Truly, it was said: Do not plan roast fowl
for dinner until you have caught the bird.

Kraigan cleared his throat, recalling Julian to present time. The tracker's face bore an odd expression;
Julian supposed he had been muttering to himself
again.

"*Dom* Julian," Kraigan said, kindly, "You'll catch
your death, standing out here alone in the chilly
dark. I think supper's almost ready; will you partake
with us, sir?"

Julian supposed he had to eat sometime. He turned
mutely and accompanied Kraigan toward the other
men, huddled around the campfire.

"How long do you think we'll be here?"

"Well, it's an early storm and apt to rage itself out
quickly. I should say—no more than three days."

"Three days! Kraigan—!"

Kraigan whirled about on his employer, who, startled, backed off a step.

"Yes, *vai dom*; three days! And during that time,
we will shelter, as any sensible man would. You are
not from these parts; you have not seen what even a
mild summer storm can do. Will you run out alone
into this wind, young man, without so much as a
guide? Because that is what you will do if you insist
on leaving any time before I say it is safe. We all
have wives and bairns at home, worrying for us."

"Presumptuous—" Julian's face darkened; his hand
fell to the hilt of his dagger. Kraigan waited stolidly,
to see what he would do.

"Here, here, don't fight!" Dakstar yelled, bustling up to them. He tried to thrust his spindly frame between the two men. Julian laughed unpleasantly, and pushed the old farmer away. "Peace, friend. I mean no ill to anyone, except my enemy."

Pointedly ignoring Kraigan, who was still staring hard at him, Julian made his way to the fire and sat down before it. The others gave him plenty of space, he noticed.

"*Dom* Julian," Carlo asked after a time, "Can you tell us why finding one particular catman is so important? If you'll forgive me for saying so, it seems almost impossible. There's thousands of leagues of wild forest out there in which he could be hiding."

"I think I have told you why before," Julian replied as he spooned up stew from the cookpot into his bowl, "but to refresh your memory: the particular one I seek was one of their principal warriors. He carries a matrix, and is skilled and dangerous in cattish sorceries. I saw him last swimming the ford of the Corresanti after he had butchered nearly a score of Guardsmen in his escape. I would have followed him immediately, but I—had a friend who required my help just then. I believe he is not simply fleeing for his life, but intends to reach his surviving kin to the north and cry vengeance. So we will have more of the devils to face next summer, if not sooner. Any more questions?"

Carlo's expression reflected doubt and mistrust. Julian supposed the lad was wondering if he would insist they follow their quarry to the banks of the Kadarin and beyond; or to world's end, whichever proved necessary.

"No, Carlo," he said, very low. "We will catch him long before that. I know it—"

"I know it," he repeated as Carlo withdrew with a muttered apology, ostensibly to tend the fire. Julian thought, *Is there something in my face that frightens the lad?*

Kraigan grumbled across the campfire, "We have no way of *knowing* as you do, *vai dom*. We are only simple men and can follow only our normal senses—not even as well as Derhi, here." He patted the nose of a dog come rubbing up against his side for comfort. "Eh, Cormac, is that lame foot of yours still bothering you?" he asked fondly of another hound nestling at his feet. "Let's see—" He was busy with his dogs awhile, comforting their hurts, adjusting the little rough boots they wore as protection against the icy terrain.

"Master Kraigan ought not to be so modest," Julian said blandly, as the tracker finished.

"I beg your pardon?" Kraigan returned, glancing up wide-eyed, as if he really did not know what Julian meant. "Well," he went on after receiving no enlightenment, "we might as well all get some sleep. If there is any chance of an early start tomorrow, we shall all be rested."

He looked pointedly at Julian, who shrugged and said, "I will keep watch for a while. Then one of you can relieve me. *Don't* tell me a sentry and fireguard isn't needed."

"*Vai dom*, my hounds are not deaf," Kraigan began, and then thought better of it. With a rumbling sigh, he rolled over in his blankets; four or five dogs ran up, to lie down beside him.

Carlo and Dakstar soon followed his example, huddling close together. Julian considered them, the boy's dark, curly head cradled against the older man's bony shoulder. He sighed, without knowing that he did so. They were not, after all, unlike some Guardsmen he had known.

"They'll stay warm, surely," Terenz said. Julian jumped slightly. The burly, coarse featured man was easy to forget; and he'd been quieter than usual this evening. Terenz poked at the fire, exclaiming, "How lucky we are, not to be caught out in the open on such a night as this! Brrr, it's cold out there! The catman may not be as privileged as we—"

"Oh, he has found a hidey-hole, never fear."

Terenz nodded. "Yes, *vai dom*, you are probably right." After a long hesitation, he said, "I hope we can start out again on the morrow. It's a fine adventure you have led us on. Whenever would lads like us get such another chance? Not with my uncle, I vow; he thinks little of us. And—I agree with you; such animals should all burn, down to the smallest cub.

"I—I had a young sister who went with her man to farm on the Alton lands, years ago. Never heard anything from them until last year, after the trouble there began. Then, one day, my wife looks up and sees a poor old ragged woman at our door; she thinks, a beggar. 'Don't you know me, Mhari?' my sister asks. My wife screams for me, and I come running from the fields. Deirdre falls into my arms, sobbing and all a-tremble. They had murdered her man and children, the beasts, and set such terror upon her that I fear she'll never be right in her mind again. She has—such nightmares; waking and asleep—

"Well—" He looked away, as if embarrassed.

"Doubtless you have witnessed worse things. I only wanted you to know—I think differently than these others, here. . . . Good night.'

"Good night, Terenz," Julian replied, surprised and touched. He had not thought Terenz revealed much of himself to anyone. "Sleep pleasantly. Sleep without dreams."

"Thank you, *vai dom*," the other whispered, drawing inside his bedroll. "I knew you might understand."

There was little sound now but the slow crackling of the fire, the rusty breathing of the men, the querulous moaning of the wind. Julian got up and prowled around the fire.

Kraigan is right; that's a hellish storm. Nor do I really need to stand guard, with these fine dogs as protectors. What is the matter with me?

The young man stared into the glowing embers, his true sight filled with visions of a laughing, freckled face, blue eyes shining with mischief and tenderness.

Oh, Julian. You are too serious and sober by far! Come, have a drink with me at the tavern when all this is over. That's a pretty woman working there; very—kissable—hmmm. Listen: did you hear the joke Domenick told about the two Terrans, the riyachiya, and the so-polite cralmac? You look as if you need a good laugh, bredu. Well, it goes like this—

"Alaric, be quiet," Julian said aloud. "This isn't the time for making jokes."

I must not think of you; or I will remember too well how you died, sobbing in my arms, your bonny face all spoilt. I will remember how long it took you to die.

I will go out again in the morning, alone if necessary. Let them all rest safe here and wonder at the madman.

Julian went apart from the others, outside the circle of light, where the wind's cold slap might wake any forlorn dreamer into a state of reason.

This did not help as much as he hoped. At last he said to Alaric's ghostly presence, "When he killed you, he killed whatever laughter was in me. It's petty for me to think this; but I hate him as much for that, as for the other killings he and his kind are guilty of."

Oh, I pray you are still alive, catman. I feast on dreams of what I shall do to you.

These prolonged faints were becoming quite annoying; particularly when one swam up out of unpleasant dreams to a more unpleasant reality. To be sure, he had been moved closer to the fire. The hands of the healer were gently stroking his forehead. Sherdra was dismayed that he could not even summon up a desire to attack again. The man gave him water to drink. He took it greedily, no longer able to withstand his thirst.

"Not even your touch can dirty the springs of life," he rasped, more for himself than the other, who could not understand. He saw the man make that peculiar movement of his mouth—a smile?—that must mean mockery. *Have I indeed fallen into his snares?* he wondered.

"I felt someone close to you die," Coryn said. Then, by the mindtouch, he continued, *I cannot understand you well. But if it were I who broke the truce between us by seeking rapport against your will, I ask pardon.*

It is the lingering fever in my mind that distorts his meaning so, Sherdra thought. He thrust the image of a spear at Coryn. *Still you talk. Talk-talk. You weary me, Comyn. Let me alone.*

I am afraid that I cannot. I see now it must be peace between us or a death. Ah, man, don't growl at me. You'd like me to think you only an animal and not worthy of my caution. Am I right?

Sherdra laughed, after his own fashion. An animal, at least, knew his enemy.

But I am not your enemy. I took no part in the wars against your people. My own kin might call me traitor, for I have dealt with you kindly.

Sherdra shut him out. He wanted to think of Ashyr, of how she must have died. He could not express sorrow, nor sing the songs of passing for her and her children, before this human. But he might gain a desolate satisfaction in planning how he would find her murderers, and what he would do to them—if only this silly child would stop talking.

"Hrrta!" He pushed the human, not roughly, away.

"Come, now." Coryn brought his knife up between them. *I do not want to use this. We need only refrain from killing each other until the storm dies down. Then, I promise you, I will be on my way. I have business more important than attending to your wants.*

Silent as cold stone, the catman glanced past him, at the swirling darkness outside the cave's mouth.

"No." Coryn moved between him and the cave entrance. "You will die out there." He tossed his dagger at Sherdra's feet. *Take it up, if it will give you comfort.*

Sherdra's broad nostrils flared; his eyes veiled as the nictitating membrane slanted across them. He kicked at the dagger, set it spinning across the floor.

Coryn fought down a surge of anger. He got up and retrieved his knife.

"Since you will have it no other way—"

The catman's head rested against his drawn-up knees. *So he will not trust me, not even in this.* It might be a kindness to dispose of him now, Coryn reflected. *And certainly a service to humankind, as my father would say.* Despite the catman's proud and continuing defiance, despite the obvious strength of his *laran*, his instincts were totally barbaric. Of course. That was the burden of the tales about such folk. They were savagery incarnate, with no affinity toward life and the living. They would drown the world in blood if they could.

And another voice stirred within Coryn's mind; a voice from out of a memory the young man usually tried to keep from his waking consciousness; Brother Stefan's gentle voice: *He dare not trust a human's kindness, ever. What must he have suffered at our hands?*

He turned as if compelled and put the same question to Sherdra.

You dare to claim ignorance of what your kind has done? the alien spat; or rather, his presence within Coryn's consciousness radiated a bitterness like the once poisoned lake where, some said, a god had walked.

I did not kill your sister, Sherdra.

No. Wolves wearing human skins. Like all of you. Go away and let me be.

Almost Coryn let him have his wish. He was deathly tired himself. And yet—

We have been blind to each other, Coryn acknowledged. *He has been within my barrers without seeing. Even as I deluded myself into thinking this a mere beast. It is time these barriers of ill will crumpled. And I, as empath, must take the initiative. Oh, Stefan, you are right: I do not wish his death. I never really did. And so I must throw myself wide open to him. No seeking, probing touch, to ruffle his*

*pride, and thrust knife-hard into all his festering griefs.
No, I must open to him in welcome, and wait. He may yet
be strong and potent in mind. Ah, he bites at his claws and
stares at me, so hard!*

*Holy Bearer of Burdens, may your image give me strength;
I am so afraid!* Coryn prayed in earnest. *This is hard,
so very hard for me to do—*

He quickly relaxed every particle of his defenses
without giving himself a chance to reconsider. Any
rational thought would only echo fear and the very
prejudice he was trying to melt away with his total
surrender. The feline would *look* at what he was
seeing, this time.

*Come now, proud enemy, and feast your fill of me. This
is who I am.*

The catman's consciousness stirred and strengthened. Coryn could scarcely believe he was yet so
vital. He waited. Something with bright, mad eyes
came hunting him on gliding, clawed feet; hunting,
scenting out his barely hidden and vulnerable life.
This is not Sherdra, but the image of my fear. And it
seemed then he looked from out of the gateway of
Nevarsin into the perplexed face of a very strange
young man; a lost young man who stood shivering in
the wintry wind but who would not come inside for
comfort. *You are welcome, stranger; come in.* He reached
out; he opened all doors, cast down all barriers and
all shields, letting his inner light well outward to
illuminate him clearly. A dazzling shock spiraled
through all the currents of his being as the stranger
touched him, and entered.

And Sherdra came; and hesitated, opening only a
small part of himself in return. *Do not be so frightened.*
To Coryn, the other's mental voice was remote,

distant. *I see this is possibly not a trick. And this deathgame must be ended.*

They do hunt you with hounds, then. But why?

It is you who must share your life with me. I will not do the same, Coryn. I cannot.

Coryn sighed. *I also dislike making myself known to such a stranger. But come; look; be with me. Here.*

Coryn tried to hold back nothing. Much there was to show, to share with a stranger who had but the dimmest conception of the ways of a human, much less his inner life. He thought first of Illona—surprising himself. He had not realized how much she meant to him; he thought, shivering on the edge of tears, of the young hill woman he had loved, but could not save from death. And Sherdra recoiled, as from a gross obscenity. *Your women are always ready to offer themselves.*

Sherdra, this is me! Can't you— Almost Coryn broke off the rapport in anger.

I thought you might do this. Sherdra began to withdraw; with something like real regret, Coryn perceived.

"No." He seized Sherdra's hands in his own. The catman did not move.

You wait with more patience than I have, for something you can understand. Very well; we've each had the experience of—growing up, haven't we?

It was not so hard, after all. Coryn shared with Sherdra what he hoped the alien might grasp. The earliest memories: waking on any given morning in a poor trapper's cottage, near the Naderling Forest. Coryn huddled together with his younger brother and sisters for warmth on one dreary sunrise after another, the littlest sister sometimes weeping with hunger as their mother scrounged outside for firewood and anything remotely edible. The lame, untidy man usually sprawled amid the better furs by the sputtering fire. The inevitable slaps and cries as he beat their mother when she came home with little enough to keep the chill out. The other children were taught to call this man father, but Coryn learned soon enough that he should not. He became glad— almost—to have been denied this privilege. When one morning his mother quietly awoke him, and, taking him where their furtive conversation would not disturb her husband, told him her news, he could not understand it. But he laughed aloud for joy, that he could leave them all. . . .

Somehow his mother had managed to send word to the Ridenow of his son's existence; and of how the shy little fellow had the disconcerting habit of answering questions before they were asked. So he was recognized, *nedestro*, and a gleaming future offered itself.

So you left her to the cruelty of her barbarian mate. I do not know how. . . . Sherdra projected in confusion.

Yes. I left my mother. Chagrin washed over Coryn. He had never seen his leaving as desertion or associated it with shame. She had given him up willingly enough. *She sold me, Sherdra.* He wondered how many coppers his father's retainers had pressed into her hands that long ago evening when they had come for him.

"Forgive us, *chiyu*," she whispered at the last, holding him so tightly against her thin, sere body that he had almost cried out in pain. "Forget us." She did not weep openly. She never did, not when her husband beat her, not even when the littlest sister had died. "Never look back."

You cry with the one you try to forget.

I had to try; I never bore pain very well, and then— You must know, Sherdra, she never had any right to me! By what chance my father came to lay with a woman so—so outside his caste—I never learned; nor cared to. She should not have kept me so long, in that place; with that man. (A child cried out in pain as he felt his mother's face break open under the force of her husband's blows; he ran at the man, striking out furiously with both small fists. The man laughed and kicked him, bleeding, into the wall.) *She—she should have done something.* (The sobbing child's image receded; an elegantly dressed Comyn lad—a later version of Coryn—regarded with distaste the spectacle his younger self had made; and began to lecture the catman on Domains law.) *I learned at Nevarsin—at my studies—that my mother had no legal basis on which to hold me from my father. The precedents are clear. I belonged to him by right, from the first. He wanted me, if only for the sake of my laran. And she, like most women, must bow to the will of any man; whatever his quality.*

Did that give the right for that— (Sherdra used a concept Coryn could not comprehend, only that it was unspeakably vile.)*—to beat and degrade the mother of his children? Tell me how this can be!*

"Sherdra, please—"

The Goddess howls in outrage. Among us, every mother is regarded as an image of the Sacred Presence. To say she has no right to her children is madness.

If so, then all the Comyn are raving lunatics.

Do you like to consider yourself Comyn?

Coryn's heart skipped a beat. Stefan might have said this to him. The rapport then was pure emotion, anger and revulsion and a bitter, bitter grief he could not fathom from Sherdra, his own emotions so mixed he could not understand them himself. (*Oh, mother . . . did he finally kill you?*)

You will never know until you go back and see. Do not cry anymore. One late tear cannot end a summer's drought. So. So. You left your mother—or never returned to help her, which is worse . . . went to your highborn father's cave-holding—house, I must say?—which earned you much gyar. And when came this Nevarsin, at which you learned such peculiar things?

Coryn reflected that Sherdra had to be close to collapse. Perhaps it would be best to end this now. "Won't you take now what you need from my hands?" he asked. "Truly, I feel your need."

No brother's truce has been spoken between us yet. Continue.

Of course, vai dom.

Sherdra made a disdainful gesture in response to Coryn's sarcasm. They might have ended then, in mutual antagonism. But Coryn whispered, "I am sorry." *Or should I say—j'dara?*

"J'sidarra," Sherdra corrected him; and did not withdraw.

Coryn continued. Indeed, Nevarsin lay at his heart's core. Serrais, the home of his forefathers, meant little to him. *And there is little to show you of Serrais, for I didn't spend much time there. I was not welcome. Nor anyplace else, it would seem. My father—* (The image of a cold-featured, sharp eyed man, extravagantly dressed, formed in Coryn's mind. He was saying something about responsibilities and duties.)

". . . A younger brother of Lord Serrais; oh, the name does not matter. We only talked once or twice. He was almost headblind, as we call it. He saw that I learned manners and swordplay. I hoped at first that he would love me. He was honest about that. ("*I am not capable of softer emotions, Coryn,*" his father said. "*Since my bredu died . . . but you are too young to understand that. Understand that I won't mistreat you, as did that peasant cur. I will see you have what you need. Some of it, anyway. And what you deserve. I am sorry, son; but don't expect any more.*") He was interested in what I might pass on to my children—the children I might father for our clan, I should say. When he learned that I was developing *laran* young, that pleased him. I guess. He arranged for me to be fostered at Nevarsin. He had one of the servants tell me of his decision."

Sherdra did not seem to understand. Coryn pulled him closer, and took him into his memories of Nevarsin. *Can you comprehend such places, such houses of the spirit?*

Yes.

Have patience. This I must show you, for it is—what made me as I am.

Coryn arrived at Nevarsin rebellious and aching. *No one will want me here, either.* But a strange alchemy began to transform him soon after he entered Nevarsin's gates. For there he experienced a variety of warmth he had never known. The harsh discipline of the monks scarcely daunted him for Coryn had never lived in ease. He regarded the pampered Comyn youths who grumbled at the cold with unconcealed contempt. They in turn mocked him for his peasant attitudes and ignorance of *casta*. He found no friends among these young and arrogant strangers, but the brothers were invariably kind. And Stefan was more than simply kind.

It was Brother Stefan who noticed the boy's loneliness and who gave generously of his free time without in any way shirking his allotted tasks. It was Brother Stefan who noticed first Coryn's developing gift of healing and who persuaded the lad to accept training in putting this to use, even after Coryn had told him that he had no kindness to give to anyone. It was Brother Stefan who touched and brought out the gentleness in the child who feared he would be as cruel as his mother's husband, as cold as his true father. It was Brother Stefan who taught him not to despise his manhood.

And there was more. There were long, satisfying talks during the period between morning meditations and afternoon devotions, when Stefan patiently answered his eager questions about the tenets of the *cristoforo* faith. Beyond the squalor of village existence and the squabbles for precedence among those who named themselves superior, there were eternal values. At Nevarsin there was more honor paid to the man who sought after truth than to the man whose pride lay in birth alone. This was a creed of wisdom that Coryn could embrace wholeheartedly. He would belong to no house but the house of the spirit.

Yet this was not to be. His father learned of his inclination toward the life of the brethren. A retainer was sent to retrieve him so that he could be safely dispatched to a Tower where he might be trained to do useful tricks for the Comyn.

He hesitated; then shared with Sherdra his bitterest memory: the day when Brother Stefan came to inform him that he was again to be uprooted. He was to lose everything; and all his hopes for a life of dignity based upon his own aspirations and newly acquired beliefs were inconsequential, it seemed.

I will not go meekly at any man's will! With a heady feeling of rebellion he formed a desperate plan.

"Tell my father's man I wish to meditate first before I go," he told Stefan. "You cannot refuse me that."

As if he sensed something of Coryn's state of mind, the monk placed a gently restraining hand on his shoulder.

"Meditate, then, upon the virtues of endurance and humility. That is the way of the Bearer of Burdens. Do not fly from destiny."

"I will do as I must, Brother Stefan." He turned his face away. He wanted to express his gratitude for those hours of communion, those glimpses of truth he had been privileged to share. But words were inadequate. How could he say what he truly felt? The holy man might misconstrue. . . . The very suspicion of abomination must be avoided. So Coryn gathered up his few possessions and exited from the brief presence of friendship in his life. The warmth of such closeness may singe the unwary.

He slipped out into the silent snows, using a few tricks he'd learned to avoid attracting attention, and entered upon an unknown fate. If Coryn wept as he ran, it was not from fear.

What Sherdra learned from Coryn's last gift of himself he did not say. One question formed and launched itself across the gap still between them. *How could you defy your elders to become a peddler?*

Caught in the most heinous crime of all, Coryn thought with amusement. Surely there is nothing worse than wandering the world with goods for sale upon one's back. Outlawry would be excusable, but never such an ostentatiously peaceful pursuit.

Do you not understand, man of the catfolk? I am free. I answer to no one's will but my own.

And you are as homeless as I am. That is something. Could two peoples hold things in common? This seemed incredible to Sherdra. *Even two clans must hold their differences at bay in order to co-exist. Yet I cannot deny what the Goddess must have shaped. She does nothing without purpose. Am I to accept you as—friend? Is that what was meant to be?*

Coryn smiled up at Sherdra as the rapport dwindled away. Sherdra had risen and was walking up and down briskly in front of the cave entrance, taking in deep steady breaths of moist, cold air.

"How have you stood up to all of this, I wonder?" he asked in simple admiration.

Sherdra's hands, claws sheathed, took him by the wrists, helped him to stand himself. The catman did not let go at once. Coryn thought it was no longer exactly an alien face that confronted him so gently.

You still carry a fine sword, Coryn. Among my people, simple traders do not do so. I think among your own people, there is a similar law. Why retain a privilege that belongs to a way of life you reject?

"Why, man, for protection against such as you," Coryn said; then realized this was not the answer Sherdra sought. The question was a final test. If his answer was satisfactory. . . .

My sword is not the only thing I retain. Sherdra loosed him; he drew out his matrix pouch. *This I obtained after testing at Neskaya. You know its significance? It is a part of me.*

I thought you must have one of those. Sherdra lifted his right hand, the one that bore *Soulseye;* for a moment Coryn fancied that the jewel flamed through its covering. *You still lack good sense, little bird; you should have tried to take this while I slept. Yes. It is something like yours. It is one of the few left to us. I have not worn this all my life; it was . . . a gift. But do not think you can touch it now, even with truce fairly said between us. If your people knew of its existence. . . .*

Coryn mentally hugged himself. Why, poor puss was actually shivering—absolutely abject in his vulnerability. *Zandru! I'm an empath! How could you believe I would lay a hand on someone else's matrix? The backlash would kill me.*

You must have no true sisters, then. Ashyr might touch this without harm.

Coryn waited for more, but there was none. "Stew's gone stone-cold; and you haven't let me tend the fire," he said at last, hoping the catman would now be willing to listen to the voice of practicality.

Dawn was breaking dimly through scudding gray-black clouds. The blizzard had barely subsided. Sherdra knew he was in no condition to steal a start on the men pursuing him. He had perceived that their camp was not far away. Well, he might decide to surprise them; would the wolves like that, the hunted turning hunter? But for now, he had no choice but to depend upon this strange outcaste human who denied his Comyn heritage. Meanwhile, he would sample what human cooking tasted like.

As Sherdra took another dish of stew from his hands, Coryn asked one last question.

"Would you really have let yourself starve when I had food to offer?"

Sherdra took a bite of stew, then carefully removed from his mouth a piece of tree-mushroom. The meat was not bad, if overcooked.

"Strengths Sherdra has that Coryn may not see yet," he replied, trying to approximate *cahuenga*.

When Coryn continued to stare at him in what Sherdra believed must be perplexity, he explained between mouthfuls. "What Coryn offered before, Sherdra—that is, I—could not accept for reasons. Many reasons. You understand? But it would not be dishonorable for me to take, while you slept."

"Or kill me, and take all you wanted."

"Please! Not necessary."

Coryn began to swear; then laughed, laughed, until he was breathless.

"What a coil!" he said. "You must understand that all my life I've been taught to be wary of—even despise—strangers like yourself. Certainly you did nothing at first to dispel my prejudices."

Sherdra handed him back the dish. "More. Then I will sleep. That is—if you are done talking?"

Coryn nodded. "We both need rest." He returned to the fire. *This time it will be closely watched, as my mother's husband so painfully impressed upon me. He warned me against furred devils lurking in the woods, too. And here I am out in the woods sharing a camp with an erstwhile attacker.*

Sherdra restrained the growl rising to his throat. "Do you have to remind me of that? What we have lost with the dark. . . ."

"Pardon me, Prince Sherdra," the human said. He made a gesture that looked almost like a proper sign of apology. "I merely wanted to say . . . what begins ill may end well with the aid of patience and good grace. So goes the cristoforo teaching. Thus man—so might we all survive."

* * *

"You see? The storm is dying with the morn. So much for your uncle's weather predictions."

Terenz shrugged at the *vai dom's* mockery. He and his uncle had never been close. Reining in his laboring horse, he surveyed the narrow, sparsely wooded valley he and *Dom* Julian had finally come upon, after a bone-chilling crawl of a descent he would just as soon erase from his memory. The icy glimmer of water, there among those scrubby trees . . . he gestured toward it.

"That looks familiar. That creek, I think, is where we went awry, got off on the trail of the poor ladycat. Perhaps she was making a rendezvous with her mate, and he is the one you seek? Doesn't seem likely. But we've nothing else to go on."

Julian was holding his starstone within his hands. "You are almost right," he said. "Almost—almost I can feel him someplace near. But the sense of him comes, then goes. I'm not particularly skilled in this kind of tracking. Perhaps a Ridenow—" He sensed Terenz's questioning eyes upon him and straightened up, with a fretful sigh.

"Yes, Terenz. I should have wakened your uncle, put the matter fairly to him, asked him again for his help. But the impudence of that fellow Carlo and the others, when they refused to follow me this morning—well, that did not sweeten my temper. It is enough that you came riding after me." He coughed as if embarrassed. "You should have known better. But it is no matter. Let's ride down and see if you are right."

"This experience will make quite a tale for the ears of my sons, if I live to speak of it," Coryn muttered to himself as he looked out, squinting, into the crystal-bright afternoon. He had slept little since the dawn meal over which he and Sherdra had wrestled night long. And his rest had been fitful, broken by dark, unsettling dreams. In one of these, as he struggled to rekindle a guttered fire before his mother's husband woke, he was seized roughly from behind by strange men with wolf eyes. They had called him traitor to all human-born. One had grabbed at the pouch which held his starstone.

He did not want to examine these fears too closely. He glanced over at Sherdra who lay almost as motionless as one dead. Coryn resisted the impulse to envy this haunted one his oblivion. *I am much better off; that is clear.*

He fed himself and Picaro; then sat considering how he might play the part of a wise man, rather than a fool, for a change. He could pack up, leave the catman sleeping; set some provisions out for him, of course—perhaps a kinder act than he deserved. *If I start now, and this break in the weather holds, I could reach Vandemyr not long after sunset.*

He got to his feet, carefully stamped out the few remaining embers of the fire, and went to check the weather again. It was definitely clearing. A kinder god had plugged the storm leak in the sky. That was a muddled thought born of sleeplessness, Coryn castigated himself. *But where will it all end? What's to be done with my furred companion now? It would be a mercy simply to let him sleep, but what of those enemies he feared? Were they only a fevered fantasy?*

His sister's death was no fantasy.

Picaro jerked at his tether and whinnied uneasily. "I know you don't like his smell," Coryn whispered, rubbing the gray horse's nose. "But soon, I promise—"

Picaro tossed his head, snorted, seemed to stare with an almost human curiosity over Coryn's shoulder.

Something caught Coryn's attention, as he turned: a flicker of movement, a flash of unnatural color, down in the scrubby woods across the narrow creek; a sound as of horsemen approaching.

"No; no. Incredible, I can't believe this."

Coryn rubbed his burning eyes and looked a second time. Surely the two horsemen now in full view were only chance-met travelers on an innocent enough errand. If these were Sherdra's pursuers, where were their dogs?

But their manner denoted some grim, shared purpose. Coryn could not like the looks of the man in green and black.

He moved backward and dropped to one knee to make himself less visible. "Be quiet," he hissed to Picaro.

Too late. The bigger man was staring in his direction. The man pointed toward the cave and muttered a few words to his comrade. The Guardsman was peering into something held between his hands. Coryn felt certain that he was using a starstone. Was he attempting to pick up mental traces of his intended prey?

It was a rough climb up to the cave entrance. Both men dismounted. The Guardsman slipped his jewel back inside his shirt. Fire, then ice, pulsing along his veins with every leap of his racing heart, Coryn strained to hear what the men were saying.

"Someone is really sheltering up there?" he thought he heard the Guardsman say.

"I'm sure I saw a man's face looking out at us—no, that cave, up there, *vai dom*. If you're so sure the cat's close by, the man may have seen something."

Their voices faded into the wind as the man approached. Coryn flashed a look at Sherdra. Still asleep, though he had begun to move uneasily, making soft growling noises. *Should I wake him?* Coryn needed no bad dreams, no precognitive gift to warn him of what might happen if those men found him and the catman together. *What's Sherdra done, to provoke such interest?*

He stepped quietly to where Sherdra lay. He considered the catman's face for a moment. There were a number of things he might do to protect himself. He shook his head. "I'll have to try that," he mumbled, yawning. "If I fail, I'll try to rouse you while there's yet time."

Laying a knife by Sherdra's hand, he prayed to his saint to protect them both, then went out to greet his visitors.

Despite his bleak mood—he seemed to have lost the sense of the cat entirely—Julian could not restrain a smile. What he had half-feared to be some desperate bandit was only a grubby, shivering wretch of a man, possibly very drunk and only a mere peddler, more eccentrically dressed than usual. As he met Julian and Terenz, the peddler dropped a flimsy, simpering bow. He stammered a formal greeting in very bad *casta*. Then, hardly giving them a chance to respond with so much as their names, he launched into a rambling explanation of how he came to be in such a place. Julian's eyebrows rose a notch. The man seemed nervous; perhaps he was a thief of sorts. Well, so were all his tribe.

"Have you really spent the night sheltering in that cave, good fellow?" asked Julian in a patronizing tone.

Momentarily the man looked annoyed. "The name is Francis, *vai dom*." Then he dropped his eyes, and scratched busily at his shoulder. "Where else might a poor peddler hide from this storm?" he whined. "As I have been telling you—and thank you so much for your gracious patience—I was on my way to Vandemyr, when that starveling bandit jumped me on the road. I drove the cur off, but not without hurt to myself." The fellow patted the marred cheek at which Julian had been staring. "And my chervine ran off during the fracas, with my pack and most of my goods. I'll have little enough to trade for my keep in Vandemyr. Ah, how sadly the world goes for a man out of luck!" He belched and wiped his nose on his sleeve.

In the past Julian might have sympathized with the man's trouble, even offered to help him. But his present concerns lay elsewhere. Zandru, he was tired! And quite out of patience with idiots.

"I'm hunting a foul, murdering cat-thing," he said. "Have you seen any trace of it?"

"A fiend indeed!" Terenz cried. Julian thanked him with a glance.

The peddler looked shocked. He made a sign of aversion. "N-not a catman?" Terenz nodded grimly. The peddler shuddered. "F-forgive me, kind sirs, but no! If I had so much as smelled one of those demons, poor Francis would have fallen down dead with fright. I'm amazed that you are both so brave, tracking such a monster, and in such a storm, too." Wringing his hands together, he glanced upward at the sky.

"And if you ask me, *vai dom*—I know you do not ask me, but perhaps I should call it to your kind attention—it looks like we're not clear of the blizzard yet. It's getting marvelous dark again. Can't you feel that wind?"

To Julian, the weather seemed no more perilous than it had been earlier in the day. He and Terenz had somehow made their way through worse. But Terenz was saying, "He may be right, *Dom* Julian. I think we're in for more."

Julian bit back a groan of dismay and turned his back on them both.

"If you've a camp nearby, noble sirs, you'd best be getting back while this lull lasts," the peddler said.

"You do think it's only a lull, then," said Terenz.

Francis nodded. "I know the signs. Pardon me, but I imagine you don't travel much in these parts. That storm will surely be pounding your ears before the sun's down, *vai dom*."

Terenz looked uncertain and gazed upward with an anxious crease in his forehead. "It may well be," he said after his examination. "That sky's like a wench that doesn't know her own mind. We'd best be searching no further today."

Folding his arms, Julian propped himself against a large rock. "By all means," he drawled. "Go right ahead, Terenz; creep back to camp and rejoin that pack of cowards if that's your pleasure. I am tired of being warned that a few raindrops may blow our way. Damn it all, man, that cat's close. I could almost— as Kraigan might say—smell him!"

"*Vai dom*, I beg you—" Terenz said.

"These past few days," Julian continued, "I've heard enough complaints about the weather to last a lifetime. Terenz, I thought you at least were with me. I thought you understood. Or was all that talk about avenging your sister—only talk?"

"I do understand. And my words were not empty

ones," Terenz replied. He paced up and down a minute, as if to keep himself from weeping in sheer frustration. Then his face brightened. He pointed past the peddler, toward the cave.

"We could shelter in there awhile, at least get warmed, until it's safe to go on. We'll lose less time that way. That is, if Mester Francis doesn't mind sharing his quarters."

"No," said Julian.

"*Dom* Julian, have some pity on yourself if not on me. You look about ready to drop. We'll find nothing but our own deaths if that storm blusters down upon our heads!"

Julian smiled at him. The peddler cleared his throat.

"You must be thinking I've forgotten my manners. But it's a damp unwholesome place, fit only in a pinch for lowly folks like me."

"And cat-hags," Julian muttered to himself.

"Of course you are welcome, both very welcome. But as I should have said before, I've a young serving-lad with me who's quite ill. At first I thought he took some hurt from the bandit and was too proud to tell me at first. But no, he's taken some strange fever. Could be catching. All broken out in ugly spots, he is." The peddler scratched his right arm again, vigorously.

"We'll take our chances, Francis. Perhaps we can help the poor lad," said Terenz. He began walking toward the cave mouth.

"I've little enough for Jamie, or myself," the peddler replied. Julian wondered why his face had grown so white. "You really would be more comfortable back at your camp."

"That's more than a half-day's journey back. If

indeed the lads still wait for us. . . . And I'm as loath to see them again soon as *Dom* Julian. We'll be glad to share what we have with you." Terenz tried to push past the other man, who very drunkenly, it seemed, wavered directly into his path.

"Would you? How very kind of you! I own, I'm half-starved. Poor Francis would be grateful, so very humbly grateful—"

"I would be grateful, man, if you'd stand aside and let us get out of this murthering cold!"

They stood arguing a few steps from the cave entrance. Then the peddler giggled and bowed. "But the *vai dom* should go in first, should he not? Manners, my lad, manners!" He wagged a finger in Terenz's astonished face.

Julian laughed out loud, to cover the vague suspicion he was beginning to feel. He joined Terenz, who looked at him with what appeared to be vast relief.

"*Dom* Julian, this discourteous fool—"

"Correction, Terenz. This lying fool," said Julian, very low.

But now the peddler was moving to one side, favoring them both with an exceptionally warm smile. "Watch your heads; the entrance is low, and narrow," he said. "Well; go on in, gentlemen."

Said the spider, Julian thought. He yanked Terenz back by the arm.

"*Dom* Julian, please," Terenz said; then bit his tongue as the Guardsman's boot came down upon his right foot.

"Thank you for your generous offer," Julian said to the peddler, in the same tone he'd use if invited into a royal chamber at Elhalyn. "But we dare not

delay any longer on our hunt; particularly since, as
you tell us, we may not have many fair hours left.
Good luck to you, Mester Francis. I hope your boy
gets well. Come on, Terenz." He hurried the other
man, who was struggling to stifle his protests away.

"I would have welcomed your company," the peddler sighed; and belched again. "But if you must go,
you must." Grandly he waved to them as they trudged
back toward their horses. "*Adelandeyo*, noble sirs."

After they had forded the creek and ridden a short
way into the covering woods, Julian indicated to
Terenz that they dismount again. Then Terenz exploded. "*Dom* Julian, what new madness is this? I
think—"

"You were not hired to think. You are to follow
me without question. That is what you promised to
do this morning, wasn't it? Or would you rather
rejoin your friends at the camp?"

"No, sir," Terenz sighed, and dropped his head;
quite hurt, Julian realized. He was sorry, sorrier
than he'd ever thought possible, to wound Terenz
so. But he would give no explanations until he had
fully considered the danger they seemed to face. If
the cat had indeed picked up one human protector,
he might have others, now following them. There
might even be watchers and listeners in these woods.

*Perhaps I am only mad, after all. The peddler may have
been as innocent as he seemed. But his manner was strange;
and I sensed something evil about that cave. The reek of
cat? I must be certain, before we venture further, that we
have the means to face the beast and several human allies.
Dry Towners, perhaps? Avarra defend us, what manner of
men can these be?*

He listened inwardly for Alaric's voice but felt only
the same empty silence as had been with him since the

morning. He also felt very lonely. *Well; I know you wouldn't agree with me, anyway.*

"Are we to make camp here?" Terenz was asking.

"For a while. Watch to see if someone comes out of that cave. I hope there are no side or back tunnels through which they may escape us. And be quiet! We may be spied upon." He drew out the pouch that contained his starstone. "I will try to contact Kraigan. I am not a long distance telepath. I don't even know if he can receive a message. But we may need him and his hounds."

"What?" Terenz gaped at him. Julian patted him on the arm.

"We may have found what we're looking for."

"It's all right, Sherdra. They've gone."

Coryn groped his way back into the cave. He could hardly see for the tears of tension and relief that flooded his eyes. "They've gone," he repeated to the two glowing pools of eyeshine that appeared suddenly out of the darkness. "They've gone." He collapsed to his knees, shaking like a man with the palsy.

I was not frightened. Neither should you be. You should be proud, and sing of your pride. We would say—you have earned much gyar.

Sherdra had relaxed his defensive crouch. He came padding noiselessly out of hiding. *I heard your warning call, as you see. Many thanks.* He touched Coryn upon his right ear, then tendered him back his knife.

"Keep it, please. Many thanks to you, also, for not attacking them." He tried to rise. His knees kept giving out. Sherdra helped him to settle down upon his bedroll.

I waited to see what you would do with the hunters. I am not strong enough yet to risk a fight. You taught me humans are not taken so easily. Yet we might have crushed them between us. I am sure of it.

Coryn lowered his head, teeth chattering. "I'm so cold. That Guardsman! I think he's mad—fit to be chained, as you would say. How he looked at me! I know he guessed the truth."

"If he is mad, then he cannot see so well."

"You may be right. But the tale I gave him would not fool a congenital idiot. The big lout, maybe, but not another telepath—I think they will be back. With the hounds." He rocked back and forth, hiding his face in his hands. "I am a fool to think that such a silly act fooled him."

I would have struck at them if they came inside this place. Meanwhile I waited for your word.

"I didn't want to see anyone killed," Coryn whispered.

"So?" Sherdra crept to the cave entrance, and looked outside. His stubby tail twitched; he made a slow hissing sound. "No watchers within sight. But that means little. You had better give me back my claw-sword, and dueling whips. I could not find them when you woke me."

The catman met him halfway as he returned to the bedroll with Sherdra's weapons. "I will take them. You sit down and rest." *Or must we argue a night over this?*

"We have to get out of here, Sherdra. Now. They may be coming back."

"What, in this weather?" Sherdra may have been smiling.

So you did hear all that was said.

Some. My clan does not run to deafness.

"It is well you leave," Sherdra observed as Coryn

began to stuff his belongings within his own pack. "Your bloodkin may indeed kill you if they learn you were helping me."

Coryn slammed down the pack. "Look here, man, surely you're not thinking of staying behind in this rat trap? If you don't mind traveling with me awhile, I know a place up in the hills where they'll never find us, I swear."

"Sherdra knows how to defend himself in caves."

"I realize that; but—"

'I owe you a debt I cannot repay. You shall not further risk your life."

"Sherdra! I've spent enough time and energy on you not to want it wasted."

"Why did you help me after I tried to kill you? You did not show me that."

"Why? Most simply—" He pictured mentally for Sherdra the horror he had once glimpsd in the southern woods, an outlaw run down by a pack of hunting dogs. He felt the catman flinch. *They said the man had murdered a child; yet I was half sick for days afterwards, remembering. Guessing this was your trouble, I was compelled to prevent it.* "Yes, there is more to this," he said aloud, swallowing. "But we really have to stop talking and start moving, as my mother's husband used to say."

Then go. Do what you think necessary for your own sake.

"But, Sherdra—"

I cannot run fast or far. If the hound-hunters scent us in the open, they may pull you down with me. I said I will not accept such a risk from you. Besides, I am very tired of running.

Sherdra fell completely silent then, sitting back on his haunches. His eyes were dim and fey, like those of the captured woodscat Coryn had once seen near

Serrais, caged for the amusement of one of his headblind cousins. The guilt had remained with him lifelong, that he had not attempted to free the poor beast or put it out of its misery.

Coryn tried several other arguments. He pleaded, cajoled, used the finely tuned tactics of logic he'd learned at Nevarsin. Sherdra remained impervious.

"Very well." Coryn got up and shoved his pack behind Picaro. "I'll stay with you just one more day, to watch while you rest." Sherdra signaled "No," but Coryn continued, grimly, "I cannot do otherwise. Do not ask me why. I hardly know myself."

"Coryn is weary himself, and should sleep while I watch."

"At Nevarsin, I learned how to withstand many hours—a long time—of sleeplessness."

"My debt to you mounts. I must think of some way to repay you."

"I want no payment."

"It is a debt. I would lose *gyar* in my own eyes were I to stint you."

"You'll pay no debts in your condition. Take my advice, for once, and rest quietly."

Sherdra stretched his long feline body out on the cave floor. *I begin to obey you as a habit,* he projected.

If that is true, you astound me. Are you learning wisdom at last? Coryn hoped that Sherdra would perceive the affection underlying his thought as the catman drifted off to sleep.

Kraigan and his hounds were stumbling down the lower slopes of the mountain when the message flashed into his mind. He reined in sharply, nearly throwing his horse. By nature he was more careful, but he was not used to this sort of thing.

A cold voice sounding within his head told him how Dom Julian had reconsidered the matter and now had need of him. The guardsman seemed pleased to learn that Kraigan was following him and Terenz after all. He did not ask for explanations of why Kraigan had reconsidered his own decision not to continue in the hunt under conditions only a madman might not scoff at. Kraigan had told himself that it was concern for his nephew that had compelled him to begin a search for the wayward hunters after he'd been wakened by Carlo earlier this morning and informed that the fools were gone. But his motives were unclear even to himself. Indeed, he had finally concluded that his search was hopeless. His hounds could not pick up any likely scent. He had begun to circle back to camp when Julian contacted him. *Most marvelous, and most strange—*

Vai dom—

Listen, old wolf. (A mental image of a hand shaking him urgently, as from a fool's unwary sleep.) Kraigan swallowed, quelled his inward reservations, and fought to hold himself open to what Julian was relaying to him.

He was shown what the guardsman had found and what he suspected; and where they might meet. *Come quickly, but quietly, very quietly. Try not to let your beasts cry out unexpectedly, whatever they may scent. They will have a bellyful of meat if we are successful. No more. I cannot—I dare not maintain this contact any longer. Yes, Terenz is all right. I'll tell him that you—*

It is certain that he's mad, Kraigan thought as the strained contact broke off. *But he seems to have read his signs correctly if there's any truth in what he says. He may be one who's sane enough when the wind's in the right quarter.*

In any case, he felt no disinclination to disobey. If all went as Dom Julian proposed, the hunt would be successful. His spirits lifted. He had never yet failed the *vai domyn* in helping to track down their lawful prey. He would never fail to finish a blood hunt, for good or ill. He acknowledged to himself that he'd always delighted, as much as any of his hounds, in pulling a catman down.

If he had been a reckless sort of rogue, he might have blown his silver horn as he spurred his horse once more onto the trail. Instead a hunter's song rose to his lips as the black hounds coursed silently around him, their eyes shining with such joy as wolves might feel.

Coryn had overestimated his own endurance. His need for sleep had become a bitter enemy. He was nodding off, but someone had to keep watch in case that guardsman. . . . That guardsman. . . . He was being brought to Serrais in a cage while he spat at his captors and tried to claw— Claw? The scene shifted. He and his father fought. Which father? The face kept changing. Suddenly he saw himself plunging a clawsword into a blackened body that came alive before his eyes and turned into Sherdra, who drove the sword back at him and shouted, "*That* for Myor," in a language no human should know. Then Coryn felt himself falling, falling, and woke up with a scream in his ears. It was not his own voice.

Coryn crossed over to sleeping Sherdra who was tightly curled and whimpering. The scream rose to a howl, then subsided again. The nightmare, or whatever it might be, had no end. He, Coryn, must have been getting snatches of the horror interwoven with his own fears. This couldn't be allowed to continue. He shook Sherdra gently awake. Sherdra clung to him and kept on crying.

Only a short while before, Sherdra had appeared so much stronger. Recovering, he had argued and joked after his fashion, even offered to return the help Coryn had given him. Now Coryn realized that he had not lanced the deepest, most subtle wound, the source of a withering poison for both body and spirit.

You dreamed? Coryn asked.

Murder. Myor. Ashyr. The Comyn hunting us down to the last. No hope. No future. Only blood.

Coryn rocked Sherdra in his arms, trying to breach the wall of despair. A part of his own mind was beginning to gibber in panic, *Run, hide!* No; no, this was not just the fear he felt in Sherdra. For there came to his ears a distant, bestial cry, as of wolves. There came to his mind's eye a dark vision of three men meeting in the woods not far off, exchanging only a few words, expectant glances, then riding swiftly toward the cave. Coryn held this knowledge back from Sherdra by a strength of will he'd never known he possessed. He must deal with this peril but for this very moment, he must comfort this poor child, who could never help him as he was now.

Child? No. The feline was no frightened infant but an adult in pain, filled with the torment of real tragedy past and yet to come. How could anyone tell this man to hope on when all hope lay in tatters? Yet without hope Sherdra could never rise to stand beside Coryn as they faced the hunters. Without hope he would never recover from his injuries. Coryn had monitored them and they could heal, but healing lies within the mind of the one injured as well as with the healer. He could not fight Sherdra himself and wrest the catman's survival against all odds. Sherdra must be made to see. . . .

They come? Sherdra's claws bit into his arm. Shuttered eyes cleared, blazed molten gold. Coryn glimpsed within the catman's mind the havoc he would wreak upon the hunters and their wolves before they pulled him down. *Soulseye* was kindling. Coryn gasped at the burning sensation in his hands. Almost, he let Sherdra go.

Forgive me, Father. For this one there is no help in your gentle creed.

Was this the answer? To recall Sherdra to himself by summoning the warrior within him? Coryn's cristoforo self rebelled against it, but there was a part of him that exulted in violence and hated the Comyn. Hated his fathers; hated his kin. To nourish the warrior in Sherdra would arouse the monster in himself. In what way then would he be better than the Comyn he despised? He would listen inward for the voices of the holy brethren. Yes. . . . It was really quite simple. If one can be moved. . . . He had seen the key before. In mind to mind sharing there is understanding, though he was no Alton to force rapport. He realized that he didn't need to be.

Again the baying of dogs was heard; but closer. Even now they must be scrambling up the hill that fronted the cave. Sherdra nudged hard at him. *O hawk; fly with me at these curs.* Coryn reached for his sword. Then he recommitted himself to his purpose, and sent his mind ranging. He encountered another of lesser strength but intent upon its goal. The Comyn guardsman must be mad, thought Coryn, to send so far and wide his hunter's challenge. Yet it was upon such madness that Sherdra's salvation depended.

Come closer. Find me, seeker.

The bristly face of one hound, snarling, looked directly at him from just outside the cave entrance. Sherdra growled back; Coryn just managed to hold on to him. The timing must be swift indeed.

Now that the trap is sprung, let me draw you in, Sherdra, to meet your true foe. We can deal handily enough with these dogs. Sherdra! Come with me! Show him your dream of fear and death.

The hunter had pounced upon the *laran* presence as the answer to his own contemptuously hurled bolt of thought, but he did not think to find what he saw. His memories of Corresanti, and what he and his kinsmen did there, were very different from . . . this perverse vision. So much slaughter, and he had been part of the massacre? *Even if they were animals, would you treat a mad dog so?* Julian dismissed the thought savagely. *That thing killed Alaric! Whatever it may be— man or animal—too great a loss! Ah, bredu!*

Two cat beings swore an unbreakable oath—hunted, ate and slept side by side—sharing in all things. *Myor, my hunting brother,* said the alien mind. Then came a dark vision of the same cat being on his knees, defeated, alone; while a humanly inhuman cruelty plunged a sword of power into the feline body as it burned and blackened—as it lay twitching. *Myor murdered,* came the bitter bleak thought.

And there was something more: something about a woman, fiercely alive, beautiful as the dawn for which she was named; a woman dancing, singing within the circle of watchfires, for joy of the new life that burned within her; something about a woman, her beauty, her life smashed utterly, the living hope she carried also destroyed; lying forever still and voiceless at the bottom of a great chasm. *You did that,* the catman said.

Just outside the cave, Julian Castamir came to a halt. "What are you waiting for?" Kraigan growled at him. Julian shook his head, bemused.

"So they too have *bredin,*" he murmured. "And that woman—his sister? The score should be equal, then. No! He is an animal. Alaric—"

"My lord! The dogs have caught the scent. No doubt of it. In there," Kraigan spat, indicating the cave's depths.

Julian flung back his head. "Take them," he wanted to say. He could not. He felt as if turned to ice. Alaric was whispering within, *No jokes now. Time you let me go, Julian. But this bloody deed you plan may chain us together forever. Something else calls me outward. It is hard to leave you, but I must. Bredu, can't you understand? There was no real malice in what he did to me. I merely got in his way as he was trying to escape us, I cannot hate him any more. For now I see. . . . Oh, how I wish I could tell you all I see! Give it up. Give up your hatred, for your sake as well as mine. Julian, please. . . .*

Julian would never know if Alaric had truly spoken to him from just inside the borders of death's country, or if his bredu's voice had only been the creation of a disordered mind. He did know then what it would mean to lose Alaric completely. Dimly he realized that Kraigan had turned away from him in disgust; heard, as if from a great distance, the tracker calling out, "Ho in there, you might as well come out and face us like men."

"Kraigan!" He pushed past Terenz and ran after the tracker, catching him by the arm as he sought to pull out his hunting knife.

"Call off the dogs," said the Guardsman.

"Call off the d— *vai dom*! Kraigan's breath hissed inward. "I thought you might do this." He shook himself free of Julian, then whistled to his nearest hound to come stand between them. "And after all our trouble. No."

Julian tried to reach him mentally; felt something more animal-like than human. He backed off a step. Kraigan grinned, showing all his teeth.

"Just stay there and let my hounds and me take care of them. You'll change your addled mind quickly enough when the cat comes out. Terenz—"

He looked toward his nephew, to command his obedience. As he did so, the heavy hilt of Julian's flung dagger struck him hard at the base of his skull. Kraigan staggered and fell.

Terenz ran forward. Julian thought that he might have to fight the big hill man also. But Terenz cuffed aside the huge hound springing for Julian's throat, pitched it sprawling down the steep rocky grade. He helped Julian to fend off and subdue the other angry, confused dogs that now swarmed about their master's unconscious body. Perhaps Kraigan had controlled them too closely. His dominant presence gone for the moment from their minds, the hounds were speedily quelled by a few harsh words and kicks from Terenz.

"I don't have his ability to compel them. But they'll obey me for a little while," Terenz said.

Bending over Kraigan, Julian assessed his injury and thought with relief that it was not serious. "Help me carry him back down the hill—gently, man, gently! We'll take him back across the creek. Never mind about the horses; they'll follow. Perhaps when he wakes, our—friends—in the cave will have flown; or at least he'll see the light of reason."

"Why?" Terenz asked as he assisted Julian. "Why have you done this. I am not like my uncle. I could never defy such as you. Still, you have hurt him. Look how his blood stains his clothes. And—all this—has come to nothing."

Julian was glancing over his shoulder, to make sure the hounds trailed them. He fancied he glimpsed, crouching in the cave mouth, a gray-furred beast, watching him with too-bright eyes. He returned his gaze slowly to the hard face of one who might have become a friend.

"Watch your step," he said, more to himself than Terenz. The tracker was heavier than he appeared, the ground uneven.

"Why, *vai dom?*" Terenz persisted.

"I lost my heart for it, man. No more."

"You must be bewitched, lord. The cat-thing's a killer."

Julian remembered clearly then some things he had seen—and done—at Corresanti. "Terenz, if you would seek for killers, you need not look so far as that."

A silence fell between them then; a silence that Julian knew would in essence deepen as they finally left this place and turned their steps homeward. They would shelter the coming night in these woods, each saying not a word to the other, each outwardly intent on Kraigan's care and comfort. On the morrow, Julian realized, he might have to face Kraigan down again. By that time the catman and his human ally might have had the good sense to move away from danger. At the very least, he would have to bear the tracker's scalding comments when Kraigan saw his hunt was spoiled, his prey safely flown. The Guardsman did not care much. He had said farewell

to Alaric. He had let them all go free. The catman.
His bredu. Himself. Nothing mattered, besides that.

Snow was falling, ghostlike, around the men as
they reached a likely shelter and laid their living
burden down. Flakes drifted across Julian's face,
streaking his cheeks with something like cold tears. *I
am too sentimental by half*, he mocked himself.

"I can't believe that really happened."

Coryn had joined Sherdra in the cave entrance to
stare after the departing hunters, their hounds trailing wearily (and sorrowfully? he wondered) behind
them.

"They treated the old hunter, the wolf that ran on
two legs, badly," Sherdra replied. "The others—ha!
They were only tame dogs, after all. But to strike *him*
down as he cornered his prey! This I cannot understand."

"We made the Guardsman understand."

"Him? Him they should have caught and chained.
And carried him home to his mother, for healing.
Truly he has—how would you say—lost his mind?"

*No; he found it instead . . . when you showed him your
dark dream; when you shared yourself with him, Sherdra.
Don't pretend you fail to grasp my meaning. We've come
together so much farther than that. Perhaps—perhaps there
is still hope for us all—hope that one day all your people
and mine will learn to look behind the skin—all of us—see
we are not so different, after all.*

He was so exhausted now he could scarcely frame
with his thought the idea he was trying to convey. He
started to explain aloud. "No," Sherdra said, his tone
like that one might use toward a child, "Too much
has happened. Too much hurt on both sides."

"One friendship pledged cannot bridge a river of blood," Coryn said. "But we have begun to build that bridge. Perhaps, in time, even this small beginning. . . ." He yawned, then swayed. Sherdra held out a steadying hand. But Sherdra's knees were buckling also. They gripped at each other for support, half crawled together back to Coryn's tumbled blankets. Presently they fell asleep—almost in each other's arms.

A reasonably fair, brisk morning dawned. Sherdra left the cave. He saw and smelled no sign of the hunters. When he returned, he found Coryn brooding over the rebuilt fire. The human's barriers were up again, and Sherdra thought he looked worried.

"Probably it is safe to leave this place now," he said. "It is good to walk out again in the wide world, taste its sweetness without fear."

"Yes. Remind me to choose a shelter more carefully next time," Coryn replied. "Not that I haven't found the company interesting. I just hate to feel—always cold; and closed in."

"This place has been good enough for me."

Coryn shrugged. He began to put things into his pack; then he took them out again, as if dissatisfied with their arrangement. Sherdra asked to see the peddler's goods he had never had a chance to inspect.

"Take whatever you like," said Coryn. "No payment needed. I should travel light. I'm unlikely to find better accommodations than this for some time."

"You just said you do not like to stay in caves."

"I can't become a cave dweller like you, by habit." The man laughed, then sobered. "I was thinking of going on to Vandemyr, where there is a cheap, comfortable inn; and a woman who might welcome me there. But I doubt I should risk going back there soon. I won't see the Guardsman again, that's sure. But those other two fellows— I remember now, Sherdra; I've seen them at the inn before. Terenz, was that his name? Will he remember me, should he see me again? What would he do? Oh, never mind, Sherdra. A very unlikely coincidence, that he and I should ever meet."

"This may be something to worry about. It may not be wise to return where someone remembers what a certain peddler did. Have you anyplace else to go?"

"Oh, yes, I suppose so. Well out of this country, I should think. Even a simple peddler makes . . . acquaintances. Though I make too much a habit out of slipping out of other people's lives." One memory, then another, brought to the forefront of Coryn's mind by a long night of struggling and sharing, flowed into Sherdra's consciousness as if they were the catman's own. Sherdra could not understand them all, but he thought he recognized some of Coryn's ghosts, the people left behind on Coryn's journey here: his mother; Brother Stefan; one or two others.

"I don't know how I can manage it; but down the road a bit, there are a few I should see again," said Coryn. "Unfinished business—" He broke off in the middle of the proverb, wih an embarrassed cough.

"A good trail to follow. But until you find it—and it may be long before then—Sherdra has a suggestion."

Coryn was shaking his head before Sherdra had finished explaining. "I see your point. It may benefit us both to travel together a day or so. But Sherdra, I really do not have the time."

"Obviously the simple passing of lights and darks is regarded as something of a goddess by you people. You will explain that to me when I have—more patience; and you—more time. Now listen, Coryn.

"By the time you return to the human countries, perhaps no one will be talking of what you did. Who would imagine, anyway, that Puss and bareskin can be—traveling companions? Or more."

He felt the other's hesitant, seeking touch upon that part of himself he always hid, by necessity as well as habit. He tried to bear this and communicate the warmth and reassurance he thought Coryn needed.

We need not go so far as you think; not so far as where the great ice river meets the Mother of all waters; where, I hope, there will be someone waiting to welcome me. I would not lead you into any danger. The Clanmother I will ask—protection? sanctuary? of—was first in counseling peace between our folk and yours. She will ask that I use Soulseye in other ways than in completing a game of vengeance. Many children will cry with hunger this season.

He saw his companion was still troubled. But he thought he recognized the beginnings of a smile, a certain yielding. This bird was nearly within his grasp. He would take it up tenderly, meaning it no harm.

No. This was not a thing to trap, to tame, to use against its will. This was a man. *Hunter, let this prey pass by.*

"Sherdra doesn't want to do that, either," he said aloud.

"What don't you want to do?" Coryn asked, after a pause.

"Give you up."

"Why, Sherdra. . . ." The human looked down at

his own feet, his hairless face turning a brighter color.

"Coryn! Whatever you may have heard of us, we do not always like to journey alone in the dark."

My brother: will you walk a little way with me?

DAW

DAW PRESENTS THESE BESTSELLERS BY
MARION ZIMMER BRADLEY

THE DARKOVER NOVELS